God When He's Drunk

KEN STANGE

BOOKS BY

KEN STANGE

Love Is A Grave (Nebula Press)

Bushed (York Publishing)

Nocturnal Rhythms (Penumbra Press)

These Proses A Problem Or Two (Two Cultures Press)

Cold Pigging Poetics (York Publishing)

More Than Ample (Two Cultures Press)

Bourgeois Pleasures (The Quarry Press)

Colonization Of A Cold Planet (Two Cultures Press)

Advice To Travellers (Penumbra Press)

A Smoother Pebble, A Prettier Shell (Penumbra Press)

The Sad Science Of Love (Two Cultures Press)

God When He's Drunk

~~

Ken Stange

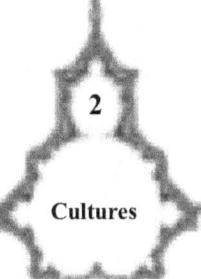

Two Cultures Press

2012

For information about permission to reprint, record, or perform sections of this book, write to <u>Two Cultures Press</u>, 970 Copeland, North Bay, Ontario, Canada, P1B 3E4

Library and Archives Canada Cataloguing in Publication

Stange, Ken, 1946-   God when he's drunk / Ken Stange.

Short stories.ISBN 978-0-9809273-6-8

    I. Title.

PS8587.T3G62 2012   C813'.54   C2012-907218-4

Acknowledgements

    "The Heart of a Rat" won the Vanderbilt/Exile prize for short fiction and was published in *CVC Short Fiction Anthology Series #1* (Exile Editions, 2011).

    Some of the fictions in *God When He's Drunk* first appeared in these periodicals:
    "An Experienced Traveller Doesn't Magnify Trivial Incidents Out Of Proportion" in *Scrivener* (Vol. 5, #2)
    "One Needs Reliable Transportation" in *The New Quarterly* (Vol. IV, #3).
    "Aqua Regina" in *Wascana Review* (Vol. 40, #1-2, 2008)

Cover Art: Ken Stange

ISBN: 978-0-9809273-6-8

For Ursula as always

(just as she has always been there for me)

"Bacchus was the god of wine, theatre and ecstasy. That makes him a likely candidate for the one true god."

—Hippokrites

CONTENTS

ROACHES

"I am a survivor. I am like a cockroach, you just can't get rid of me."
—Madonna Ciccone (Attributed)

It may or may not be true of white folk, as a black friend of mine maintains, but it certainly is true of all those doors that lead to apartments over small businesses: they all look alike. Sandwiched between laundromats and restaurants (or bakeries), these entrances have a faceless anonymity house doors can only dream of.

.

Long ago I learned that life is one surprise package after another, so I shouldn't have been surprised, but I was: I just didn't know which of the two faded green doors flanking the bakery led to our old apartment. That I'd forgotten the exact address, okay, but that I was incapable of even recognizing the door, this was unsettling. Christ, you'd think one could never forget the appearance of the portal to one's old private purgatory, no matter how much time had flowed down life's dirty drain.

.

So since I didn't know which bell to ring, I decided to go into the bakery to see if it rang any mental bells. Only faint ones, it turned out, although there was loud jangle from a metal clanger over the door. The place was only vaguely familiar, like a man you pass on the street in a foreign country and you feel, while thinking it unlikely, that you've met him years ago.

.

I sniffed the warm, thick air. It was so heavy with the smell of baked goods, I couldn't detect that acrid pesticide stench that I knew must lie beneath its surface, like a heretical, licentious message hidden below the religious text of a medieval palimpsest. I tried to remember what days the exterminators came. Tuesday and Friday? This was Monday. But, of course, it was absurd to think that the spraying schedule hadn't changed in twenty years.

.

I was examining the cracks in the worn, wooden trim along the floorboards, expecting to meet the pinprick gaze of a roach staring out at the dangerously lit daytime version of his nocturnal terrain, when my concentration was interrupted by a young woman's voice.

.

"Can I help you with something?"

.

A quick embarrassed response in the negative and I was out the door. And then, standing there back on the street, feeling foolish, and my body remembering that when I used to go for fresh bread in the morning, I'd always turn to the right when leaving the bakery. So the door with the 971 stencilled on it had to be the one—no matter how unfamiliar it looked.

.

I gazed up at the second story window. Drab, faded beige draperies blocked any glimpse into the interior. But what the hell, even if the drapes were drawn open, from my position I'd only be able to see the living room ceiling. Real meaningful, that would be.

.

The sun was dipping below the horizon, shadows lengthening. Soon it would be dark, but there were no lights on in the apartment. Probably no one was home.

.

The girl from the bakery came out and looked at me suspiciously and then hurriedly pulled an accordion security grating across the front of the storefront, secured the padlock, and, casting one final glance at me, nervously strode off.

.

So what to do now? In fact, why was I here at all? What exactly had I expected to see? Ghosts? So I could exorcise them? There are no ghosts. There is death, but there are no ghosts. There are no ghosts because there is death: final, irrevocable, unequivocal, unambiguous, omniscient—but invisible. Nothing to cast a shadow on the living.

.

I suddenly remembered an ad for roach trap called The Roach Hotel: "They check in, but they never check out." That's also what we used to call our little matchbox of old marijuana butts that we intended to recycle into new joints—a 'roach hotel'.

.

Press the bell, I told myself. Steel yourself and press the bell. I'd worked out an intricate song and dance about my sentimental need to visit my old apartment that might, just might—if the current tenant was soft-hearted—get me into my old hell, my old shell. No harm in trying.

.

Unfair, really, that it should be so difficult for me, a fairly smart guy, to gain access to what once was my home—yet so damn easy for the stupid cockroach: even the fattest of roaches can flatten their bodies and wiggle through a crack thinner than a dime.

.

(The advice for the infested is full of warnings about roaches' uncanny ability to slither and scurry into one's apparently safely sealed hermitage. 'Retrofit aluminum screening for vents and windows, and be sure to caulk around the edge of the screen to make a tight barrier.' 'Caulk, paint or seal potential roach harbourages with whatever material is appropriate to the location.' And knowing that houses and apartments are virtually impossible to seal, the advisors go on. 'Store food in containers that close tightly and that roaches cannot chew through, and remember paper and cardboard boxes should not be considered roach-proof.' 'Place waste from the clean-up or preparation of meals in plastic containers with snap-on lids, and snap the lid on firmly after every use.')

.

I wondered if the present tenants had problems with roaches. Almost certainly they did—because the bakery was still there. Where there is a bakery there are roaches. (This is the Second Law of Insect Dynamics.) It's a dirty little secret that all bakeries need at the very least weekly visits from the exterminator, reason being that the filthy things love carbohydrates and are damn near indestructible. Roaches have survival skills well-honed by evolution: they can do without or make do with almost anything. They can live up to four weeks without food and almost two weeks without water, but rarely have to—because they'll gladly eat just about anything: food scraps, garbage, sewage, decaying organic matter, leather, hair, the glue in book bindings, the toothpaste residue in your toothbrush (of which they are particularly fond), each other's excrement, each other (cannibalistic by nature), even, in extreme cases, human flesh. They can survive radiation up to 12 times greater than humans can. Unlike us fragile mammals, they could easily survive a nuclear holocaust.

They are the meek who shall inherit the earth.

Roaches have inhabited the earth for more than 250 million years, so it'd be very naïve to expect the exterminator's twice weekly assault on the bakery to ever wipe them out—even with the very newest agents of chemical warfare. Yes, traces of these chemical pesticides in our buns and bagels and biscuits may eventually do in us highfalutin species, but they're nothing more than a minor setback to Roach Civilization.

When Sharon and I had first moved into this place, we never expected cockroaches. The neighbourhood was good. Working class, yes, but far better than some of the areas where we'd lived back in Cleveland. And never before had we had a problem with bugs.

Our second night in the place I woke in the middle of the night and went for a drink of water. I nearly pissed myself when I turned on the kitchen light. The sink and stove were alive: an undulating shag carpet of roaches. Within seconds, of course, they were gone. I blinked: they were gone. It could've been a hallucination. (Especially then, it could've been a hallucination.) But it wasn't.

The next morning I called the landlord. The landlord, although friendly, was not especially sympathetic.

"The exterminator does the bakery twice a week, and them roaches no fools. They head for cover whenever the Man shows up. Cover, that means your apartment, Mr. Maddock. When the Man's downstairs, they move upstairs. So don't you worry, them roaches don't mean you're dirty or that you're leaving food out. They just looking for a place to stay till that DDT dust clears. Besides, roaches cleaner than houseflies. There was a piece in the Star said so."

I remember feeling an idiotic satisfaction that the landlord didn't think we were "dirty". I also remember what an insecure, unassertive, and pathetic fool I was back then.

Incidentally, our landlord was misinformed about roaches' cleanliness. True enough those ordinary houseflies are filthy, feeding, as they do, primarily on the nutrients left in excrement, but cockroaches aren't any better, having an even less discriminating diet. Many people get sick from roaches contaminating food with bacteria that cause gastroenteritis, food poisoning, and diarrhoea. Also, many of us over-sensitive humans have severe allergic reactions to the dust created by cast-off cockroach skins, dead bodies and droppings. And the evil little creatures have even been implicated in the spread of tuberculosis, leprosy, cholera, dysentery and typhoid.

.

I didn't know all this back then, but what I did know was that the mere thought of roaches made me feel sick to my stomach. They gave me the creeps, made my skin crawl, disturbed my ability to sleep. Each night I imagined them emerging as soon as the light was out—and crawling over my body as I drifted from consciousness. So I began to insist on sleeping with a small light on, although Sharon said this made it difficult for her to doze off. Even with my night light, often I wouldn't be able to drive the thought of the damn roaches from my mind unless I had a few drinks—or even went so far as to smoke a joint.

.

We couldn't afford the dope or even my few drinks. We couldn't afford to move. We couldn't afford anything. We were barely more than kids—suddenly with a kid of our own: Billy was only three months old. Sharon had to stay home to take care of him. And, hell, I wanted her to stay home and take care of him. Unfortunately, I wasn't making enough money to support the both of us, never mind an infant.

.

Before Billy arrived we'd felt rich. With both of us working (albeit at poorly paying jobs), we had nothing to worry about except which brand of cheap wine to buy or what 'happening' was worth attending. We'd felt more affluent than ever before. ('Ever before' being three years of marriage while I finished university and Sharon worked split shifts at the phone company.)

.

Our 'affluent' working-poor stage lasted two years. When Billy came on the scene, suddenly our income was cut in half, and I had another human being to support. This tiny, fragile creature both delighted and terrified me. Getting married is nothing. It simply means you get to spend all your free time with someone you love. Having a child, on the other hand, means you've signed a pact with God (who is even more demanding than The Devil) to support another human being for the next two decades. It is no wonder Mother Nature wires us to breed so easily when we're young and foolish. Few sane and mature adults would so casually mortgage a quarter of their lives in this way.

.

(Incidentally female cockroaches make an even greater lifetime commitment: the males impregnate them with a 'package of sperm' that may keep them pregnant for their whole adult lives. The males, however, don't much worry about anything after they've had their way with a momentarily receptive female.)

This is not to say I regret the 'foolishness' of having Billy or the responsibility it entailed. My son has turned out to be more than worth it all—even the year spent at 971 Hell Road.

Well actually it was 971 Samsan Road. The significance of the address only struck me as I stood there twenty-one years later, trying to get up the courage to ring the bell to our old apartment. I'd missed the irony in the name back then. Nor had I made the connection of the number with the year I spent there: 1971.

1971. What a year! 1971 was more 'the sixties' than any date starting nineteen-sixty-something. The pungent aroma of marijuana and the burnt cordite smell of revolution were in the air. The 'sixties' only happened to most people after that decade was actually over, and its self-righteous, hedonistic philosophy had wafted down from on high (Mount Berkeley and Mount Frisco and other oracular heights) to the urban canyons and valleys where most of my generation lived.

Everyone was reading the Whole Earth Catalog, although it was closing up shop. Altamont and Manson were supposed to be signalling the end of the naïve, sixties fantasy of love and peace, but people were still going on about Woodstock (now a movie for the deprived majority who hadn't attended) and if Morrison was dead because the dream had become a nightmare, few seemed to notice, being far more interested in writing sentimental eulogies (now that he had redefined 'poetry' as what they don't bore you with in college) than in looking closely at what a total fuck-up the poor guy really was. And, at least with my friends, The Stones and getting stoned were still both big.

Drugs weren't to blame for my descent into Hades that year, but they were what the social scientists like to call 'a contributing factor'. You might say that roaches, both kinds, were my Virgilian guides. I began my descent, my purgatorial tour, because a friend of a friend of a friend named Mark, a graduate student at the university, was doing a 'study' on the effects of marijuana on short-term memory. I'd agreed to be a subject in the experiment.

Even in those days I smoked dope only occasionally, for it wasn't (and still isn't) my recreational drug of choice. I much preferred drinking (which at that time was contemptuously referred to as 'juicing'). Beer perked me up. Dope usually just made me sleepy—unless I'd already been drinking, in which case it made me silly and hungry. But most of my friends were happier with a toke than a drink, and it was bad form to turn down a free high.

The experiment was being conducted in the Psychology Lab, which was located in the sub-sub-ground level of an ugly concrete building. All cinderblock and fluorescent-light, the place had a coldness that did not recommend it for drug experiences. Everyone knew about the importance of "set and setting". (The acidheads talked of little else when they were trying to convince someone to 'turn on': bad trips never the drug's fault.)

Half of the subjects in this experiment were to smoke a placebo and the other half the real thing. Of course, who got which was determined randomly, and the subjects weren't informed whether the 'good shit' they were smoking was really any good at all. I was feeling out of sorts when my number was called, so I was actually hoping I'd get the placebo.

I didn't. The stuff was lethal. (I'm sure my short-term memory was non-existent and serious-researcher Mark got what are called "statistically significant differences".) Mark was reading numbers to me, and I was responding with any phone number that popped into my head. He was trying to be the serious researcher, but I could see him smiling to himself.

I wasn't amused. I was wasted—and not happy about it. I'd just butted the research roach, when my heart started racing, as did my thoughts. I'd occasionally had mild paranoia or anxiety attacks and even tachycardia from smoking, but nothing as severe as this. As I looked at Mark's suddenly sinister smile, I became convinced the Narcs would at any moment raid the lab. I was equally convinced that my heart would burst if I didn't 'stimulate' myself.

"You okay?" he finally asked.

"No," I replied, "I'm freaking."

"It's clean. USP THC. Supplied by a lab."

.

"Don't care. I'm freaking."

.

Mark called a cab. I think he was anxious to get me out of the lab before I did something outrageous and endangered his research project. He volunteered to accompany me home, but I declined his offer. He seemed relieved.

.

When I arrived back at 971, Frank was there sipping a coffee while Sharon boiled some pasta. Frank and I had been friends since our high school days back in Cleveland, where we'd competed with each other in the chess club.

.

My paranoia was waning, but my mania was increasing. I was delighted to see him and my wife, neither of whom looked sinister, but I couldn't stand still, never mind sit down. "Let's play a-couple simultaneous games," I said, searching around for all three of my chess sets, two of them magnetic pocket things. Once I found them, I told Frank to set up the pieces and then went to turn on the TV. Then I turned on the stereo. Frank and my wife looked at me as if I'd just landed in from another planet—but they said nothing. Their concerned expressions spoke for them.

.

"Need some stimulation." That was my explanation—seemed adequate—and they pretended to accept it as reasonable.

.

I played (and lost) all three games while watching Kirk seduce go-go-girl aliens on Star Trek reruns while frenetically tapping my foot to first the Stones' Sticky Fingers, then CCR. I was asked several times if I was okay. I always said yes.

.

I wasn't.

.

Frank said he had a couple roaches in his wallet. Did I want to have a toke to chill out?

.

I didn't.

.

When Sharon said the spaghetti was ready, Frank said he had to go, probably knowing there wasn't enough for three. Pointless: I couldn't eat anyway. I couldn't even stay in my chair. Sharon looked mildly concerned, but then Billy woke from his nap, and she went to check on him.

•

I was pacing about the kitchen when I spotted a roach peering out from behind the cheap linoleum splashboard. Cockroaches are most comfortable when they have pressure on three sides of their body, which is why they keep to cracks and crevices except when, because of the need to feed, they absolutely have to venture onto flat surfaces such as kitchen counters. This creeper was obviously secure, but also obviously hungry—or he wouldn't have been peering longingly at the stray spaghetti noodle that lay on the edge of the sink.

•

I had a fit of shivers. I don't think I have ever felt such disgust and hatred for a creature in all my life as I did for that goddamned cockroach scrunched in a greasy crack by our sink, his antennae fibrillating with gluttonous anticipation. The cockroach has no brain. The cockroach is pure instinct driven by a neural system down in his body. If you decapitate a roach, it will walk around without its head for over a week before it dies of thirst.

•

I called to Sharon that I needed a walk. Then I said (*sotto voce*) "Fuck You" to the cockroach and went out.

•

The world out on the street didn't look right. It looked unreal. Life is not real: That is the thought that dominated my thoughts as I wandered the streets that night. This idea and the corollary that Only Death is Real came to be my dominant thoughts over the next several weeks.

•

I finally wended my way home just as dawn was graying the horizon. The light was on in the kitchen. I didn't see any cockroaches. I went to our bedroom and collapsed.

•

I was less manic the next day, probably because I'd only had two hours sleep, and managed to do my job without screwing anything up or having a major panic attack. But there is no question that the panic bird had nested in my gut.

•

As the weeks went by I became more and more morbid. There was a funeral home next to my subway stop. (I'd always wondered at the choice of words: funeral home? Whose home? Everyone's? The ultimate home? Eventually it comes time for all of us to go home.) I'd walk out of the station and see this place (Martin's it was called), and I'd experience a despair that was as deep as a well. Why even bother to go to my temporary residence at 971? Why not just go home? Because 'home' terrified me.

.

Sharon was a very good mother, and because she was too busy being this good mother, she didn't seem to notice that her husband was losing it. And of course I was too busy trying to be a good father and provider to draw her attention to my own problems: I kept my morbid thoughts to myself. My salary was chicken shit, and the bills were piling up—which didn't help. I began to wonder how they would live without me, for I now believed my death to be imminent. (The cause varied from day to day, although a stroke, a heart attack, an aneurysm, some kind of catastrophe in my circulatory system was the most frequently imagined deathblow.)

.

The only thing that took my mind off death was an obsession I had developed: the god damned cockroaches. I took books out from the library and read up on their disgusting habits. I learned about the different varieties.

.

Consider the American Roach Periplaneta americana, also known as the water bug: the largest house-infesting species; about one and one-half inches long with reddish-brown wings with light markings on thorax; considered very aggressive, prefers warm, damp areas. Or the German Cockroach Blattella germanica (our particular problem): about five-eighths inch long; light to medium brown, with two dark longitudinal streaks on the thorax; nocturnal, primarily infesting areas close to food, moisture and warmth; the most common roach found in and around apartments, homes, supermarkets, restaurants—and bakeries; eats almost anything; females produce one egg capsule every 20 to 25 days, each capsule containing from 18 to 48 eggs, the newly born becoming adults in as little as 36 days and can live up to one year. Or the Brownbanded Cockroach Supella longipalpa: about five-eighths inch long; wings with two brownish-yellow bands; nocturnal and can fly; may be found throughout any structure, but prefers dry, warm areas, high locations, and inside furniture; sometimes confused with the German cockroach; often hides egg capsules in furniture; not as dependent on moisture as other species.

.

I learned that cockroaches are basically nocturnal, and if you ever do see any during the day, they were likely forced out by overcrowding, a sign of severe infestation. (Not something I wanted to know.) I learned that they, like me, liked beer. (And sure enough I found several in the case of empties in the corner of the kitchen.) I learned that cockroach eggs are naturally protected from insecticides. (So much for ever hoping to be rid of them.) I learned that their blood is yellow and they have no true circulatory system: the blood just sloshes around inside their body cavity. (Cockroaches are physiologically incapable of dying of strokes or aneurysms.)

Only my cockroach studies (and making sure I was never alone for more then a few minutes) allowed me to stagger on along the precipice of sanity for months without toppling off.

Then one day I came home from work and Sharon was sitting at the kitchen table, a pile of crumbled Kleenex in front of her. She looked up at me with red, swollen eyes. Her father had had a heart attack. He was in IC and his condition was listed as critical. She'd already booked a flight to Cleveland for seven that evening. She was taking Billy with her, because she knew I had to work.

I wanted to cry out: "Don't leave me, please! I'll die if you leave me alone!" But even in my madness, I knew this would not be comprehensible to her, would hurt her and make her misery even worse. I tried to comfort her, although I could feel my heart racing in my chest—and the terrified child in me screaming in my mind: "We're both going to die. Your father and me. At least the hospital will be taking care of your father. I'll be alone. I'll die alone. Please don't leave me to die alone. I know it is a selfish, horrible thing to ask, but I beg you. Don't leave me!"

Still I tried to comfort her and somehow kept gagged the terrified child within me. Sharon flew off to Cleveland on the last flight that evening.

I knew that night was going to be a nightmare, for I knew, with a certainty that I had about nothing else in the world, that I'd never wake if I went to sleep. I'd die in my sleep, and the roaches would come out. Several nights later when my body had begun to stink, they would break into the apartment. When they snapped on the bedroom light they would find my bloated corpse matted with scurrying roaches, reminiscent of fur blowing in a breeze.

I would not go to sleep. I turned on the TV. I tried to distract myself with a movie, but almost all movies have people dying or reference to people dying. I finally found a pathetic 'comedy' that, while not funny, kept me from dwelling on death for at least a few minutes at a time.

When the movie ended, I got up and flipped through the channels, but all the other stations were already off the air. I snapped off the snow and hiss, and silence flooded the room. I could feel tremors threatening to take over my body. I knew that the time had come at last: that I was going to die. I knew my heart was going to stop. And I knew I didn't want to die alone.

I flung open the apartment door and bounded down the stairs. There would be people on the street. At least I wouldn't die alone. God, how I wanted to live, but how can you live when you are constantly terrified of dying? You can't protect yourself by moving into an intensive care ward and having your heart monitored constantly, your vital signs kept under constant surveillance. Hospitals mean death. Hospitals kill. There is even a term for it: iatrogenic.

It was past two, so of course the street was deserted. Every few minutes a car would whiz by, but really I was just as alone here as in our apartment. That they'd find my body sooner—that was the only difference. That, and that I was away from the roaches. I stood shivering in the cool night air. The shakes were getting worse. This was it, certainly. The end.

A man came around the corner. His walk was unsteady and his head was down. As he drew near I could see that his clothes were very shabby.

Suddenly he looked up and shook his head as if to clear it. He did a double take when he saw me standing there, quivering like an aspen.

"What's the problem, friend?" he said.

I felt a mixture of hostility and appreciation for his presence.

All I could think to do was to ask him who he was.

"Name's Roach," he replied. (I swear that is what he said. It isn't something you forget.)

"I'm going to die!" I said. As I spoke, I realized that this was the first time I'd ever confessed my fear to anyone. I'd made an odd choice of confessor.

"What?"

"I said I'm going to die."

He seemed totally unconcerned. "Yeah? Aren't we all?"

"No, I'm going to die now!"

"Really? Great! Never seen anybody die. It should be an in-ter-est-ing experience." He took a few more steps toward me and studied my face with his rheumy eyes. I could smell the stale liquor on his breath.

"You think it's funny?"

"Funny? I don't know. Like I said, never seen nobody die. Maybe it's funny, maybe not."

"I didn't want to die alone."

"No one does, but can't be helped. We all die alone."

His remark irritated me, sobered me. "A philosopher of the bottle, are you?" I said. He was getting on my nerves.

"Don't have to be a philosopher to know we all die alone."

"Shit!" I said. Damn, he was annoying me. I noticed I'd stopped shaking.

"So, c'mon, do it! Die! Get on with it. I ain't got all night, my friend."

And then I was really angry. "Oh fuck you, you goddamn wino!"

He pulled himself up and straightened his shoulders. "No point in getting mad. As my mum used to say: 'Shit or get off the pot.' So c'mon, let's see some writhing, some blood and guts and screaming. Some dying. Let's see your soul go poof in a puff of smoke. I ain't got all fucking night. Got places to go, people to meet."

It was then I started to laugh.

It was all so incredibly absurd: this wino berating me for taking so long to die. And here I was twenty-two years old and not even sick—except in the head. He'd need more than "all night" if he were to wait around for me to die. A phrase popped into my head: "I laughed so hard I thought I'd die." This made me laugh even more.

.

I left the drunk standing there and went back to my apartment. Exhausted and giddy, I had no trouble getting to sleep. In the morning I woke with a shitty grin on my face, and a feeling of incredible well being. I saw a roach scurrying along the floorboards—and just said Good Morning to him.

.

I won't claim that after that night I was completely cured. But certainly it was what doctors call the crisis, the turning point. After that whenever an anxiety attack or a fit of morbidity would start, I'd very consciously script and perform a worse case scenario on the stage of my imagination. And just offstage there'd be this wino calling out "C'mon, let's see some writhing, some blood and guts and screaming. Let's see your soul go poof in a puff of smoke." And I'd end up laughing to—and at myself.

.

We moved to a different city a few months later, and I got a job that paid a bit more. But that wasn't what allowed me to regain my sanity. It was this tactic of using my imagination to push my fears up against the wall of absurdity until they were crushed—like a bug.

.

The anxiety attacks still came now and then, albeit with less and less frequency—up until my son Billy's sixth birthday. I remember thinking as we blew up balloons and strung streamers that I'll never again have these attacks. One doesn't have to be a psychoanalyst to understand this. My own father died when I was five, and I have no memory of him whatsoever. All my life I've been convinced that if he'd lived one more year, I'd have a few mental snapshots to treasure.

.

.

1992. The door to 971 opened. A young man stepped out, glanced up and down the dark street.

.

He had longish blonde hair and appeared to be in his early twenties. His t-shirt had the silhouette of a marijuana plant emblazoned on the front with a flippant slogan I remembered well: "Reality is a crutch, use drugs!"

When his eyes met mine they at first flicked away—but quickly returned to lock onto mine. His eyes looked furtive, even frightened.

For several seconds we stared at each other. I felt a bit like I was looking at a ghost of my younger self. We couldn't have been three feet from each other, and the air between us microwaved. There was terror in the kid's eyes. Even in the fading light I could see his sea-blue pupils were grossly dilated.

I felt protective, fatherly. He looked much as I imagined I must have looked that night twenty-one years ago when I'd come out of my apartment to confront death on a public street. So I was moved to speak to him, knowing, even as I spoke, that my words would probably seem foolish and pompous.

"Don't be afraid," I said in a voice that came out sounding inappropriately harsh. "Fear is just a waste of time."

The young man's response was unexpected. He slowly put his hands up—as if I were pointing a gun at him.

"Easy," he said in what was clearly intended to be a soothing tone, but was edged with hostility. "Ya don't have to get heavy."

It was me he was afraid of!? I had no idea why.

Then, behind him, the door began to open again and the young man suddenly shouted: "Narc! Split, Greg, run, man, run!"

What happened next is a blur. Over the boy's shoulder I saw a second young man, with a shaved head, emerge from the doorway. Then suddenly the blonde lad charged past me, shoving me hard. I stumbled back over the curb and fell on the street. My head hit the asphalt just as I heard another male voice, shrill and agitated, screaming: "What the fuck, man!?"

I lay still for a few seconds and then struggled to a sitting position. I had to get out of the street. I crawled back on to the sidewalk, closed my eyes and took several deep breaths. I was just about to try getting to my feet, when a car stopped on the street and a man wearing a black, silk shirt that made him look like a priest leaned out the passenger window. "You okay pal?"

15

.

"I'll live," I said. Then I started laughing hysterically. Because I knew I would. At least for a while longer.

.

The man frowned and shook his head. He undoubtedly thought I was either stoned or crazy. Reasonable assumptions. The car drove off. One taillight was burned out; the other looked like a hot ember fading into the distance. Behind the dark windows of the bakery, it was dinnertime.

~~~~

PLAYING HOST AT TRINITY GARDEN

"Night is the best time to visit suburban gardens, for the dark makes even Eden ominous and interesting."

—Hippokrites

Enter here.

.

> *You must of course enter*
> *softly . like a slug*
> *trailing your slime of humanity*
> *over the patio stones.*

.

A vector is carrier of a pathogen from one host to another. Host and Holy Ghost. Three vectors. Call them: Lover; Seducer; Trespasser. Three converging vectors. Choose your poison. You are observer. You play host tonight.

.

Enter now. Carefully. Or you'll crack the fragile porcelain of this nocturne. Move as quietly as a shadow or some unmentionable creature of the summer night. One must always move slowly, ever so slowly, when in a monochromatic landscape. Submerge yourself gently into this murky typography where all sounds are shades of gray, all colours muted. Here perverse Four O'clocks are in full bloom, but what should be a rich burgundy is only a circular darkness. Decorum. It is a matter of decorum. Light flashes, but night crawls, so behave appropriately.

.

Lester inhaled deeply as he sauntered along. The air tasted like cool, spring water. It'd been a long time since last he'd been permitted to drink of the clean night air. (And if his father discovered that he was missing from his bed, it would be a long, long time before he'd ever be permitted to do so again.) Strange that the bed he'd slept in for most of his first fifteen years should now cause insomnia—one 'problem' he'd never suffered from during his three years at Harkness.

Most of the house windows were dark, which was a bit disappointing, for one of the things he remembered most fondly from his earlier days of freedom was the glimpses lighted windows offered of other people's homes. He used to love to sneak out for walks at night, so he could view the illuminated lives of other families. He didn't know what it was like in the city, but here in the suburbs a surprising number of people didn't bother to draw their curtains after dark. There was something sensuous about watching people moving about their brightly lit rooms, oblivious of their exposure to a watcher in the night. You got to see people with their defences down, relaxed and secure in the familiar context of their own home: the old man slouched in his chair picking his nose as he stares at the Tube; the old lady in her bathrobe casually scratching her ass as she walks from living room to kitchen; the little boy at the kitchen table pretending to do his homework; and the little girl—but best not to think about the little girls.

Lester stopped at the corner and looked up at the street sign. Oak and Greenview. He didn't recognise either name. The night air was intoxicating, as was his freedom, and he'd let himself become disoriented. Not that it mattered, really, for he knew all the major streets. If he just kept walking until he hit a thoroughfare he'd be able to get his bearings again. He wasn't stupid. Hell, he'd eventually fooled even old Dr. Vincent, hadn't he?

"Susan, it's a stupid idea, a really stu-pid idea."

"You're just saying that cuz you're afraid."

"Afraid! Afraid of what? Boogie men? There's nothing to be afraid of."

18

"Right, so why don't we do it?"

.

"There's nothing to see."

.

"It'll be spooky, Karen, real spooky."

.

"No it won't. How can it be spooky if there's nothing to be afraid of?"

.

"Well the heck with you then. I'm goin' to do it. If you want to watch from the window or just cover your head and go back to sleep, I don't care."

.

"Susie, you're crazy. If Dad catches you sneaking out into the yard at two in the morning, he'll have you locked up in the loony bin."

.

"Yeah, yeah. Just go cover your head Karen. I'll see ya later."

.

"Su-san, why are you doing this?"

.

"You know what Daddy's always saying?"

.

"No, what?"

.

"You're only young once."

.

"Je-sus!"

.

Tom opened his bedroom door and listened for the sound of his father snoring. It was fainter than usual; the old man sounded like he had his head buried in the pillow. Tom tiptoed out into the hall.

.

They'd made the pact three days ago. Three musketeers on a mission of vengeance. The twerp had ratted on him to Mr. Mitchum, and Tom's buddies had all had trouble with her, too. It was time she was put in her place. Billy had had the idea: a week long campaign of nightly sabotage. Billy had even volunteered to go first, and Monday, good to his word, he'd stolen the Henderson's porch light. On Tuesday night James had let the air out of the tires of their station wagon. The twerp had been late for school this morning because she, poor thing, had had to walk. Tonight it was his turn to assault the Henderson household.

The stairs creaked, but Tom knew where to step to minimise the noise. Once he reached the ground floor he felt relatively secure. He'd slipped out at night twice before without being detected. His raid wouldn't take long, so he figured his chances of getting caught were pretty slim. The Henderson's lived on his side of the street seven houses down, and he could reach their garden by travelling through backyards. It would be especially easy since none of the backyards on his block was fenced, except the Henderson's—which just figured. The whole family thought they were special. As soon as they'd moved in they'd put the fence up; it was like a sign saying: "Keep off, we're special and you guys can't be trusted." And the twerp, oh was she something else! Some of the boys thought she was pretty, but nobody liked her. You could tell by the way she walked that she thought she was God's gift to Oakville Senior Elementary.

He slipped back the bolt on the back door and stepped out into the night. For mid-August it was surprisingly cool. Damp too. He shivered. For a second he was tempted to go back into the house; he could snitch some of his mother's carrots from the fridge and use them as 'proof' of the success of his mission. But no, his buddies hadn't chickened out.

A vector is a line representing a physical quantity that has magnitude and direction in space. Three vectors. Call them: L; S; T. Three converging vectors. L is an unknown quantity. S and T are of relatively small magnitude, but will grow. Between some of the vectors there is an attraction; between others, repulsion. Place U at the point of conversion, for the sake of observation. Like an immutable constant. Now of course you must first go there to be there.

You must of course enter
softly . like a slug
trailing your slime of humanity
over the patio stones.

Cross the lawn, wading in its ooze of silence,
creep past the primroses melting in the moonlight
and stealthily invade the vegetable patch.

Crouch down by the compost . (warming to its own decay)

and don't let the slow . heavy . breathing
disturb you;
it is only the rhubarb exuding night
and those are not fingers . rising from dirt—
merely asparagus tips.

.

Lester was thinking about the way his father was treating him since they'd let him return home, when a car passed on the street. A cop car.

.

And it was pulling over to the curb further along Greenview. Lester felt his heart jump in his chest.

.

Without changing his pace he casually turned up the next driveway. He could remember only too clearly his last encounter with the police: the name calling, the threats, the looks of contempt and disgust, the graphic descriptions of what happened to 'his kind' in prison. Thank God he'd never had to go to a real prison!

.

Of course he wasn't doing anything wrong. There was nothing illegal about going for a walk. But it was late and he knew they'd run a routine check on him. And then...

.

He reached the garage and quickly ducked into the shadows. His best chance would be to get a few houses away and hide somewhere, maybe under one of the decks that extended out from so many of the house in Oakville, till he was sure the cops were gone.

.

There was no moon, and the backyard was considerably darker than the street. He peered into the capacious blackness. The yard wasn't fenced, nor was the next one or the next. He began to run back the direction he'd come.

.

Suddenly his foot caught on something and he sprawled onto his face. The grass was wet with dew; it felt slimy. His left hand had squished something—probably a worm. He wiped it off on his trousers.

.

He lay still listening, the dew soaking through his clothes. Everything was quiet. He got to his feet and proceeded at a slower pace. He came to a yard that was fenced, and just beyond the chain-link barrier stood a large, aluminum shed. A perfect hiding place.

It was only as he began to vault the fence that it occurred to him to wonder why this yard and only this yard was fenced. As he went over the fence a large, vicious German Shepherd leaped in his mind.

He landed in soft earth, in the answer to his question: a garden. Of course. The family had a backyard garden, and the fence was to protect it from stray dogs and kids. The owner of this property was a gardener. Almost half of the yard was devoted to orderly rows of plants. He could smell that special lush and slightly acrid aroma of tomato plants. In fact the air was heavily laden with both strange and familiar smells, rich vegetable smells. There was what could almost be called a texture to the air, a richness like heavy brocade. It reminded him of something he couldn't quite put his finger on, something so natural it seemed unnatural. Something rotten. Something so thick and fecund and moist, he could actually taste it. A musty and rank taste, but with something most definitely pleasant about it, something, well, sensual.

Lester felt a funny stirring in his gut. Suddenly he felt like he had to piss. Or no, not so much that he had to piss, for there was no pressure, but more like that he—well—wanted to. Like it was the right thing to do. And he also felt frightened, strangely, inexplicably afraid—more so than when he'd seen the cop car.

He shook like a wet dog to drive back these odd emotions and turned toward the shed doors. They were the sliding type and there were two holes drilled in their handles for the insertion of a padlock—but there was no padlock. He slid them open as quietly as he could, stepped into the blackness of the shed, turned around, and was about to slide the doors shut behind him, when he saw the screen door at the back of the house swing open.

Susan stood outside the back door, peering into the dark. The robe she wore over her pyjamas offered little protection from the cool, damp air. She got goose bumps and her nipples became erect. Suddenly the whole idea did indeed seem stupid. The problem was Karen, who was no doubt watching out their bedroom window; there was no way to save face now except to go out into the yard where her sister could see her.

But it was silly to just walk out into the middle of the yard and then turn around and flee back into the house. She had to do something, make some sort of gesture of bravado. Otherwise it would look like she was chickening out.

.

Ah, she had it! Her father kept a small cache of Penthouse magazines hidden in the shed behind his peat pots. She and Karen had discovered them last month. She'd go into the shed and steal one of the magazines to show Karen. Her sister would think it funny, for she'd sure laughed a lot when they'd browsed through them last time. Yes, that would be the perfect gesture: just a bit naughty—and yet quick and easy.

.

Susan set out across the lawn. The wet grass quickly soaked her slippers and made her wish she'd never had this crazy idea. It was spooky out. It felt like there were strange things creeping about in the darkness.

.

When she reached the border of the garden, she turned and looked up at her bedroom window. It was impossible to tell if Karen was up there watching, but surely her sister wouldn't have really just gone back to sleep.

.

.

Tom jogged along toward the Henderson's. To control the fear that was knotting his stomach, he imagined himself a cat burglar. He'd read about them in one's of his Dad's magazines. They were real professionals—unlike the dummies who held up liquor stores and that sort of thing. You had to have nerve and strength and co-ordination to be a cat burglar. There was also something really weird in that article: it said that cat burglars often left something to show their contempt for their victims. They, ha!, often took a crap right in the middle of the floor. Geez, it'd be a laugh to leave a pile in old man Henderson's precious garden. They say it's good for the garden. Ha!

.

But he knew he didn't have the guts to do it. What if he got caught with his pants down? It's one thing to get caught stealing a few carrots, quite another to get caught crapping on your neighbour's vegetables. But it sure would be the perfect gesture to express his feelings toward snooty Susan Henderson and her family. Maybe he'd tell the fellas he'd done it. There'd be no way for them to ever know if he was lying.

.

As Tom approached the Henderson yard, he tried to make his movements sleek and confident. But his stomach still hurt. He reached their fence.

.

.

Susan entered the garden. The shed was in the back corner. The shed doors were open—which was odd. Her Dad had a fit if anybody left the doors open. About ten feet from the shed she stopped. The inside of the shed was like a giant, black maw. And there was something a little lighter, floating right in the middle of the dark maw. Like a tongue.

.

She stared. Like a tongue? Or like a shirt. Like a light coloured shirt. A man's shirt. As she stared it began to look more and more like there was a man standing there in the darkness, a man wearing a light shirt and dark trousers. A man standing, waiting. It was impossible, she knew, totally impossible. Her eyes were playing tricks on her. She was just getting spooked. Still she felt a tremendous urge to turn and run.

.

But Karen! Karen was up in their bedroom window watching. And would she ever laugh if she saw her little sister turn tail and run. But Geez, it sure did look like a man standing there in the darkness, perfectly motionless, facing her, surely staring right at her.

.

Then she heard a noise: the chain link on the fence at the other side of the yard rattling. She turned in time to see a small figure vaulting up, onto and over the fence. A boy. Apparently he didn't see her, for now he was walking confidently down the rows of vegetables. Then he crouched by the carrots. It was one of the neighbourhood brats, maybe the same kid who had let the air out of their tires the other night. By his size she judged him to be even younger than she was. The little jerk was going to steal their carrots!

.

She looked back at the shed. The light spot seemed to have disappeared. Of course it had just been a trick of the light. There wasn't anyone in the shed. What would anybody be doing in their shed? It'd just been an optical illusion.

.

But there was someone in the carrot patch. That was no illusion. Now he was creeping down the rows bent over as if he were inspecting them.

.

Susan made a decision: she wasn't going to let anybody steal from her father. The neighbourhood was full of the most incredibly bratty boys, and she'd make sure that at least one of them would learn a lesson about the Henderson family. She'd get a rake or something from the shed and go scare the living b'jesus out of the little thief. Susan took a deep breath and started toward the shed.

.

.

You must of course enter
softly . like a slug
trailing your slime of humanity
over the patio stones.

.

Cross the lawn, wading in its ooze of silence,
creep past the primroses melting in the moonlight
and stealthily invade the vegetable patch.

.

Crouch down by the compost . (warming to its own decay)
and don't let the slow . heavy . breathing
disturb you;
it is only the rhubarb exuding night
and those are not fingers . rising from dirt—
merely asparagus tips.

.

Spend the night;
you are there to enjoy growth.

.

However . if you are extremely lucky
you might also glimpse
innocence:

> *a boy*
> *stealing carrots*
> *a girl watching*
> *both gloriously unaware*
> *of the omnivorous nature of earth.*

.

.

"Daddy, wake up! Wake up!"

.

Frank Henderson propped himself up on his elbow and tried to bring his older daughter's face into focus. "Good Lord, Karen, what's the matter?"

.

"There's a man in the shed and ..."

.

"What?"

.

"A man! There's a man in the shed. And Susan's out there!"

.

"Out where?"

.

"Out in the yard. Susan's out in the yard!"

.

"You had a bad dream, honey, just..."

.

"I wasn't asleep, really! Please listen! Susan wanted us to sneak out into the backyard cuz it'd be scary but I wouldn't go so she went by herself. I watched out the window and saw a man go into our shed. And then I saw Susan come out and start walking toward the shed. I saw her! Daddy, really!"

.

Frank Henderson was an orderly man. Some might even say compulsive. Some would even say, wrongly, paranoid. He was just cautious. He had a fenced yard. He had an expensive alarm system on his house. He had a deep, perhaps overly protective, love for his two daughters. He had a handgun locked in the drawer of his bedside table.

.

.

Lester stared in disbelief as the girl once again started toward the shed. She had long blonde hair that shone in the starlight. She walked with the innocent grace that he'd always admired in girls her age. She seemed to be very, very pretty. She was coming to him. She was wearing a bathrobe; she had come from her bed. Why was she coming to him?

.

He imagined he could already smell her fresh soapy scent penetrating the dank atmosphere of the shed. She was walking boldly toward him now. She'd hesitated when she first saw him, but now she was coming to him confidently, without fear. It was like a dream.

.

But it was wrong. Wrong! He knew it was wrong. It was hard to understand how such cleanliness, such innocence, such wholesomeness could be wrong. But he knew it was.

.

"I want you, too" he whispered loudly as she approached the

threshold. "But no, please no! No!"

.

Then she was screaming. Why was she screaming?

.

He brushed against her as he staggered outside. She smelled sweaty.

.

A parallelism: on opposite sides of the garden two figures at the encircling fence. On each side, a leg rising to the aluminum rail. Both figures male. Both figures going up, over. Two vectors moving in exactly opposite directions into the compressing night—or one vector with two heads. Another vector moving perpendicular to the movement of the double-headed vector. Ahead of this third vector, cutting the way, a jagged scream like a lightning bolt. And a point: you. In the middle, watching.

.

A vector becoming a girl becoming a part of her father's arms becoming a sobbing, a whimpering. Becoming at last a silence.

.

Silence. A suburban silence. No gunshot. (Thank God!) No more screaming. If any sound, just that of breathing, heavy breathing. Silence and breathing. And the sound of the good earth waiting. (With you.) In the experienced dark.

~~~~

A CONFIDENT MAN NEEDS FAITH

"All you need is ignorance and confidence and the success is sure."
—Mark Twain

In my case it might be the other way around.

.

She had the long, dark, silky hair that graces so many Asian women. Were I the poet I once wanted to be (instead of a so-called 'public servant' shuffling papers when not defacing them with bureaucratese prose), I would be able to compare her lovely mane to something that would express its incredible sensuousness—but whatever poetry I ever had in my soul atrophied while I made a living scribbling out Ecological Impact Reports for a government that couldn't care less about the ecology.

.

And if her perfect hair wasn't enough to make a man crazy, she was slim and willowy as a reed, with delicate facial features and perfect skin. And then, most importantly to me, she also had the penetrating intelligence that I, despite the political incorrectness of it, also associate with women from the Far East. She rarely spoke in class, but when she did it was always to ask a surprisingly perceptive question that hadn't crossed anyone else's mind. It was this last characteristic that pushed me over the edge from banal lust to exquisite longing. I always found a seat in the lecture hall from where I could discreetly ogle her.

"Go on, ask her!" Scott's face was boyishly eager, despite the fact he was pushing forty and most times looked it—at least it.

"She's with friends," I said.

"Makes it easier. Ask them all to join us."

I glanced over at her table. She had a mug of beer in front of her—which seemed somehow inappropriate for such an exquisite creature. She was sitting with three other young women, none of whom was particularly attractive. I had to wonder once again about Scott's motives. I'd known him for close to a decade, and in all that time, only once had I seen him make what could be called 'a pass' at a woman. He was married, so one might think this a sign of an honourable nature or of a deep respect and love for his wife, but, frankly, I know that's not it. Enough dinners at his place have made it obvious to me that his marriage is of the typically tepid, suburban sort. He likes his wife probably more than most married men I know, but it is still a lukewarm affection—nothing more or deeper. And with all due respect to Scott, I don't think he'd pass on the chance to cheat on his wife were the opportunity to avail itself to him—which it never seemed to do. Sad to say, I'm sure his fidelity has more to do with shyness and cowardice than any higher motive.

"C'mon," Scott moaned. "Why are you suddenly so shy? You've told me she really turns you on." Scott had an occasional nervous, barely perceptible, twitch in his left eye whenever he got excited. I tried not to look at it.

If I did invite Li-Ming and her friends to join us, Scott wouldn't start flirting with her or try charming her. He'd want me to do that, while he just sat there quiet and deferential. He's confessed to me several times that he lives vicariously. I'm sure that is one of the cornerstones of our friendship. If I were to suddenly stop 'sharing' my sexual experiences with him over a few pints at The Lion's Den, I fear it might so weaken the foundation of our friendship that the modest edifice would collapse.

Yes, I kiss and tell. But only to Scott, for I totally trust him never to pass on anything I say to anyone else. Again, this is not as much to his credit as it may seem at first glance. No, his lips aren't sealed by integrity: it is simply that he treasures my experiences too much to pass them around. Vicarious Scott, hoarding his second-hand 'memories'—like those people who collect yellowed photographs and daguerreotypes of total strangers and hang them on their walls.

.

Being prone to probe for motives, I have thought not just about other people's, but also given a lot of consideration to my own. I'm forty-one years old, and it is very adolescent to brag about one's 'conquests.' But that is not what I'm doing when I talk to Scott about the women that come and go in my life. I never think of my sexual experiences as 'conquests', and I'm not a braggart. Were I as sleazy as all that, I would want him to blab to others, spreading my reputation—or I would do so myself. And I'm not married, so I've no fearful reason to keep my mouth shut; and, at least in the case of some of the women I've known, it wouldn't matter a whit to them if I spoke of my relationship with them. A few, at least, I strongly suspect would even like it. A surprising number of women have an exhibitionistic streak in them: I've been taken aback many times by a woman's desire to make love in public places, to blow me on public transport or fuck me on the grass in a park. (Or—to my way of thinking—the far worse desire to recount the intimate details of their previous relationships.) But even if I am a male slut, I'm the paragon of discretion—with the one exception of private, beery conversations with my buddy, Scott, who might as well be an encrypted personal diary.

.

So what motive do I find in myself for my candour and volubility with Scott? It sounds like a rationalization, but I honestly believe it is largely just a desire to share. I'm not pretending to some high-minded generosity toward my shy friend with a dull sex life. No, I don't 'share' out of any altruistic motive, but rather, more selfishly, because sharing increases one's own pleasure in anything. Sunsets are lovelier, the aesthetic experience deeper, if you watch them with someone else—even if that someone else is a mere acquaintance. Or perhaps a more apt comparison is how we all try to get other people to read a book we really liked. It isn't that you want to make these other folk happier, or enrich their lives, so much as it is that if they in the end are equally enthusiastic about the book, it somehow mysteriously increases your own pleasure in it. But, no, that's probably a flawed comparison: I'm not encouraging him to have sex with the same women I've enjoyed. Oh, I just don't know.

.

Maybe talking about something adds to the reality of it, more firmly embeds it in memory. Wake up and tell your dream to someone—or else it will fade forever. I like my memories—most of them, most of the time.

.

And then there is my need to understand my experiences, which seems only possible in the expression of them. I'm a 'verbal thinker'.

.

.

"What are you thinking about?" Annoyance was creeping into his voice. Scott really was determined to have me invite Li-Ming to our table. His eye-twitch was becoming more noticeable. "C'mon, exercise your charm!"

I smiled and stood up. Frankly, I was ashamed of myself for not having made a move sooner. I'm usually more confident and assertive.

.

.

The next week Li-Ming wasn't in class. It was the first time she'd missed class. It made me realize how much her presence contributed to my conscientious attendance. The Prof had her good days (nights actually, it being an evening class) and her bad ones, but not a strong enough ratio of good-to-bad to keep me coming even when I had a cold. Scott and I were both auditing the course, and auditors are notorious for casual attendance. We were both getting points at work for just auditing the course; we didn't have to produce any grades or records of attendance.

.

During break, Scott expressed his dismay with Li-Ming's absence: "It's like they've turned down the dimmer switch this week. She lights up that class."

.

"Maybe she's staying home to nurse her professor." The night at the bar when I had successfully lured Li-Ming and her friends to our table, she had mentioned that she was living with a History Prof at the school who was down with the flu. She only graced our company for half an hour before she said she felt she had to go home and check on him. (Her friends, however, sat with us until closing time.)

.

"Horrible thought," Scott replied. "Do you know the guy?"

.

"Yeah, but just to recognize in the hall."

.

"What does he look like?"

"Like he'd be prone to catching the flu."

"Ha! Sickly looking fellow? Another one of those inexplicable pairings—beautiful woman hooked up with a nerd."

"I was just being a smart ass. He's a rather ordinary looking guy, kinda skinny maybe, probably closer to our age than hers. I've heard, though, that he's a brilliant teacher."

"So she loves him for his mind?"

I took a sip of my coffee instead of responding.

"You going to make a move on her?"

"Scott, give me a break. She's with some other guy."

"Like that's stopped you before!"

"Bad judgement on my part. Or they made the first move, not me."

"Not always," he said, smirking.

"Scott, can I ask you something?"

"Sure."

"Why does it matter to you?"

"I wanna see my buddy happy."

"She's beautiful and desirable, but it wouldn't make me happy."

"Oh, c'mon! Why not?"

"I'm think I'm losing faith."

"I don't understand. What do you mean? You losing that famous self-confidence of yours?"

"No, actually that's the problem."

"I still don't understand."

"I don't either."

When I'd gone over to Li-Ming's table that night, I knew she'd agree to join us. There wasn't the faintest shadow of doubt in my mind. This was reflexive. My confidence is reflexive. I'm a confident man— a conman.

One time the government sent me to this Eco-Conference in B.C. Most of the people there were dull as dishwater, tree-huggers with leaves in their hair, wearing faded khakis. But I hooked up with this one crazy fellow from Ireland. He was a good-looking, muscular guy—boisterous and a drinker. His name was Liam, and he had that much spoken of—but in my experience rarely encountered—Irish charm. I'm sure Scott would've admiringly pegged him as a 'lady-killer'.

We both skipped a seminar on "Alternatives To Clear-Cutting" and went wandering around downtown Vancouver. We found this seedy tourist shop and both bought t-shirts inscribed "Join The Army, Travel to Exotic Places, Meet New And Interesting People—And Kill Them." Our plan was to wear the t-shirts to the windup dinner and dance—and offend all the puckered assholes we'd had to put up with at the conference. The plan was probably ill-conceived because, despite the constipation of the conference attendees, most would probably be sympathetic to anything making fun of the 'military-industrial complex'.

The conference was at the University of British Columbia, so after our foray into downtown, we went back to campus and searched out a student pub to toss back a few brew before the scheduled evening social. The place was almost empty, probably because it was summer break, so this one young woman sitting alone in the far corner was very conspicuous. I thought her only moderately attractive, and that more because of her youth than her features, but Liam honed in on her.

"What a dish," he said, ogling her rather obviously. "We should invite her to the wine and cheese tonight."

"Sure," I said. "Go for it."

.

Then, to my surprise, he showed the same reticence I associated with Scott. "I can't just go up to her and ask her to be our date at a conference do!"

.

My friend Scott is not homely; he is just the kind of guy that no one notices, who could attend a party and afterwards no one could say for certain he'd been there. But my new acquaintance Liam was downright handsome, rather larger than life, robust and full of piss and vinegar, so I was startled by his response.

.

"You don't strike me as the shy guy sort," I said, laughing.

.

"Okay, wise guy, you go pick her up."

.

"Sure," I said. I went over and politely asked her if she'd like to join two lonely out-of-towners for a drink. She agreed.

.

After sitting with us for twenty minutes, she'd also agreed to be our guest at the conference wine and cheese reception that evening.

.

Walking back to our rooms at the UBC dorm, I told Liam I hoped he 'got lucky' tonight.

.

"Me too," he said. "You're a pretty smooth operator. What's your secret? You ain't that good looking." He grinned.

.

True enough: I'm not. Not ugly, okay, but I'm no Brad Pitt. Sometimes when I shave, I think to myself: "Hey you're not a bad looking guy." But other times I see snapshots of myself that aren't flattering and feel like tearing them up. So it sort of balances out. I don't really think about my looks that much.

.

"My 'secret', pal, is no secret." I said. "It's just confidence. No matter what the polls in women's magazines say, it ain't your buns or your social status or your sense of humour. It's confidence. I think women can smell it, some kind of pheromone."

.

He stopped walking. We were standing under a huge pine, and the sky was threatening with dark cumulus clouds. "So from where the confidence?"

.

"Dunno. I guess it came about gradually. Just lucked out the first few times and then it just started building on itself. Never been turned down."

"Never been turned down!? I'm sure even Richard Gere has been turned down. Gimme a break."

"Really. It's the truth," I said.

"Selective asking?"

"Perhaps. I don't know. I know I can tell when there's chemistry. But it's not like I only come on to lonely or homely women. But now I've just come to expect acquiescence."

"Acquiescence! Nice word! So now you feel you can just go up to any woman and ask her to fuck and she'll spread her legs. And she does?"

"You're being crude. I didn't say that. It's just never happened that I've had my advances rejected—and a lot of women come on to me." Thunder rumbled in the distance.

"Bloody sweet life you've lived! Must be nice! Does this apply to married women and girls half your age and all those stuck-up lovelies that hang around upscale bars teasing horny men?"

"Yeah, I guess it does."

"Must feel good."

"Less so as time goes on," I said as the first drops started falling. We jogged back to the dorm.

.

I haven't mentioned Li-Ming's legs, have I? She was back in class the week following her absence, and for the first time she wore a skirt, a short skirt. I just knew her legs would be beautiful, but even my imaginings paled by comparison to the real slopes and curves of her lovely lower limbs. The woman was physical perfection, an oriental Aphrodite.

The girl from the bar did come to the Eco-conference's wine and cheese reception, and what happened was not to my credit. Liam seemed revitalized, and made a concerted effort to get her to go back to our residence with him, tossing his very masculine Celtic charm around with such abandon that I noticed several other women eyeing him. He should've noticed and changed his focus, for our guest was clearly not taken with him. Nevertheless, I left them alone, hoping Liam would win her over, and just wandered around being superficially sociable.

.

It was getting late and things winding down, when Liam wandered off to the restroom—and the girl approached me.

.

"I have to go soon," she said. "Where are you staying?"

.

"They put us up in the grad student's residence."

.

"What's your room number?"

.

I looked at her, into her eyes. It was there. Again. It didn't feel right, but I gave her my room number. And immediately felt crummy for doing so.

.

She split before Liam got back.

.

"Where'd she go?" he asked.

.

"Home. Said she had an early class."

.

"That sucks," he said.

.

We left shortly thereafter.

.

The next morning, sometime before eight, I heard a knock at my door. I let her in, but then I let her down. Her offers were explicit and tempting. She told me about things she liked her boyfriend to do to her. As she unbuttoned her blouse, she talked dirty in the way I suppose they do on those pay-per-minute sex-lines, while I just sat on the edge of the dorm bed in my jockey shorts, getting hard and trying not to notice it. Maybe it was the early hour and my slight hangover or maybe it was because she looked so goddamn young and innocent despite the far-from-innocent words that were tumbling from her mouth or maybe it was that I felt doing anything would be a betrayal of my new friendship with Liam. Whatever the reason, I sent her on her way after telling her that her breasts were beautiful, but she should put her blouse back on, for I had another relationship going and couldn't be unfaithful. The latter statement was a lie, but she really did have nice breasts.

.

Unfaithful. Loss of faith. Not loss of faith in myself. Loss of faith in women.

.

.

I haven't turned down amorous offers often. Why should I? I sincerely like women, their nature, not just their bodies. And, god knows, I like making love. I believe I always behave like a gentleman.

.

I definitely haven't been short-changed by The Fates regarding opportunities. So what happened with Li-Ming was deeply disturbing. She was Chinese. Appropriately I think it is a Chinese curse: "May all your desires be fulfilled."

.

When she returned to class, Li-Ming started having coffee with Scott and me at break. Ever since that first time she came to class in a skirt, I knew what was going to happen. Now, for some reason she was almost always wearing a skirt to class. So during these brief mid-class coffee breaks I was so distracted I could hardly carry on a coherent conversation with her. I tried to sit where I couldn't see her legs. Scott, of course, was no help. He just sat there with a glazed look in his eyes—the poor deer caught in headlights.

.

But as the term progressed, our coffee breaks with Li-Ming became more comfortable. She was a great conversationalist, knowledgeable about the most esoteric things, but never pompous or pretentious. And she had that knack some people have of asking questions about you that don't seem prying, but nevertheless are very personal—and make you feel important. In short, she was as graceful socially as she was physically. I began to want her like I haven't wanted anyone since I was a teenager caught in a hormonal hurricane. It wasn't just her legs that were special.

.

The only problem was that she would frequently make casual reference to Fred, the Prof she was living with. And they were always affectionate remarks or references to something he'd said that was relevant to what we were discussing. I've learned over the years that women who are coming on to me almost never refer to their husbands or boyfriends—except in less than favourable terms. (To their credit, women on the prowl are less inclined than men to play the my-spouse-doesn't-understand-me tune, but anyone who keeps affectionately talking about their lover or husband usually isn't sending out availability signals.)

Yet somehow at the same time I was getting the definite feeling that she was attracted to me, and I knew that although I was being extremely proper, she could tell I was attracted to her. I can sense these things. I don't think I've ever been wrong. Certainly, whenever I tested my intuition, it's been confirmed.

"You're doing it again, you bugger," Scott said as we walked out to the car after the penultimate class of the term. "She's hot for you."

"She's obviously in love with her Prof-boyfriend. She's just being friendly with us."

"Are you getting old and stupid, my friend? I can see the way she looks at you. I don't know how you do it, but you're doing it again. I can't understand what you're waiting for. She's even more gorgeous than Suzanne."

Languid-limbed Suzanne of the sky-blue eyes was indeed gorgeous and Scott was right about one thing: Li-Ming amazingly made my former darling Suzanne seem almost ordinary by comparison.

"C'mon," Scott said in his what's-with-you voice, "Are you really going to let this opportunity pass? What is it? Have you just discovered you like little boys?"

I gently punched Scott in the shoulder. "You're a good liberal," I said. "You should have at least one friend who is sexually deviant. And don't knock little boys until you try them."

Last class and Scott wasn't there: he was in hospital. The poor bastard's appendix had exploded. They got him to emergency in time, but he was in pretty rough shape.

So at break for the final class I was alone at the cafeteria table with Li-Ming.

"I've enjoyed the class," she said. "Almost feel sorry it is over."

"Yeah, it was good. She's a great lecturer."

"Would you like to go out for drink afterwards? You're not a regular student, and I might not ever see you again."

"Sure," I said, my voice as calm as my heart was not.

"So," Scott said, lighting a Galois cigarette. "You have to tell me the details. I know from Jimmy, who saw you two there, that you went to Winslow's after the last class."

The bar was exceptionally crowded and noisy and smoky. "Should you be smoking that thing after being so sick?" I asked.

"Stop avoiding the question. What happened?" Grinning, he blew smoke in my face.

"Damn it, Scott," I said. "Maybe just this once I don't want to talk about it."

I don't think I ever saw such unadulterated glee on his face. His eyes became saucers. His grin threatened to crack his face wide open. "She turned you down," he said, such unsavoury satisfaction in his voice that I wanted to shove the stinky French cigarette down his throat.

"I wish," I replied. And watched his face collapse into confusion.

Li-Ming and I had gone to Winslow's Pub & Eatery after class. We'd stayed for about an hour, talking about the class, then about my cushy but boring government job as a so-called "ecological consultant", then about her plans to become a biologist. We almost had to shout, because they had a bad bar band that was trying to compensate for their lack of musical quality with quantity—of decibels. The one good thing about the situation was how close we had to be to hear each other.

"Let's go back to my place," she said suddenly. "It's a lot quieter and cosier, and I could put on some good music at a reasonable volume."

I was by this time incapable of anything but acquiescence. She could have suggested we drive my car into a brick wall at a hundred miles an hour, and I would've nodded agreement.

.

Fred and Li-Ming's apartment was surprisingly devoid of books. Most academics keep a few books around, if just for show. It was also small and almost Spartan. The furniture was undefined Moderne.

.

Li-Ming told me to have a seat on the sofa and went off to the kitchen, returning in short order with a bottle of Burgundy and two glasses. (We'd been both drinking beer at Winslow's.)

.

"Where's your boyfriend?" I asked bluntly as she filled our glasses.

.

"He's in New York. Some conference." She sat down next to me and looked into my eyes very intensely.

.

.

I've never understood love. Oh many a time I've thought I just might be in love, but always afterwards I realized it was just lust or infatuation or affection. I've seen love, grew up with it. I know my parents loved each other. They got to celebrate 51 years together before they both suddenly became ill. But how they found this thing I don't really understand called love—or rather how they cultivated their initial infatuation and lust and affection into the thing called love. That I do not understand.

.

One thing I think I do know is that they trusted each other completely, and I find it impossible to imagine that trust was ever betrayed. Maybe I'm wrong: children don't really see their parents as anything but wallpaper until often it is too late. But, nevertheless, I find it impossible to conceive of my mother betraying my father. Perhaps I could see my Dad falling victim to a one-night temptation on one of his numerous convention trips. It seems unlikely, but it is at least conceivable. But my mother ever having been unfaithful is totally inconceivable. How many kids say it? My mother was a saint! Well, damn it, my mother was. If you can't trust a saint, who can you trust?

.

So here I am at forty-one, looking for a saintly woman, looking for a woman to refine in the fiery forge of time my lust and affection and infatuation into a tempered-steel sword of love. I've had more than enough sex with more than enough women. I'm ready for love.

.

I'm blessed, Scott would say. Women lie down for me if only I ask. Often I don't even have to ask. Young women. Beautiful women. Married women. It sometimes seems almost any woman I want. What a blessing! But what does it make me think of women? Would a confident man, a confidence man, like myself, have been able to con my mother into his bed? I don't want to think about that. I have developed this strange need, the strangest sexual need of all: I need to be refused.

.

.

Li-Ming and I both took a sip from our wine glasses and then put them down on the coffee table. I put my hand up, palm toward her. She pressed her hand against mine, her palm warm and just slightly damp. Then she stood up and walked into the bedroom. I followed. We made love in her and Fred's, The History Prof's, bed. It was exquisite. We lay in each other's arms for a while and then we did it again. I went home at four in the morning, although she wanted me to stay. I had to be alone to think.

.

.

I'm not exactly sure why, but I don't see much of Scott anymore except at work. We went out once just after he got out of the hospital, but when I wouldn't talk about Li-Ming, he became distant. So we haven't been out for a drink together for several months.

.

Li-Ming has broken it off with Fred and moved in with me. We make love every night; and her beauty, her mind, her grace still takes my breath away.

.

But I'm still needy.

.

The other day I happened to see her chatting with this guy on the street. He had this confident air about him I didn't much like.

.

A man's got to have faith. Unfortunately, I think I've lost it.

~~~~

RECLAMATION BY THE SEA

"for whatever we lose (like a you or a me)
it's always ourselves we find in the sea"
          —e.e. cummings ("maggie and milly and molly and may")

It was after the big earthquake of Jan '94 that I moved in with my brother Rob and his wife Denise. Even at the time I suspected it wasn't going to be a good experience, but I was one very desperate woman. The local emergency shelters were packed, and I couldn't very well sleep in the park like some bag lady. It doesn't make me nervous at all to sleep out in the bush (I've done that since I was a kid), but L.A. parks are prowled by far, far more dangerous animals than one finds in the deep woods.

That quake really rattled me (no silly pun intended). Perhaps because I come from cosy little Bell Haven in Northern Michigan, I didn't handle it as equably as the California natives. Bell Haven is indeed a haven—a haven from Mother Nature's nasty side. We don't have earthquakes, tornadoes, hurricanes, flash floods, brush fires, mud slides. We do have snowstorms, admittedly, and it can get damn cold, but winter weather doesn't wreck buildings and nobody dies from it, except old fools with bad tickers who are too cheap to hire someone to shovel their driveways. Hell, we don't even have any dangerous animals. Even our bears out back in the woods, being timid black bears, almost never bother anybody. Nor do we have human-nature disasters—no race riots, gang wars, muggers, serial killers or mass murders. No madmen with Uzis walking into MacDonald's and killing everyone in sight. Hell, Bell Haven is so small it doesn't even have a MacDonald's! That is small. The last big news crime I can remember was some high school kid who held up Safe Haven Quik Mart with a baseball bat. But I'm getting silly and sentimental about home, sweet home. One other thing Bell Haven doesn't have, and Los Angeles does, is employment opportunities.

.

And the ocean. The ocean. Which is the real reason I'm here in LaLa Land. I've been attracted to the sea since I was a kid. Some primitive instinct, I guess. I once read a book by some radical evolutionary theorist who maintained we didn't climb down from the trees, but, instead, crawled out of the ocean. It was probably nonsense, but even conventional science admits life originally began in the primordial sea. I believe that somewhere down deep we remember this, our original home, our original evolutionary womb. I think it's called an archetypal memory. I know that it was when, at age eleven, my folks packed us kids into the old VW camper and drove us to California for a special extended vacation, and I first swam in the ocean, that I felt like I had come home, felt I was in my natural element for the first time in my life. It was nothing at all like swimming in Trout Lake back home. Swimming in fresh water is work. Swimming in the ocean is effortless: the water does not struggle with you, it supports you, it caresses you. It's sexy. And afterwards, aptly, your skin is salty.

.

Since I moved here, I've spent as much time as I could at the seashore and it makes me very happy. But in every other way the City of Angels is a land of fallen angels, a hell on earth. Except for its proximity to the ocean, L.A. has nothing to recommend it, and except when I'm being pacific in the Pacific, I am profoundly homesick. I hate the traffic snarl, the choking pollution, the endless sprawl of 'ranch' houses, the loonies. Especially the loonies. There just has to be more nut cases per capita here than anywhere else in the world. Perhaps crazy people are more in touch with their evolutionary past, and that is why they are drawn to the coast. (Yes, I'm quite aware what this implies about me.) Perhaps it is the cumulative effect of all these crazy people dancing the St. Vitus on the tottering edge of the North American land mass that causes the tectonic plates to shift, that causes the earth to open up and try to swallow them.

.

Yes, another problem with living at the edge (of sea and land, of sanity) is the lack of stability inherent in such places. It makes sense on many levels that the earth opens up where the sea presses against it.

.

.

It was five a.m. when the quake hit. Everyone says the timing was fortunate, for had it occurred during the daylight hours, there would've been many more casualties. Probably true, but waking up from a deep sleep to find your books falling off shelves, your fridge moving across the linoleum like some strange blocky animal, your bed shaking like a scene from The Exorcist—is, well, extremely unsettling. (Oh, here I go again unintentionally punning, but 'unsettling' really is the precise word.)

What do I, a naïf from the north woods, know about earthquakes? I know to bundle up if I'm going out in a snowstorm, but I didn't even have the sense to realise my bed in a third floor apartment was not the best place to be during an earthquake. I just pulled the covers up over my head and waited for California (and me) to fall into the sea. If Juan, my landlord, hadn't come pounding on my door, telling me to get my "pretty little ass" out of the building, I'd probably have spent the whole day like that, waiting for the—to my mind— inevitable final end, each aftershock pushing me closer to clinical shock.

.

Well, it turned out that my apartment building was one of many promptly deemed unsafe for human habitation. We didn't need the official inspection: the massive crack in the foundation was a dead give-away. (You could fit your fingers in it—if you were so inclined.) So I called my dear brother, Rob.

.

After the "You okay?" "Yes, you?" "You sure?" routine, I asked about his house, my ulterior motive transparent as glass.

.

"No damage at all, thank God! I'm so broke, I couldn't even afford to call a plumber if a pipe burst." (Rob had moved west several years before me and was now a 'home-owner', which in L.A. means tenant on a property owned by a bank.)

.

"How'd your building hold up?" Rob asked.

.

"Not so good."

.

The offer to shelter his little sister came, as I'd hoped, immediately. I offered to pay rent. He graciously refused.

Rob's house is a very small, two bedroom bungalow. Pink stucco. Cactus shrubbery. Very working-class Californian. He and Denise don't have any children, so he uses the one spare bedroom for a 'study'. As far as I can tell Rob doesn't study anything in it, any more than he ever studied anything back at Jamieson High, but the room is furnished with a huge desk on which sits a super-charged computer: the latest Pentium processor with a god knows how many meg video card and all kinds of other multi-media cards, including some super sound card. I envied him the system, but I was more than a few paycheques away from getting one myself. My brother and I are very different and really have only ever had two common interests: computers and camping. However, he seems to have lost interest in the latter since moving out here, just as I've lost some interest in computers since my last relationship with a computer nerd. But Rob seems to have lost interest in everything since he moved out here— since he married dear Denise.

Anyway, I got the so-called study. They didn't have a spare cot, but that didn't matter. I like a firm bed, and you can't find a much firmer bed than a sleeping bag on hardwood floors.

The first night there was a blur. I'd sweet-talked my landlord, who fancies himself a Latin lover and is always coming on to me, into lending me his pickup. I didn't think I had a lot of stuff, but it took two loads to get my personal possessions moved to Rob's. (Most of it went into the backyard shed, including my humble computer.) I left my pathetic furniture behind, hoping the building would collapse on it and I'd get some insurance money. Driving in L.A. is always a bad dream; after the quake it was a full-blown nightmare. The Santa Monica was closed, and twelve miles on L.A. side streets, as clogged as a fat old man's arteries, is a journey through hell. So that first night I crawled into my sleeping bag and passed out by nine.

It was the second night when I realised I had made a bad move. I'd gone back to work. My company wasn't fazed by the earthquake any more than a Bell Haven company would be daunted by a bad snowstorm. So just one day after it going past six on the Richter, it was business as usual. I arrived home about six-thirty. Rob was in his study, my temporary home, updating his computer games database. He collected pirated computer games like he used to collect baseball cards. He asked if I minded if he finished what he was doing before he gave me "my room" back.

.

"Of course not."

.

"Denise is out. We'll have to have TV dinners. Okay?"

.

"I'll turn on the oven," I said.

.

"Microwave."

.

"Oh, then I'll wait till you're done."

.

I went into the living room. It was a mess. There were at least a dozen empty beer cans lying about. Ashtrays full to overflowing. A pile of dirty laundry on one of the chairs, undergarments on top. (My god, Denise wore panties with the days of the week embroidered on them!) The carpet was stained in several places and fuzzy with dog hair. My brother, like me, has always been obsessively neat, so the first time I visited his new home in L.A. I was amazed to find what squalor he tolerated. He didn't smoke. Denise did. He didn't drink. Denise did—a lot. I remember telling my sister at Rob's wedding reception that his was a marriage made in hell.

.

She'd said, always the tactful one in the family, that "one or both will adjust". At least as far as cleanliness goes, clearly Rob is the one who 'adjusted'.

.

I resisted the urge to straighten up. It seemed presumptuous and implicitly judgmental. I sat down on the sofa and bent over to pick up an old Time magazine that was lying on the floor.

.

The magazine quivered like some living thing waking up.

.

Nothing more than a small aftershock, I realised..

.

And then the front door was flung open and Denise came in. This was a more substantial aftershock.

.

She looked like she had been sleeping in the park. Denise was once quite pretty, with the sort of slender figure that looks like it could never thicken. I'm in fairly good shape, but only because I work at it. (Raymond's Gym thrice a week, veggie meals more often than not, plus swimming in the ocean whenever I can.) Denise swigs beer like a dock-worker, with elbow-bending her only regular exercise, but never seems to add a pound. But even if she doesn't put on weight, her life style has exacted a toll.

.

It'd been several months since I'd been over for a visit. (I had been busy having, and then terminating, a relationship with a Silicon Valley guy who turned out to be the male equivalent of a Valley Girl. Besides, I really didn't much enjoy spending a whole evening trying to make small talk with a drunken Denise and a sullen Robert.) Those couple months had aged Denise several years. Christ, she was only thirty-two and she had crow's feet around her eyes! Her skin had that sallow look I've always associated with old men in smoky bars. Furthermore, she looked dirty, like she hadn't changed her clothes in days.

.

A man followed her in.

.

"Hi," she chirped. "Want ya to meet Hans, he's a quake victim."

.

The quake victim looked the part. He also looked like one of those seedy, crazed men who hand out pamphlets about the end of the world to people who couldn't care less—simply because tomorrow is irrelevant when you're just trying to make it through today. (I'm convinced that 'making it through the day' is the raison d'être for most urbanites.) The man's wardrobe was graciously supplied by Salvation Army. Hair styling by Blunt Scissors Of Hollywood. He had a five o'clock (actually more like a five day) shadow. He also had something disgusting hanging from the hairs in his left nostril.

.

I said hello.

.

The alleged quake victim rushed up to me so fast I involuntarily became rigid.

.

"We're all going back to the sea!" he declaimed, staring at me with eyes as demented as any I'd ever seen.

.

"Sure," I replied. Not exactly a profound reply, but what was I to say? I would have liked to go back to the sea, but only if he wasn't to be a fellow bather.

.

Robert came out of my room, his study.

.

Denise did introductions. "Honey, this is Hans. He is a quake victim. I told him he could stay with us until this mess is over."

"It will only be over when we return to the sea," Hans said.

"Hmm," my brother muttered and then turned around and went back into his 'study', my room. I guess he wanted to finish updating his games database.

I suggested I'd put on dinner. Denise didn't object. I found the freezer stuffed with TV Dinners. I dug out four of them and set to microwaving them. I tried not to think about where my sister-in-law was going to billet her 'quake victim'. Robert's study did not have a lock on the door.

Dinner was strange. Hans and Robert didn't say a word, both working at their meals like men who hadn't eaten in weeks. But Denise was determined to engage me in conversation.

"Did you know that Nostradamus predicted this?" Denise asked, her mouth full of the Swanson conception of 'mixed vegetables', tiny differently coloured cubes that all tasted exactly the same.

"Predicted what?" I asked.

"That California will fall into the sea."

"Oh."

"Many of his predictions have been confirmed."

"Yeah I understand he even predicted the Blue Jays winning the World Series last year." My sarcasm was lost on her.

"Don't know about that, but he predicted a lot of important things. Kennedy assassination. Vietnam. Stuff like that."

It seems Denise had blown the dog whistle: Hans, her quake victim, suddenly shifted his attention from his 'Salisbury steak'. He aimed his gone-nova gaze at me. A bit of 'gravy' was dripping from the corner of his mouth. He still hadn't blown his nose. "Yes, Vietnam. I was in Vietnam."

"Really," I said.

"Mei Chin."

"Really," I said, looking at the gravy oozing down toward his chin.

"The gooks know about the sea."

"Really," I said.

"You don't know shit," he said, suddenly belligerent.

Everybody stopped eating and stared at me, as if it were I who had just said something rude.

"Really," I said, after a long pause.

"Yes, really!" he replied, glaring at me with his nasty, beady eyes.

.

I slept poorly that night. Hans had been set up on the sofa. I imagined him getting up in the middle of the night and coming into my room to teach me about Nostradamus and gooks and the sea. Since the door didn't have a lock, I positioned my sleeping bag in front of it. If the creep tried to open the door he'd have to shove my sleeping body to get in, and then I'd scream like a banshee. My brother may have become withdrawn and strange, but he wouldn't allow his sister to be attacked by some nut case his wife had brought home.

To make matters worse, I had a roommate: their dog Ralph, a Heinz-57 breed, long in tooth and short in brains—with a flatulence problem. It seemed that Hans, who was sleeping vulnerable on the couch, didn't trust dogs. The door to Rob and Denise's bedroom was out of true, perhaps from a previous quake, and didn't shut tight; Ralph could paw it open if he tried. So the only place to securely pen Ralph for the night was the study, my room. The good news is that if this Hans didn't trust dogs, Ralph was some kind of protection. The bad news is that Ralph was a restless sleeper, prone to wandering about in the middle of the night, looking for something to do—such as licking the face of a woman sleeping on the floor or loudly releasing toxic gases. The mongrel also had fleas, and, when scratching himself, loudly thumped the hardwood floor, which

49

became the sound track for a recurring dream about the earth opening up and swallowing me.

.

Generally speaking I like dogs, but I made an exception for this flea-bitten mutt. Like Hans, Denise had found this beast on the street and brought him home. Apparently anything Denise brought home my brother unquestioningly accepted as an addition to the household. Not too long ago they had three dogs and two cats. (I'm not sure whether these other animal tenants had died of neglect or had the sense to run off, but one bestial roommate was more than enough.)

.

I soon settled into a routine. In the morning I'd get up before everyone else, be off to work by seven, where I'd have a greasy eggs breakfast in the company cafeteria. After work I'd go apartment hunting for a few hours, a rather futile effort, since the quake had made the whole city a greedy landlord's dream. (The rents they were asking for tiny, filthy rooms were often greater than my salary. So much for rent control!) I'd get home sometime past eight and put some TV dinners in the microwave. Somehow, it seemed to have been implicitly decided that I would earn my keep by 'cooking' dinner. I really can cook, could have bought some real food and made some real meals, but I was damned if I was going to put any culinary pearls before these swine.

.

That sounded unnecessarily nasty. I certainly didn't mean to suggest my brother was a swine. He was, after all, putting me up, even if allowing stray dogs and people into his house apparently was commonplace and no sign of especial concern. But Denise and her quake victim were definitely getting on my nerves. And nobody seemed to give a damn when or what they ate.

These TV dinings were always surreal. My brother rarely said anything. Denise gibbered. Hans ate sullenly until some key word triggered him. I just—well, I'm not sure exactly what I did. I was stressed out, was a bit emotionally labile. I get sarcastic when I'm on edge.

.

Example 1:

.

Denise at me: "Why are you so negative about everything?"

.

"I don't know what you mean."

.

"You think everything is a joke."

"No, Denise, I don't. I just don't take seriously the same things you do."

Hans: "The sea is the negative from which the land is developed."

Denise, quite serious: "Deep."

Me: "The sea isn't deep off the coast of California. It is, most appropriately, rather shallow."

Hans: "It is you who are shallow, woman. Ocean waters run deep."

Example 2:

Denise at me: "You don't like me very much do you."

Me: "I've nothing against you, Denise. I really appreciate being able to stay here."

Denise: "I'd do the same for anyone."

Me: "Obviously." This was a dumb thing for me to say. It just slipped out.

Hans: "Those of the land will die on the land. The sea will reclaim its children. Take them to her bosom."

Example 3:

Denise at me: "It is hard to imagine that you are Robert's sister."

Me: "Who knows? Mother was promiscuous." (This was a bad 'joke' that would have appalled my dear, rather prim and I'm sure totally faithful mother.)

Robert, looking up with disgust: "Really, Denise!"

Hans: "The sea is the mother of us all."

Me: "Well she's sure had her way with more than a few sailors."

Hans, staring at me with pity: "The sea forgives even those of her children who blaspheme."

Much as dinner conversation seemed to have the sea as recurring motif, I hadn't had time to get to the beach since the quake. A dip in Southern California's 'winter' sea (which is actually warmer than most Michigan lakes in June) would've have been a welcome ablution, but I just didn't have any time. I wasn't sleeping well, partially because of my roommate, restless Ralph, the mutt from hell. Also Denise and Hans were really getting on my nerves. My brother was like a vague shadow on the wall.

My seventh night as house guest, I was poking around in the fridge, looking for something to snack on before retiring, since my microwaved Hungry Man Chicken (allegedly chicken) Dinner hadn't quite satisfied this Hungry Woman. My brother, complaining of a headache, had gone to bed. Denise and Hans had gone out to a Save The Whales (or penguins, or something) meeting. The fridge, unlike the freezer, was virtually empty. There were five jars of various hot sauces, seven kinds of mustard, two different barbecue sauces and a bottle of ketchup—but nothing upon which to apply these fine relishes and condiments.

Suddenly I felt a hand on my shoulder. It scared the bejesus out of me.

I spun around. It was Denise. Standing behind her was Hans. He had his right hand on her shoulder. His fingernails were dirty.

"You must come with us," she said. Her voice was slurred.

"Come with you where?"

"To the sea." She lisped the word sea: to the thee.

"Denise, it's ten-thirty, and I have to work tomorrow. I don't want to go to the beach."

"Better we go now than wait for it to come for us." Her breath could pickle an egg right through the shell.

"Denise, I don't think you're in any condition to drive."

"I just drove home, but okay, you drive."

"Sorry, but I really do have to work tomorrow."

"There will be no tomorrow."

"I'm sure there will. Get Hans or Rob to drive you if you really feel the urge to go to the beach."

"I don't have a license," Hans said.

"Rob is sleeping," Denise said.

"Shit," I said.

I really don't know why I agreed to drive them that night. It was stupid of me. Maybe I was still feeling guilty for taking advantage of my brother's hospitality. The poor guy had enough problems with his wife and the strays she brought home.

Hans and Denise sat in the back seat. Ralph, who Denise insisted join us, sat next to me, peering out the front window and drooling. Hans imperiously called out directions. Shut up, you idiot, I thought. It's not hard to find the ocean: You drive west. However Hans seemed to have a particular stretch of coast in mind. We drove north for quite some time before we finally headed west. I became more and more annoyed, but nevertheless drove on.

Our destination turned out to be, not a beach, but a small roadside park and ocean lookout. There was one other car in the parking lot, a VW bug, and although I couldn't see any heads, the car was moving slightly. The sea is an aphrodisiac.

Hans got out of the car and strode purposefully toward the cliff overlooking the Pacific. Ralph followed, sniffing the ground. Denise stumbled after them. She was obviously very well lubricated, so well lubricated her joints were slipping. Me, I wasn't lubricated: I was grating. So much so that I was going to just sit and wait until they had done their sea gazing and were ready to go home—but then I worried about Denise. The lookout had no protective fence, and she was dangerously drunk. After a few minutes, I flipped off my seat belt and got out and followed them.

.

.

Hans stood at the very edge of the cliff and raised both arms, hands outstretched and started intoning something I couldn't understand. Denise stood, swaying, beside him. Ralph lay between them, his head on his paws.

.

I peered over the precipice. Around L.A. the Pacific Ocean merges with the unpacific land mass in gently curving beaches. Not here. The drop was sheer, and below, the ocean was crashing into some very nasty looking rocks.

.

"The animals will be the first." Hans said.

.

"First what?" I muttered.

.

"First to sense it."

.

"Earthquakes?" (Why was I even talking to this lunatic?)

.

"Yes, but more. They sense when the time has come."

.

"Time for what?"

.

"Time to return to the sea."

.

Before I could think of a reply Denise suddenly leaned against me, put her head on my shoulder, and sighed.

.

"If Ralph jumps, I jump," she mumbled and closed her eyes.

.

"Denise, you're not a god damn lemming," I said. I wasn't too worried. The dog had more sense than my sister-in-law. Ralph wasn't going to jump off a cliff. In fact, he looked like he'd gone to sleep. Apparently he found it easier to sleep here on a windswept precipice than he did in my room.

.

Suddenly I felt the ground quiver slightly beneath us. It was a bit like the vibration of a subway train approaching. It was almost imperceptible, but I took it as a warning from Mother Nature to get the hell off this cliff. Denise took it as a sign of a different kind. Suddenly she pulled herself together and spun on me, her eyes screaming: "See, I told you so."

"The time has come," proclaimed Hans in a stentorian voice. Then with his foot he booted poor, mangy Ralph off the edge.

The dog didn't bark or howl or make any sound at all. He just was gone. I could hardly believe he had even been with us a few seconds before.

I don't know why, but I didn't grab Denise and run. I just stared at this fucking madman, Hans, her quake victim, who thought we should return to the sea.

He stared back, and in his eyes I saw something that terrified me. People are always saying they can see this or that in someone's eyes—all that silly 'the eyes are the window to the soul' jazz. Even I say things like that, but this was different. I swear I really thought I did see something in this man's eyes that was more than sclera, iris and pupil. I really was staring into a window, and outside the window was the ocean, fathomless, eternal, extending to a curving horizon.

We stared into each other's eyes for long seconds or minutes—I don't know. A long time.
Finally, a mental image of Ralph spattered on jagged rocks, the sea lapping at his blood, blocked out all other visions. I screamed. "You god damned asshole! Why don't you go back to wherever in hell you came from!"

And then he did.

He stepped off the edge. And like Ralph, disappeared without a sound.

The only sound was the waves far below crashing into the rocks.

Eventually I turned to Denise. She had her eyes closed and was swaying. I took her arm and guided her back to the car. She slept all the way back to the city, snoring loudly.

The police didn't make nearly as big a fuss as I'd expected. Denise was so drunk she didn't remember a thing after talking me into driving them, so she could offer no corroboration of my story. Nevertheless, my version of what happened was accepted at face value. Hans was not an important person. (I don't think they ever even found out what his full name was.) And apparently lunatics jumping off cliffs into the sea is not a particularly unusual occurrence in California. I had three interviews with cops, always surprisingly casual and cordial—and then was never contacted again.

My brother didn't seem to take a great deal of interest in the whole affair. Although he'd accepted Ralph and Hans into his home, he had never developed any abiding affection for either of them. He just went on reorganising his hard drive and updating his database of games.

Denise just went on being Denise. Maybe drinking even more than she did before—if that is possible. I think that because she didn't remember anything, she just dismissed the whole incident as one would a newspaper report.

My new—criminally overpriced—apartment, in an allegedly 'quake-proof' building, is nice enough, but I've decided to move back east, to back off from the ocean. I must hear reference to 'the big one' at least several times a day, and it unsettles me. I don't, of course, really believe California will fall into the sea when the 'big one' finally comes. But, to be completely honest, some perverse part of me rather wishes that it would—albeit only after I've gone home to Bell Haven. Afterwards, after the land stops quaking, and North America has fresh, new, and stable, western coast, perhaps I would move back. It would be nice to live on a newly defined—and unpopulated—edge of the sea.

~~~~

THE VERY PRIVATE LOVE LIFE OF KTTG

"You can tell a true friend everything, but a true friend never asks that you do."
—Hippokrites

"Although he was morally weak, he did love his children."

"What?" Bill said.

I read the line again: "Although he was morally weak, he did love his children."

"Jesus!"

"Yeah, this is the eulogy from hell."

"Sarah's contribution, no doubt."

"Well, I certainly don't think Andy wrote that line. There are a few others just as bad. That woman is like one of those vicious little terriers. She can't stop nipping at his heels even after he's dead. What kind of person attacks her husband in what is supposed to be a eulogy?"

"Correction: ex-husband. It's a good thing Andy assigned you the job of final editing of his eulogy. I trust you're removing all his mother's editorial contributions. Can you imagine what the funeral service would be like if Sarah were organizing it!"

"Even as it is, it's going to be a very uncomfortable affair."

"Interesting choice of words," Bill said, smiling wryly.

As far as I could glean there had only been three women in Kendall's life. And only one was present at his funeral.

I don't how true it is, but I'm told that in France it isn't, or at least wasn't, uncommon for both the wife and the mistress to attend a man's funeral. The French are noted both for their discretion and their tolerance in matters sexual, so it seems entirely plausible. But it would've greatly surprised me if Angela had showed at Kendall's funeral. And if she had, I can't imagine Sarah behaving with tolerance and discretion. Of course, Kendall wasn't noted for his discretion either. But no, actually that's not true: Kendall was in some ways very discreet. In some ways. And in some ways not. He was a bit of a paradox. Or maybe it just seems that way to me because, although I know he considered me one of his few close friends, I can't say I really knew him.

But then Kendall was hard to get to know. In the days immediately after his sudden death, I'd spent a lot of time trying to figure him out. I'm sure that's not unusual. When friends are alive, you just accept them and all their mysteries and paradoxes, but when they die you're suddenly confused about who they really were. At the funeral you want to go up to the coffin and lean over and whisper: "There is something I've been meaning to ask you…"

Professor of Musicology: Kendall T.T. Gifford. Hell, I didn't even know what his middle initials stood for. I only knew what Bill, who liked to play with anagrams and acronyms and such, decided would be a good nickname for someone of somewhat simian characteristics and the initials KTTG: "Knuckles To The Ground".

Kendall was short and stocky and did have long arms and walked with a slight stoop. And his lower jaw was as prominent as his brow was not. But it wasn't this slight physical resemblance to one of the great apes that inspired Bill. It was Kendall's indiscreet and crass expression of animal lust toward young co-eds. Once the seed had been planted in my head, it was difficult to exorcise the image of my friend transformed into a hairy ape, lumbering through the hallowed halls of Academe, dragging his knuckles as he trailed after feminine temptations.

.

Fortunately Bill was discreet, so he only shared the meaning of this somewhat cruel acronym for our friend with me—although he would refer to Kendall as KTTG so frequently in front of others that everyone always knew who he was talking about. I even eventually heard other people occasionally—and quite innocently—also refer to Kendall as KTTG.

.

Kendall was in his fifties and although certainly not as gross as Bill's acronymic nickname, it was unimaginable that any of the young women he taught could've found him attractive. His lust was quite transparent whenever talking to any even slightly attractive female. So one had to think that his students, like his colleagues, just considered him a dirty old man, albeit a very smart dirty old man and—I should add—a basically very decent human being. So the scandal with Angela left everyone I knew shaking their head in total disbelief.

.

Angela was one of the most physically attractive young women ever to grace our campus. She also was an honours student and a talented violinist. Her beauty, however, was not intriguing—at least to me. It was more like 'pretty' raised to the nth degree. It is just that she was just so very, very pretty that it seemed wrong to apply such a moderate word to her good looks. The same could be said of her intelligence and her musical skills—they were somehow 'ordinary' even as they were at the same time truly exceptional. You would not describe her as a 'brilliant student', even though she maintained a GPA that was in the top 1 percent. And although she was an extremely accomplished violinist, applying the adjective 'gifted' to her playing seemed wrong. When I'd tried to explain my take on her to Bill, he just laughed and said I was like the kid whose parents don't get him the fancy bike he wants and so says "that bike ain't really that special!" It's true that at least putatively she wasn't available, being recently married, but I can honestly say that I did not lust in my heart for her.

.

I knew Angela spent a lot of time in KTTG's office, since my office was right next door. This wasn't at all suspicious since he was her advisor for her Master's thesis—and he always kept his door open. Besides, as I've mentioned, she'd recently married a young man she'd known since high school. In retrospect, I suppose what was suspicious is that Kendall never made lustful remarks about her to us, and Kendall was always making lascivious comments about the young women in his classes.

.

Still he had two very different personas. In front of class he was as dignified and professorial and seemingly sophisticated as imaginable. Out of interest, I'd sat in on his course on the history of Western 'concert' music. (He refused to use the term 'classical' which he reserved for a specific period from the death of Bach in 1750 to around 1820.) He would stand in front of class in his neat cheap suit and wax poetic on the subtleties and intricacies of the sonata form without even glancing at his notes. In fact he often actually closed his eyes as he spoke. (And he was such an effective speaker that only rarely did his students also close their eyes.) But apparently he had his eyes open enough of the time. After class I'd go to his office for a coffee, and he would transform from Dr. Jekyll (AKA Dr. Gifford) to Mr. Hyde (AKA Mr. KTTG) and talk about the "hooters" of some young woman in the class.

.

Bill and I had decided shortly after we first got to know Kendall that the 'real' Kendall was the somewhat nerdy, even prissy, musicologist, and the KTTG side of him was just over-compensation for never being one of the boys when he grew up. We figured he liked hanging around with us because we were, in his very limited experience, more worldly. And the fact that his wife, Sarah, didn't much like us probably made our companionship even more attractive.

.

One time we took Kendall to a strip club on the outskirts of town. Clearly it was his first time in such an establishment. When he started in with his juvenile comments about the 'hooters' of one of the dancers, Bill arranged for him to have a table dance. This was before the days of lap dancing and so-called VIP private rooms. One just went over to where the dancers sat while not on stage and asked the woman of your choice for a so-called 'table dance". She'd come to your table and for five bucks—and a three-minute song—dance naked by (not on) your table. When the young woman 'with the great hooters' KTTG had expressed admiration of came over, we indicated the dance was for our friend. When the song started and she removed what little she was wearing and started to gyrate, I'll be damned if Kendall didn't whip out his half-lens reading glasses! For the whole dance he sat there, an almost puzzled look on his face, studying the dancer's body like it was the score of a new, just recently discovered, Mozart sonata.

Friendship is based on intimacy and trust. Male baboons will greet other male baboons by shaking—not hands (originally a sign that no weapon is in one's hand)—but each other's penises. In fact, not just shaking but actually fondling. To put what is in evolutionary terms your most valuable—and vulnerable—asset in the hands of another brute who is competing for the same females may seem insane. The explanation is that it is done as proof of trust. By two primates making themselves totally vulnerable to each other a bond of trust is formed that is essential to social existence, especially in a violent and volatile primate society. Which is why we only share our dirty secrets with those we trust—and in doing so bond with them at a deep level. What's that saying? "Friends help you move; real friends help you move bodies".

So Bill and I felt a bit hurt that Kendall never told us about Angela. We all believed his relationship with her was purely professorial and avuncular. He'd pulled the wool over everyone's eyes, even Sarah and Angela's husband. Angela would even look after Sarah and Kendall's house if they were away.

Some younger profs had reputations for breaking the frequently broken taboo on relationships with their students, but even if the age difference was a decade—or even two—it didn't surprise anyone. But, as I've said, to imagine Kendall and Angela engaged in coitus was too—too, well too unimaginable. When in KTTG mode, one might just be able to conceive of him making a pass—although even that required an exceptional imagination. Having it be a successful pass—and with a woman like Angela!—that was just inconceivable. It had everyone shaking their head in total disbelief.

Well, Kendall never discussed it with us—even after his divorce. He never even mentioned Angela's name again after the shit hit the fan. On this he remained in discreet mode. Bill and I never asked. I'm not sure our own discretion was nobly motivated; it may have had more to do with our pride. Besides we, almost everyone, knew the basics anyway. Angela's husband had come home unexpectedly to find her and KTTG flagrante delicto on the newlyweds' bed. The sordid details of the subsequent scandal are not important. In the end, Kendall's tenure, academic reputation, and status as full professor, combined with Angela's husband's surprising willingness to forgive and forget, left things a year later almost much as they were before.

KTTG kept his job, although not his house or his marriage. (Sarah was not the forgive-and-forget type.) Angela and her husband remained married and eventually moved out west.

.

.

Kendall's three sons seemed to take all this in stride. I got to know them slightly when they stayed with him on school holidays. Kendall would frequently have us over on a Friday afternoon for a few drinks at his new bachelor pad. The elder son, Andy, who was studying architecture at U of W was exceptionally mature, and it fell to him to write Kendall's eulogy. Out of respect for his mother, he passed it on to her for her additions--additions which turned out to be all somewhat nasty and inappropriate. Knowing I taught in the English department, and that his dad considered me a close friend, he passed the penultimate version to me for final editing. I cut out or toned down Sarah's additions, and the final product, if I say so myself, was quite respectable.

However the eulogy still remained strangely impersonal. Even his son didn't seem to really know his father. I suppose that is not uncommon. We are all very much defined by our sexuality, and few fathers have the kind of intimacy with their sons that involves sharing that part of their lives. (And probably few sons would even want that kind of sharing.) But Bill and I were his closest friends, and we, one would expect, should be privy to that part of Kendall's being. But we weren't.

.

.

Oh my friend, I—when I paid my last respects to you, lying there with your eyes closed, just as they were when you lectured passionately about some aspect of your much beloved music—I so, so much wanted to beg of you: "Speak! If I'm really your best friend, explain it to me, explain you to me. If I really was your friend why did you never expose yourself to me." Maybe he would've replied: "Real friends don't pry."

.

.

It was a couple years after the Angela affair that we started to hear about Suzanne. Once again Kendall was not exactly forthcoming about this new woman in his life. He'd met her on the internet. She lived in Montreal. She was very attractive. (But he didn't talk about her 'hooters'.) She shared his passion for 'serious' music. And that was about all he had to say about her. We'd somehow been conditioned not to be too openly inquisitive. Kendall being discreet meant KTTG was caged away. Kendall would tell us what he wanted to tell us, and it seemed somehow indecent (especially since the Angela scandal) to pry. That he wasn't being KTTG about her, just as he never had been about Angela, made us think this was serious, and we were just happy to see our friend getting lucky again. This time, presumably, with a more appropriate woman. Surely, we thought, she couldn't be another beautiful youngster.

.

Naturally Bill and I speculated about this mystery Montreal woman. Suzanne was a French name, and Kendall spoke passable French. We figured she would probably be our friend's age or a little younger, probably a widow, no looker but no troglodyte either. He'd never mentioned her occupation, so she probably wasn't an academic and most likely had some conventional white-collar job, but we figured she'd have to be well-educated and quite intelligent to keep Kendall's interest—or be interested in Kendall. We quietly and complacently assumed he'd finally found someone more suitable. For all we knew his only previous relationships had been with his ex-wife, Sarah, who he'd married while still in grad school and Angela who was quite a spectacular compensation for a largely celibate life, but obviously never destined to be more than a short-term flash in a pan that was usually just sitting unused on the stove.

.

.

I got the phone call from the SQ, the Quebec cops, on my cell phone—which I normally leave turned off since only a few friends have the number, and they know that. It was just as I was heading off to bed after watching a mediocre so-called romantic comedy on the tube. Did I know a Kendall Gifford? Yes, I did. What was our relationship? I was his friend. Then the cop told me our friend had bought the farm. Heart attack. They'd found my number on a scrap of paper in his wallet.

.

Kendall had just left for Montreal the day before—for a long weekend with his Suzanne. According to the cop he'd had a sudden heart attack while having dinner with a certain Suzanne Laframboise in her apartment. Did I know next of kin? I'm kind of obsessive about maintaining my electronic address book, so I actually was able to find Andy's number. I thought it more appropriate for them to contact him than Sarah. It's only after I'd hung up that I wondered why this Suzanne didn't know how to contact any of Kendall's family or friends. For almost a year he'd been seeing her whenever he could get away to Montreal.

.

.

So at the funeral, we didn't expect to see Angela, but surely there was no reason for this new woman in Kendall's life to stay away. As far as we knew Sarah didn't even know her ex was seeing anyone—or have any reason to care if he were. But the only woman in my friend's life that was there to say a final farewell was Sarah, and one had the impression she wasn't there so much to say goodbye as to say good riddance.

.

So when three months after the funeral I was going to be in Montreal for a conference, Bill said I really should look up this mystery woman whom no one ever heard from—even though KTTG died at her dinner table—or more likely, we suspected—in her bed. Bill said he had what he believed to be her phone number.

.

.

It was spring and warm and sunny and I was on a second floor terrace bar in the university district admiring the constant stream of lovely young women from McGill and Concordia parading along below me. Being above them I had an exceptional perspective on what KTTG would call lovely 'hooters'.

.

I punched in the number on my cell phone. Then I paused a few seconds, rehearsing what I was going to say before pressing the dial button.

.

Her voice surprised me. It sounded younger than I expected, and if she had a French accent, it was barely detectable.

.

"Hi, I'm a close friend of Kendall Gifford. I happen to be in Montreal, and I was hoping we could get together for a drink to talk about our mutual friend."

.

"Oh." It was a very non-committal 'oh'.

.

"It would mean a lot to me to meet you," I said, sounding silly.

.

"Okay." It was a very unenthusiastic 'okay'.

.

"At your convenience of course."

.

"Now's okay."

"I'm downtown at a bar on Crescent. Would that be convenient?"

"I live in the village," she replied.

"Would someplace on St. Denis be better?"

"Yes, I'm a couple blocks from The Magellan on Ontario just off St. Denis." Her voice was totally lacking in expression.

I told her I knew the place and could be there in half an hour. She agreed. I told her I was wearing a blue Adidas jacket.

"The place is small," she replied.

The Magellan is modestly upscale, a nice, unpretentiously elegant resto-bar. I was there in 25 minutes, but there were no single women present. I ordered a Boreal Russe, which they have on tap, and had just had my first sip when a woman walked in. She was in her forties, dressed in an expensively tailored pants suit. Moderately pretty and friendly face. Kendall did okay, I thought.

I met her eyes and smiled. She smiled back and then walked right past me and sat at the bar. I was nonplused. I stared at the back of her head, not sure what to do. After she ordered her drink, she turned her head, met my gaze and smiled again. Strange game she seemed to be playing.

I got up and walked over to the bar and introduced myself. "I'm Jonathan. You, um, prefer to sit at the bar?"

"Hello, Jonathan, pleased to meet you. And since I'm sitting at the bar, it is rather obvious that it is where I prefer to sit." Her voice was ironic but friendly. She didn't sound as young as she had on the phone, and the French accent was heavier.

I sat down on the stool next to her, and she raised her eyebrows and gave me a wry smile.

"You left your beer back at your table," she said.

65

"Right," I muttered and got up and almost collided with a young, tall, and stunning brunette wearing an extremely short skirt and tank top—which revealed a belly ring.

.

"You Jonathan?" she asked. I instantly recognized her voice from the phone call.

.

"You don't waste any time, do you?" she said in her strangely inexpressive voice. The woman at the bar was looking at me with a very bemused expression.

.

"Case of mistaken identity," I muttered.

.

.

Suzanne ordered a vodka and tonic and then opened her purse and took out a pack of Du Maurier. I lit her cigarette for her. I was still feeling like a fool and didn't know how to start the conversation. That the woman was so young and attractive didn't help matters. Jesu, I thought, old KTTG must have excreted some pheromones that other males couldn't detect. First Angela and then this angel. The eternal mystery of what women find attractive in a man! But then I remembered how in high school I was always wondering at how some of the most incredibly nerdy boys managed to hook up with girls that I wouldn't dream of approaching.

.

So my first inane remark was: "So you're a classical music buff, eh?"

.

"Not really," she replied in that unnervingly unemotional voice.

.

"Oh, I thought Kendall said you shared an interest in music."

.

She said nothing.

.

She was rattling me. Talking to her was like what I imagined it would be like talking to a non-directive psychotherapist. So I sort of lost it and blurted out: "I'm sure you had a good reason you couldn't attend his funeral."

.

"Reason? You're kidding, right?" Her voice finally took on some expressiveness: sarcasm.

.

"No. I mean you were with him when he died."

.

"Yeah," she said, "and it was probably the worst experience of my life."

"I, uh, can understand…"

"Oh, I don't think you can." Now she was getting quite expressive. She was staring into my eyes in a way that made me feel very uncomfortable.

I started to mutter something when she interrupted me: "So what is this really about? Do you want to know if he really collapsed into a plate of spaghetti while having a romantic dinner? Or do you want to confirm your macho fantasies that he blew his wad the same time he blew his aorta."

I was speechless. Who was this woman?

She stared at me with eyes that were cold as cold can be. Then unexpectedly her face softened dramatically and she smiled sadly and looked down at her drink.

"Look, I'm sorry," she said, looking up again. "I gather you really were his friend. You look too innocent and hurt to just be some jerk looking for vicarious thrills. So, I'll be frank. Yes, he did die in bed, not over pasta. You happy now? I had to sweet talk (and tip) the paramedics to have it reported more discreetly. Which, of course, was best for all concerned."

"Sorry, it must've been…"

"You don't know!" There was no longer any lack of expressiveness in her voice.

"I guess that is why you didn't come to his funeral. You were too…traumatized."

"Whoa! I was 'traumatized' alright, but why on earth would I want to go to his funeral anyway?"

"Christ," I blurted out indignantly. "He was your lover!"

"Lover?!" she said, shaking her head. "Sweetie, he was just my client!"

.

.

Kendall, if you can hear me, I'm sorry. Real friends don't pry. Real friends are discreet.

.

When I got home I told Bill the phone number he'd thought was Suzanne's was out of service.

~~~~

CALL WAITING

"Get that long distance feeling!"

—Bell Telephone Advert

Monday, 9:02 p.m.

.

The phone rang, more insistent and demanding than any other (mechanical) thing in the world. Frank's wife was out at a meeting of the Windsor Entrepreneurs' Club, so he had to answer it, really had to, much as he'd have preferred to let the damn thing ring itself out. His wife frequently received important (urgent!) calls and had asked him (most imploringly) not to turn on the answering machine when he was home and to take messages "in person". It was a small thing to ask, so he complied, but it annoyed him. She was asking him to be her receptionist, even though she knew he absolutely detested talking on the phone.

.

"Hello, Carter residence."

.

"I just can't believe you people worship the Queen of England! Have you no pride?" The high, always slightly hysterical, voice was only too familiar.

.

"Hello Hedda." Frank's voice was like a long, deep sigh.

.

"This is the twentieth century. How could you move to a country which worships a queen, and not even your own queen?"

"We don't worship her. She really has nothing to do with this country, except as a figurehead. Besides, your country has a queen, doesn't it?"

"The United States does not have a queen." Her voice was slurred. He could almost smell her breath over the phone.

Frank sighed. "I know the United States doesn't have a queen. I meant Sweden."

"They don't worship her. Sweden is a democracy."

"Canada is a democracy, too."

"No it isn't. I just read about it. It's a monarchy. England owns you."

"England does not own Canada."

"Yes, it does. The queen makes your laws."

"Parliament makes our laws." Frank could never understand how Hedda managed to lure him into these insane arguments. If someone calls you up and informs you that the moon is made of green cheese, you don't try to change their mind; you try to get them to see a shrink. It must be all the years of teaching grade school. It always took several lunatic exchanges before he could finally resist trying to correct Hedda's misconceptions, no matter how demented. But she wasn't a confused child. She was a middle-aged nut case married to his brother.

Hedda was ranting on. "...and your tax dollars going to support all those big castles and fox hunts."

"Fox hunts!?"

"Cruel. It's not bad enough that you kill all the buffalo and beaver and baby seals — and penguins."

He firmly withdrew from this mad hatter discussion. "How's Jake?"

"Why don't you ask him. He's just getting out of the bath."

"Jake refuses to talk to me. You know that. He's got this crazy idea about us..."

.

"Well, your idiot brother's the same as always. Hateful. Spiteful. We're getting a divorce."

.

"You've been telling me that, on and off, for several years."

.

"He won't give me a divorce. I'll have to kill him or maybe I'll kill myself."

.

Frank began to wish they were still discussing Canada's subjugation by England—or the recent immigration problem of Antarctica penguins seeking refugee status in Canada. When Hedda got started on her murder/suicide theme — which lately she'd been doing more and more often — his stomach knotted up. He told himself it was bullshit, no more than hysterical histrionics. His sister-in-law was unbalanced, but not dangerous. But then, on the other hand, it was true that Hedda's brother had committed suicide.

.

"...tore the phone out of the wall and threw it at me."

.

"I can't imagine my brother doing that. He is not a violent man."

.

"What do you know about him? You don't live with him. You don't even talk to him."

.

Frank rapped his knuckles loudly on the kitchen doorjamb. "Sorry, Hedda, I've gotta go. Someone's at the door."

.

He doubted the deception was convincing, but for some reason he couldn't make himself just hang up on her, even though it would be the reasonable thing to do. Why should one accept phone calls from a woman who insists on telling you what a bastard your brother is? Was it because he subconsciously wanted to hear someone say these things? No, he couldn't believe that of himself. It was just that he wasn't the kind of person who can hang up on someone. Unlike his brother.

.

Tuesday, 7:23 p.m.

.

The phone rang, for the seventh time since he'd gotten home from

71

work. Frank truly hated phones. His wife loved them. Frank liked answering machines, because it meant he could avoid talking directly to anyone who called. His wife hated answering machines and believed everyone, except her quirky husband, felt the same way. This was perhaps the only major incompatibility in their marriage. (Proof, he often thought, that they had an exceptionally good marriage.)

.

It was a family trait, this dislike of telephones. His parents, admittedly very eccentric, refused to have a phone in the house up to the day they died (ironically, in a car accident, running a chore they could've handled over the phone). They had passed their values, if not their no-phone-in-the-home policy, on to their children. Frank's sister Helen also hated phones. As did his brother Jake. Jake, of course, had the best reason of the three of them. His monthly phone bill was greater than his rent, thanks to Hedda's frequent and totally unrestrained calling of everyone she knew (including her family and 'friends' back in Sweden).

.

Frank realised that this shared familial distaste for phones was extremely inconvenient, since Helen lived in L.A., Jake in Chicago, and he himself in Windsor, Ontario — but they coped. Every Sunday Jake would call Helen. Then Helen would, in turn, call just to give a brief (very brief) update on her life — and Jake's.

.

Frank loved both his sister and brother, but only his sister reciprocated his affection. His brother Jake had one day, several years ago, without feeling any need to explain, abruptly severed the sibling connection. Jake's sudden refusal to even acknowledge his older brother's existence was so unwarranted, so misguided, it was like a long, sharp splinter in Frank's heart. It was also, he strongly suspected, Hedda's damn fault. Hedda was a chronic liar, but Jake believed anything she said.

.

"Hello, Carter residence."

.

"You and your queen are killing all the trees in B.C. You're ruining your land. It's a good thing we are doing something about it."

.

"Hello, Hedda. What are you talking about?"

.

"You call us tree-huggers. Mock us. It doesn't matter. It's a war. Well, we have our ways to stop you!" She was trying to make her voice threatening, ominous, but because it was so high-pitched and slurred, it only sounded silly and hysterical.

"Ways? You mean things like tree spiking?"

"If it works, why not? No one is going to put a chainsaw to a tree if he knows it might hit a spike and backfire!"

"Backfire? You mean kick back and maim or kill some poor guy just because he's trying to eke out a living for his family. Yeah, Hedda, tree spiking is a great idea. The tactic could be expanded for use in other areas. You know about all the baby seals we—and the Queen—kill? Maybe you could spike the seals too. That would teach those blood-thirsty seal hunters." Frank felt embarrassed. It wasn't his nature to be sarcastic. Teaching Grade Three had taught him patience, but Hedda would try the patience of Job.

"You don't care about the seals either, do you? You're just like your brother."

He was tempted to interrupt her with a riddle he'd heard recently. Question: What do the Swedes have that neither the Norwegians nor the Finns have? Answer: good neighbours.

Instead he just listened to her prattle on.

"Nobody cares about life. Plant, animal, human. No matter. Nobody cares. It makes life not worth living. I don't see any point in..."

Oh, oh. Frank just wasn't going to listen to more suicide talk. He rapped the doorjamb so hard he hurt his knuckles.

Wednesday, 11:30 p.m.

The phone rang. Frank was just about to go to bed, about to flip on the answering machine. His wife had left for some heavy-duty business conference in Toronto that morning, and he'd been sorely tempted to leave the answering machine on when he got home from work. Only some misguided sense of duty prevented him from giving in to the temptation. And he now regretted his stoic resolve, having logged twenty-two (!) damned calls in the four hours he'd been home. You'd think his wife would have informed some of her

73

business associates that she was going to be away for the week. Well, tomorrow night was going to be his own, he was going to leave the answering machine on (sorry dear, it was an oversight), settle down and watch a movie, without interruption.

.

Frank picked up the phone, praying it wasn't Hedda, The Gabbler, again.

.

"Hello, Carter residence."

.

"Your brother is a bastard. I'm going to art school."

.

"Hello Hedda."

.

"I told them I didn't have a degree. Saved twenty dollars. It's fifty dollars if you have a degree, but only thirty if you don't. Do you think Jake was grateful?"

.

"Really." Frank knew (from Helen) that twenty bucks was considerably less than an average day's long distance charges on his brother Jake's phone bill. And it was hard to imagine any legitimate 'art school' with a mere two digit tuition.

.

"He doesn't give a damn. I start on Monday."

.

"That's wonderful, Hedda. Thirty dollars is a very low tuition fee." Unbelievably low. Surely even match pack correspondence courses in repairing air-conditioners must cost more.

.

"You don't think they'll check up on me and find out I have a degree?"

.

"I doubt they'll call Sweden." Hedda had always claimed to have "the equivalent" of a university degree from her homeland.

.

"Why is your brother so uncultured? Are all Americans uncultured?" Hedda also claimed to be from an "aristocratic family."

.

"Jake isn't uncultured."

.

"He thinks art is a waste of time. He's just a factory worker. I'm going to kill myself."

.

Frank rapped his knuckles on the doorjamb, assuming that if Hedda would call at this hour, it wouldn't strike her as odd that he was having visitors this late.

.

.

Thursday, 5:35 p.m.

The phone rang within five minutes of his walking in from work and turning the answering machine off. Frank had decided to break the promise to himself he'd made the night before. His wife's successful business paid more of their bills than did his salary. Besides, she called him every night just after eleven to collect any messages he'd taken 'personally'. (She collected those picked up by the answering machine during the day by dialling in regularly and putting some little beeper to the receiver.) Anyway, point is, if he left the machine on in the evening, she'd know—and not be pleased.

.

Frank picked up the phone before the answering machine kicked in.

.

"Hello, Carter residence."

.

"I quit. What's the point in art? All I want is a life. I don't need classes. I can draw. I won a prize once—in Sweden, where they understand art. Still, it would've been nice, but oh what's the point? They won't give me my money back. You think Jake cares. He doesn't care. I paid good money, but Jake doesn't care. All he does is whine about the phone bill."

.

"Hello Hedda," he said. This was an all time record: calls from his demented sister-in-law four days in a row! Usually it took a few days for her to work through her little black book. Maybe the other victims of her calling were hanging up on her, speeding up the cycle.

.

"All your damn brother cares about is money. All I hear is the phone bill, the phone bill. I speak five languages. I have family in Sweden. Your mother is dead. What do you know about being homesick? My mother is sick. Is it wrong to want to talk to my mother during her final months?"

.

"I didn't know your mother was sick. I'm sorry to hear that."

.

"Jake doesn't know either. Well, yes he does. He just doesn't care. He is uncaring. I could kill myself and he wouldn't even get out of the tub. He'd just keep on sitting in the bathtub reading his damn spy novels. I will kill myself."

"Please don't talk like that."

"Why not? You know that my brother killed himself?"

"Yes, I know. Um, sorry, Hedda, but my wife's expecting an important call and I'm getting the call waiting signal. Been nice talking to you."

It had come to him at work: the call waiting excuse was more plausible than someone always knocking at his door. And his wife certainly did get a lot of phone calls.

Friday, 11:02 p.m.

The phone rang just as he was removing his coat. It had to be his wife. Frank had gone out for dinner and drinks with Jim, one of the only other male teachers at Marshall Elementary, and had stayed out longer than he'd intended—and drank more than he'd intended. (Still, it had been good to spend a whole evening in a phone-free environment.)

He rushed to the phone in the living room hall, desperate to intercept the auto-answer. She'd be annoyed if she got her own pre-recorded voice.

"Hello, Carter residence."

"I'm going to pretend to dry my hair."

Frank cringed. "Hello Hedda."

I can't take it anymore." Her voice was even more slurred than usual.

"Listen, Hedda, I'm expecting my wife to call. She's in Toronto at a..."

"You have call waiting, remember?"

"Oh." So much for his new excuse. "Yes, that's true."

"I'm going to drop the hair dryer in the tub.'

"What?"

"That'll do it, won't it?"

"Hedda, what are you talking about?"

"He loves his baths. He hates me."

"If Jake hated you, why would he stay with you? When Jake decides he no longer cares for someone, he cuts the connection, no halfway measures. Believe me, I know. Now you really should calm down, Hedda."

"How like an American! No politeness. Always telling other people what to do. People don't understand when I'm always so polite."

"Yes, you're very polite, Hedda, and I'm being rude, but really, it sounds like you should go to bed now."

"I will — after I electrocute your bastard brother."

And then she hung up.

Frank could not remember Hedda ever being the one to break the connection. It frightened him more than what she'd said. His palms sweating, he hurried down the hall to the spare bedroom that his wife used as an office and looked up his brother's number on her computer. The number, a jumble of sevens and sixes was totally unfamiliar, but then it had been years since he'd last dialled it.

The familiar, unpleasant, ringing sound. Once, twice, three times. Then a click. Then silence. Then a pre-recorded voice: "I'm sorry the number you have dialled is no longer in service." The voice volunteered no alternative number, so he hung up.

This was odd. Frank didn't think Jake had moved. The Christmas and birthday cards Frank still sent his brother would've come back. Besides, Helen would have mentioned it.

Helen, of course! She'd have Jake's number.

.

As he reached for the phone, it rang. It was his wife. Frank spontaneously confessed he'd been out all evening, and she'd have to get the messages off the machine. He didn't say anything about Hedda's call.

.

To his surprise, his wife said she'd get her messages in the morning. "I'm beat, honey. I'm going to bed. I know you hate talking on the phone, so I'll just ring off okay?"

.

It was more than okay with him.

.

He looked up his sister's number, dialled — and got Helen's answering machine. It was four hours earlier in California, so she was probably out. He left a message for her to call back, no matter how late she got home.

.

Then Frank dialled information for the Chicago area code. Carter was a common name. There were eleven(!) J. Carters listed, none at the correct address. Suddenly Frank was really frightened. He asked for all the numbers. The operator said she was only permitted to give one number. "Which one did he want?"

.

Frank pleaded with the woman, but she was adamant. He hung up. He dialled information again, figuring that he probably get a different operator. He did. She told him he could only have one number. He pleaded, said it was an emergency, very urgent. She gave in and read him the eleven numbers in an annoyed voice.

.

The first one he called was answered by a Hispanic woman who barely spoke English. What kind of Spanish name is Carter, he thought, then realised it was probably the woman's married name.

.

The second number he called rang and rang and rang. He then realised the futility of what he was doing. Panic struck him. Hedda was crazy and drunk, crazy and drunk enough to really do something stupid.

.

Frank dialled information again, this time for the number of the Chicago Police Department. The operator wanted to know which district.

.

"I don't know, god damn it!" He realised he was shouting at the poor woman. He tried to get control of himself.

"The main station. Give me the main station," he said in a somewhat calmer tone of voice.

As he dialled the number, he realised he was glad (for the first time) that they had call-waiting service: if his sister tried to call back, he would know.

The desk sergeant, policeman, receptionist, whatever he was called, whoever took the call, had a slight but distinct lisp. This was just too absurd, and Frank, to his profound embarrassment and surprise, emitted a short, aborted laugh. By now his panic was affecting his voice and he knew this inappropriate laugh did not help him sound sober and sane and concerned. Actually, truth be told, he wasn't entirely sober.

"Uh, I'm calling from Canada." he said, trying to sound important. "I was talking to my sister-in-law. She lives in Chicago." Frank paused, unsure how to continue. "Uh, we were talking on the phone."

"Presumably." Apparently the cop had not only a lisp, but an attitude as well.

"This is serious. She was drunk and said she was going to electrocute my brother. Then she hung up."

"Electrocute?"

"He was taking a bath. She said she was going to throw her hair dryer into the tub."

"Has she ever made threats against your brother before?"

"Yes, but..."

"Has she ever carried through on any of these threats?"

"No, but..."

"How many times has she made such threats."

"Damn it, I don't know. But this was different."

79

"How so?"

"She hung up."

"She hung up?"

"She never hangs up."

"I see."

Because of the cop's lisp it sounded like he said 'I thee'. Frank took a second to translate this in his mind then said: "This is serious!"

"Sir, I am taking this seriously." The cop sounded stern, but he lisped the 'seriously' which took the edge off. "Did you try calling back."

"Well, that's the problem. I don't have the number."

"You don't have your brother's number? How did you manage to call him in the first place?"

"I didn't call him. His wife called me." That didn't sound entirely proper.

"I see. But it is strange you don't have your own brother's phone number, while his wife calls you — regularly, I assume?"

"I do have his number — but, uh, the service has been discontinued."

"Then how could you be talking to his wife? Are they separated?"

This was not going well at all. Frank decided to start over from scratch.

"My brother refuses to talk to me. I don't like it, but I respect his wishes. I haven't called him in years, and it seems that I must have an old phone number. His wife is a bit unhinged. She calls me all the time to complain about my brother. I don't encourage her, but she does it anyway. She drinks a lot. This last call was different. I think she was serious about killing him. So maybe instead of interrogating me, could you just please send a cruiser out to their place to check that things are all right?"

"I'm not interrogating you, sir. I'm just trying to get the relevant information. Before I send a patrol to investigate a domestic, I think it makes sense to speak to both your sister-in-law and your brother. In fact it's now policy. I need your name, their names, and their address. We will call and speak to both parties. If there is no answer or anything seems suspicious, we'll send out a patrol to investigate. Is that satisfactory?"

Frank almost told the cop that there was no J. Carter phone listing for his brother's address, but then, foreseeing another verbal song and dance, stopped himself.

"I am Frank Carter. My brother's name is John, and his wife's name is Hedda. I believe they still live at 6503 North Lakeview, Apartment 3."

"I'm going to put you on hold, Mister Carter. I'll have someone check this out."

There was a click followed by a Musak version of "A Hard Day's Night". Apparently the Chicago police now played Musaked Beatles for all their distressed callers.

After what seemed an eternity, the lisping cop came back.

"We can obtain no phone listing for a John Carter at the address you gave us. The current residents at 6503 North Lakeview, Apartment 3, are a Mr. & Mrs. Martinez. They moved in two months ago. We spoke to the landlord. He says your brother was the previous tenant but moved without leaving any forwarding address. I'm sorry, but I can't see what else we can do for you now. If your brother does show up as a victim of violent assault, you will be called."

"Wait, how can you call me. You never asked for my phone number?"

"All incoming calls are automatically logged. Good night, Mister Carter."

Frank listened to the dead line and wished he hadn't vetoed his wife's suggestion that they get the 'who is calling' service now available to everybody. At the time he'd argued it was Orwellian, creepy. But if they'd taken the service, he'd now have his brother's number.

.

The phone rang. It was some damned telemarketer. He didn't even bother to tell him to fuck off. He just hung up.

.

Saturday, 9:01 am.

.

The phone rang, in his dream. The receiver was jumping up and down in its cradle, like in cartoons. He kept trying to grab it, but it avoided his grasp like some quick little animal.

He woke up. The ringing continued.

.

He rolled over to his wife's side of the bed and grabbed the phone on the night table.

.

"Hello."

.

"What's this, no 'Carter Residence'? Did I wake you up Frank?"

.

"Sis! Thank God! Yes, I was up very late last night."

.

"Is everything all right? I didn't check my messages until this morning. Why did you want me to call you in the middle of the night?"

.

"I need Jake's phone number."

.

"You are going to call him? What's going on?"

.

"Hedda called me last night and she really frightened me. I think she's losing it completely."

.

"She lost it a long time ago."

.

He could hear his sister flipping pages.

.

"Here it is. 776-7666"

.

Frank's hope dropped as he heard all the sevens and sixes. "I'm afraid that's his old number. When did you call him last."

"Can't remember. He always calls me. Every Sunday. You know that."

"Tomorrow."

"Yes, Frank, tomorrow is Sunday. Are you sure you're all right?"

"Fine, probably just over-reacting. Call me as soon as you hear from him."

"I always do."

"Bye, Helen."

"Bye"

Sunday, 11:05 p.m.

The phone rang, finally. Finally! It had been atypically silent all evening. What a damnably contrary thing. For once, he is actually waiting for a call, and the phone clams up.

"Hello, Carter Residence."

"Hello Frank." It was his sister's stilted phone voice. In person, she tended to be almost embarrassing flamboyant and garrulous, prone to much gesticulating, but on the phone she always sounded like a hostage with a gun to her head, reading a prepared script.

"Helen. I've been waiting for your call. It's late."

"I wanted to wait until I'd talked to Jake."

Frank held his breath. Please, he thought, please please say you spoke to him.

"He didn't call," she said. "I think you'd better tell me exactly what is going on."

Frank gave her a short version.

"I have a calendar," his sister said after a long pause.

.

"What?"

.

"A calendar from Accu Tool & Die."

.

"What?" Was his sister losing her mind too?

"Last year Jake sent me a calendar from the company he works for. I don't know why. It's ugly as sin, unless you find bimbos in bikinis holding wrenches aesthetically pleasing. But it has a phone number on it. You could call him at work, tomorrow morning. Then we'd know he's all right."

.

"Go find it."

.

.

Monday, 9:05 am.

.

The phone rang, just as Frank was reaching for the receiver to place a call to Accu Tool and Die Company.

.

"Hello, Carter residence."

.

"Hello, Mister Carter. How are you today?"

.

"Fine"

.

"I'm sure you enjoy fine dining, don't you, Mister Carter?"

.

"Yes."

.

"Well, we would all dine out more often if it weren't so expensive. Don't you agree?"

"I don't want any whatever it is." Frank said. And hung up. Hung up without waiting for a reply. It was the first time he'd ever hung up on anyone. It felt good.

.

He dialled the number of his brother's employer.

.

"Accu Tool and Die." The male voice was gruff, unfriendly, annoyed. Frank imagined a big, burly man with grease on his arms. He always

84

tried to visualise the person at the other end of the line. Disembodied voices distressed him.

"I would like to speak to one of your employees."

"Who?" Frank could visualize the man frowning. He had coarse skin, wrinkles, blackheads.

"Jake Carter."

"He's working."

"I assumed that." Why, oh, why did he always encounter such hostility when he spoke to people over the phone? In person, he got along with everybody.

"We don't permit personal calls." Bet the guy was wearing a cheap blue shirt with grease stains. He'd just been promoted to foreman and thought himself real important.

"This is an emergency."

After a long silence: "Who should I say is calling?"

"Helen"

"You don't sound like a Helen." The sarcasm dripped. This guy's new found power felt it gave him the right to be rude.

"I'm placing a call for his sister Helen."

"Her dialling fingers broken?" God, this man had an attitude!

"Please I need..."

"Just a second."

Damned if a tinny Musak version of "Paperback Writer" didn't come wafting out of the receiver, a thousand-and-one-strings type rendition. Why play strings over the phone? The frequency response of a phone headset cuts off and distorts even slightly high-pitched sounds.

"Hello, Helen?" His brother's voice, but strangely unfamiliar.

.

"Hello, Jake, this is Frank."

.

"What the hell!? Has something happened to Helen?"

.

"No. I just used her name to be sure you'd take the call."

.

"Nice. You always were deceitful. Well, bye now."

.

"No wait! Please. This is serious."

.

"You always were serious. So what do you want? I'm working. I can't tie up this phone."

.

"Are you okay?"

.

"Of course, I'm okay. You called to see if I'm okay?"

.

"You didn't call Helen yesterday. You always call on Sunday night."

.

"I called her this morning. I couldn't call yesterday, I was sicker than a dog. Food poisoning, I think."

.

"You still could've called. No matter how sick you were, it doesn't take much to lift up the receiver and dial..."

.

"Don't preach to me. I don't have a phone. I wasn't well enough to go out to the pay phone at the corner — not without taking a port-a-potty with me."

.

"Oh."

.

"So now that you know I'm okay, can I get back to work?"

.

The little beep indicating a 'call waiting' started.

.

"Hold on a second, Jake. Please! Some one is on the line."

.

Frank switched to the incoming call.

.

"Hello."

.

It was his sister. "Hello, Frank, I just wanted to let you know that Jake called this morning."

.

"I'm talking to him now. I'll call you back."

.

He switched back.

.

"Jake?"

.

"Yeah, I'm still here."

.

"What do you mean you don't have a phone. Where's Hedda?"

.

"I mean just what I said. I don't have a phone anymore. And I don't know where Hedda is. But if you want her, you can have her. Now I've..."?

.

The damn beeping again.

.

"Just a second."

.

It was his wife. He told her he'd call back.

.

"Jake?"

.

Silence.

.

"Jake? You there?"

.

"What are you doing? Manning a switchboard?" His brother's voice lacked any warmth, but the touch of sarcastic humour was somehow comforting.

.

"Sorry. What do you mean you don't know where Hedda is."

.

"Exactly what I said: I don't know where Hedda is. She left me when I had the phone disconnected months ago. Since then I've moved. I don't know where she is and she doesn't know where I am. No problem."

.

"But she's been calling me everyday all week!"

.

"Well that should make you happy."

"Jake, I don't know what you think..."

"Listen, I don't want to hear about you and Hedda sharing that long distance feeling. If you want to know where she is, why don't you ask her next time she calls? Now I really have to get back to..."

The call waiting signal started beeping again.

"Sorry, Jake, just hold on one more second." Before he switched lines, Frank heard his brother mutter "shit".

Damn, why was it so hard to ignore that insistent little beeping!

"Hello," Frank growled into the receiver.

"I can't understand why you people don't break off with the Queen of England! You must..."

He lost control.

"Go screw yourself, Hedda!" Frank yelled into the receiver. "Take your phone, or whoever's phone you're abusing now, and stick it where the sun don't shine!"

He could hear her gasp in shock. Then he disconnected her. When he flipped back to his brother, the line was dead. His brother and learned some time ago the useful skill of hanging up.

Frank set the receiver back in the cradle. A few minutes later, the phone started to ring.

He ignored it.

~~~~

ONE NEEDS RELIABLE TRANSPORTATION

"We are survival machines."

—Richard Dawkins (*The Selfish Gene*)

"Don't trade-in, trade-up!"

—User car dealer slogan

"You know, honey, I was reading somewhere that you could look at organisms as if they were nothing more than survival machines— complicated, protective shells to carry our genes. The real urge to survive is in the genes. The body is just a device to that end: a vehicle on the evolutionary road. It's all about genes."

.

"Natalie, you read too much. Stop gabbing and take your jeans off. I want to go for a ride in your mean machine."

.

"You're a pig, John, a real pig." She said this affectionately and began unbuttoning her blouse. Outside in the motel parking lot, the sound of a starter-motor failing was making an irritating screeching sound.

.

.

Harold Uzzell directed his legs to carry him forward to the only comfortable looking chair in the room. Tip, tip, the old sodium pumps pumped. His huge bulk lumbered. Input poured up along the afferent pathways. Output down the efferent. Vesicles opened, dumping acetylcholine into the synaptic spaces, the neuromuscular junctions. Feedback loops looped. Corrections were made. Adjustments. He struggled with the controls up in his head. He lumbered forward.

.

He reached the armchair and sat down. Heavily.

.

Waited.

89

The shrink entered the room. "Mr. Uzzell?"

Harold Uzzell activated his speech centres in the frontal and temporal lobes, initiated a reply.

They had a chat—that cost seventy-five bucks.

Dr. Spiel lit his pipe first, then asked June if she minded if he smoked. And so although she didn't, she was for a moment tempted to say yes she did—but instead she shook her head. The man annoyed her, but he'd come highly recommended.

"I spoke with your father."

"Well?"

"You know, Mrs. Hanson, your father's condition isn't really all that unusual. Quite a number of overweight people start to think of their bodies as separate entities. Usually the metaphor is one of an old, rundown, and gigantic mansion. It's a result of feeling one has lost control. The extremely obese person often feels trapped inside his body like a frightened child trapped inside a haunted house. That your father suffers from this sort of dissociation is actually a good sign, an indication that he desires to regain control."

"He doesn't talk about his body as being a house. If anything, he seems to think of it as some kind of motorized machine. The other day he was having a hard time getting out of a chair and he said something like 'the controls on this damn tank are jammed'. It's disturbing."

The psychoanalyst laughed lightly.

"I don't find it amusing, Doctor."

The doctor smiled patronisingly. "I understand. Of course you're concerned. But really you mustn't treat this too seriously. I found your father an amusing man, a witty man. He is well-educated, is he not?"

"He used to teach high school biology." She really didn't like this pompous ass.

.

"Well, please understand me: I don't mean to minimise the importance of his losing weight—for his physical well-being. I am an MD, and although I'm not his family doctor, his obesity concerns me. However, I want to reassure you that he is not psychotic or likely to become so. He is quite sane. Yes, a little therapy is suggested, but his metaphor about his body being a tank suggests that he desires to have more control, and desire always precedes action."

.

"Dr. Spiel, he doesn't want control. He wants to get out."

.

"I beg your pardon?" The doctor raised his eyebrows.

.

"Out, he wants out. He tells me that every day. He said yesterday— and these are his exact words—'I'm only going to drive this old clunker until I find a nice new machine at a reasonable price.' He wasn't talking about his car. He was talking about his body. That does not seem sane to me."

.

Dr. Spiel smiled, set his pipe down, leaned forward. "Homunculus," he said.

.

"What?"

.

"Homunculus. Old philosophical and psychological problem. Descartes. Mind/body dichotomy. Homunculus means little man. We all, every one of us, feel that we are inside our bodies—usually located a few inches behind our eyes—running things, directing and controlling what our bodies do. If this 'I' behind my eyes..." (He hesitated and smiled to himself at his pun.) "...if I think it is immortal and immaterial, I call it my 'soul'. In fact there is a theory that physiologically-caused psychosis is a failure of the body as 'vehicle' while the 'driver' is perfectly sane. Imagine the body as a car and the soul as the driver. Imagine how an alien, thinking cars are living creatures, would interpret a car that suddenly went off road, through a guard rail, and into a ditch. He would think this was an earth creature gone mad. But this would only be true if the driver aimed for the ditch. However if the steering mechanism failed—that is, a part of the 'body' broke down—then this would be a totally wrong inference about the driver—that is, about the soul."

.

"This is all very interesting, Doctor, but my father wasn't being witty

91

or clever or philosophical. Damn it, he was serious! What the hell am I supposed to do with a father who talks about trading in his body? I came to you to find out if he needs hospitalisation, if he might hurt himself."

.

"Oh no! Not at all. As I said, he really is fine. All he needs is to go on a diet and have a few hours a week in therapy. And you, Mrs. Hanson, if you'll forgive me for saying so, you should try to relax. Quite frankly, you seem much more tense than your father."

.

.

The old man was asleep on the sofa when John Hanson arrived home—and that was a relief. Hanson found it harder and harder to talk to the old bastard. Everybody had trouble with their in-laws, but not everybody had to live with one. The old guy was getting soft in the head. Senility city. Those fat choked arteries of his were hardening, and his brain was drying up. One didn't need a shrink to figure that out. Sure, the old man wasn't really all that old, but he was so bloody fat his insides were probably those of a man ten, twenty years older. It was disgusting how some people let themselves go.

.

Unfortunately it probably ran in the family. June was starting to put on weight too. Whenever he suggested she take up tennis again, she'd glare at him like he was insulting her. But then what the hell did it matter? He had Natalie, slim, firm Natalie. Let June and her father grow old and fat together, visiting shrinks and consoling each other. Shrinks weren't cheap, but the cost would be worth it to keep both of them out of his hair.

.

Hanson went into the kitchen and popped open a light beer. He looked out the window over the sink at the expansive backyard. It needed mowing, but he had a soccer game today. Priorities. The lawn could wait.

.

"Hello, John."

.

Hanson started. He turned around. His father-in-law stood in the kitchen doorway looking like one of those "soft-sculptures" that were such a rage in New York.

.

"Did I startle you?"

.

"It's okay. Want a beer?"

"No thank you. What I want is to talk to you."

"Sure, but I don't have too much time."

Harold Uzzell laboured over to the kitchen table and deposited his body on one of the chairs. His bulk made the chair disappear from view. He was just a doughy mass floating by the table.

Hanson remained standing. "What'd you want to talk about?"

"You're a shit, John, a real shit."

"Hey now, wait a minute! I don't have to listen..."

"It's funny, you know, that a shit like you should have such a nice body. I guess that's what lured June into marrying you."

"That shrink you went to last week, what'd he tell you? That it'd be therapeutic to insult your son-in-law?"

"No, he was quite useless. Anyway, I'm not insulting you. I'm telling you that I admire you for the way you take care of your—your body. You received an especially nice one, and you've kept it well-tuned and very well-cared-for. I must give you credit for that."

Hanson stared into the old man's eyes, eyes almost concealed by the adipose tissue of his cheeks.

"I know about your mistress, Natalie," Harold Uzzell said after a prolonged silence.

"Natalie?"

"Don't play stupid; you're stupid enough already."

Hanson wanted to simply walk out, but he was held by curiosity. Was he about to be blackmailed in some fashion?

"You treat my daughter rottenly. I hate you for it. I loathe you."

"I know you never liked me. But you're wrong: I don't treat June badly at all."

"I've developed a theory. Would you like to hear about it?"

"Do I have a choice?"

"Everybody is given a body at birth, but most of us drive the same one for all of our lives, only switching to a new one in our next reincarnation."

"You used to teach science, Harold, so what kind of crap are you talking now?"

"Some of us, however, get stuck with lemons, and decide to trade up. Now, it's not easy to trade. A person needs two things to get out of his body. First, he needs to believe. Nothing can be done without faith. You know what it says in the Bible about a mustard seed. Faith is a difficult thing to achieve, but it is also a very powerful thing once achieved."

"Your brain has gotten soft, Harold. You've got a lot of nerve calling me stupid."

"Now, faith alone is not sufficient. It is necessary but not sufficient—as the philosophers are so fond of saying. One also needs tremendous psychic energy."

"I guess that leaves you out, doesn't it? You haven't got the energy to walk across the living room without getting winded."

"You're wrong there, John. One can get this energy from any intense emotion. Fear, love—even hatred. The hatred I have for you is a great source of energy for me. And so, you see, I have everything I need to trade up."

"You're cracked, Harold. The fat has invaded your brain. I'm going to my soccer game now. When June comes home, tell her I'll be back before midnight." Hanson started for the door. As he passed Harold Uzzell, the old man grabbed his wrist and glared up at him.

"I want your body," Harold Uzzell hissed.

Hanson laughed. "You're not only crazy and fat as pig, you're turning into a fag as well."

June Hanson took a seat in front of the desk. She crossed her legs and tried to compose herself. This was not going to be easy to talk about. She wished she liked this doctor more.

"Well, Mrs. Hanson, I didn't expect to see you again."

"This time I'm not here because of my father."

Dr. Spiel tactfully suppressed a smile. I could've deduced that, he thought, but aloud he replied in his most soothing tone: "I'm terribly sorry about your father. As I told you last time you were here, being overweight is a very serious physical problem."

"I was his only child."

"It was his heart, wasn't it?"

"Yes."

"Are you here because you're having a difficult time dealing with your grief?"

"It was six months ago. I'm done grieving. I'm here because of my husband."

"You show admirable concern for the men in your life." He hoped the irony in his tone was well-concealed.

June Hanson fidgeted.

"Well?"

"My husband was with my father when he died. They didn't get along that well, and I guess seeing my father die has affected John."

"Affected him how? Has he become hostile? Withdrawn?"

"No, no, he's very affectionate. More affectionate, in fact, than he's ever been before. He's very—what's the word—protective. When we were first married he was the sort of guy that took care of himself and expected everybody else to do the same. He's changed."

"Well, it's natural you know. With your father gone, it's easier for him to assume the role of your protector. Not only is it natural, but it is good. It is a sign of his emotional growth."

"Is it also a sign of emotional growth that..." (June Hanson's voice rose hysterically.) "...that he refuses to make love to me! Absolutely refuses!"

"Oh," Dr. Spiel said, reaching for his pipe. He had a client.

Natalie ran her fingers lightly over his pectorals. "You know, honey," she said, "I used to think there couldn't be a better lover than you."

"Oh? And now?"

"Natalie propped herself up on one elbow and surveyed the muscular terrain of her lover's body. "Well, since your father-in-law's death, you've been very different."

"Oh. Am I to worry about where this is leading?"

"No, no. What I'm saying is that you've made even your former self seem—cold by comparison. You've outdone yourself."

"Really? Well, thank you."

"You make love with such passion, such pleasure in your own body and what it can do. It's like your father-in-law's death has freed up some part of you. You're like a new man."

"Indeed."

~~~~

IN A BLAZE OF GLORY

"Some say the world will end in fire,
Some say in ice.
From what I've tasted of desire
I hold with those who favour fire."

—Robert Frost ("Fire And Ice")

A few weeks after the funeral I was in this rather upscale bar on Rush Street, drowning my sorrows, as they say, when this expensive suit on the stool next to me starts up a conversation. Since my divorce and when off duty, I'll talk to anyone almost forever. So soon we did what lonely souls on barstools do so easily—but families find so difficult—got to know each other.

.

I like classy bars because the people are more interesting, although my 'colleagues' think I'm uppity because I don't want to drink at their cosy little cop bar. But c'mon, I know all their stories. When I'm off duty I want a change. And I see enough cops (and lowlifes) at work to want to relax with a different class of people.

.

Well, anyway, this guy was a shrink, although he didn't like the word. He kept insisting that shrinks were doctors, and he wasn't a doctor. He was a psychologist. I still have his flashy embossed card, and it says Dr. Krantz, so that makes him a doctor in my books. He talked like a doctor, a doc with a good bedside (and barside) manner. I understood that he didn't do surgery or write prescriptions for pimples, that he wasn't a med-school graduate, but I couldn't see why that was such a big deal with him. You'd think he wouldn't have a superiority complex about not being a real doctor. I really couldn't figure out if he didn't want to be mistaken for a regular M.D. because he didn't want to seem pretentious—or because for some reason he held M.D.s in contempt. Whatever. He was paid to help sick people, and to my way of thinking that is doctoring, so he was a doctor. Some doctors treat broken bones. Some treat broken brains—and some broken hearts.

Anyway, we got to talking about being nuts. After my third rye and coke I started talking about something I don't normally talk about, started telling him about my little brother, his kink, his pathology. Dr. Krantz wasn't surprised—which surprised me. It was like he'd heard it all before. For example, he said that cops and criminals have similar "personality profiles". Both are fascinated with crime. Whether you become a crook or a cop is almost a matter of chance, he said. It's the fascination, the obsession, that counts. He must've been a good psychologist, for he seemed to know I wouldn't—and I didn't—take offence. After thinking about what he'd said for a few moments, I told him that since my fate was crime, I was glad my coin came up heads. Being a cop ain't easy, but I've seen enough to know that being a crook, with a few notable exceptions, is a lot worse. And trying to be both at the same time is even worse still. I've seen that too. Bent cops aren't exactly a rare commodity. The man had a point.

"Your brother just took a different take on what fireman means," he said. "Ever read *Fahrenheit 451*?"

I told him I'd heard of it, but hadn't read it. They'd made a movie based on it.

He ordered another round, and suddenly I wondered what he was doing here, listening to my troubles for free—just to avoid being alone? What wound was he trying to sterilise with alcohol? Never did find out. In fact, never saw him again. But that night he did a little pro bono therapy, helped me understand a little bit more about Jimmy, and really lent a sympathetic ear. Bless ya, Dr. Krantz, wherever the hell you are.

As far back as I can remember my little brother wanted to be a fireman. A lot of young kids say they want to be firemen or policemen when they grow up, so Jimmy and I weren't exceptional in our occupational plans—not for seven-year-olds. But most kids outgrow this hero-career mentality, stop taking themselves seriously by the time they're teen-agers. In our high school, almost no one had anything that could be called 'occupational' plans. We had the hots. We had the cool scams. We had plans for Friday night at Richie's. But we didn't have 'career plans'. Harper High was a one-day-at-a-time and whatever-will-be-will-be kind of place. Yeah, but Jimmy and I, we hung on to our childish dreams. Our mother, had she still been alive, probably would have tried to discourage us, but the Old Man seemed to like the idea of his boys having macho, 'heroic' jobs. He'd worked all his life as a tool and die maker.

My brother's ambition was the greater. It wasn't as easy to become a fireman as it was to become a cop. In those days any punk could get into the police academy, and a lot of punks did. There was this all night restaurant at the corner of Ashland and 63rd called The Red Apple, and all the baby-coppers would hang out there. "What ever happened to Spike?" somebody would ask at lunch period at Harper. "Haven't seen him in months. He drop out?" "Check out The Red Apple tonight. Bet ya a fiver he's sitting there in his cute cadet outfit, practising his coffee drinking." The Red Apple was full of losers, half of them trying to become cops. And more than half of them made it. That's another reason why I don't drink at cop bars. Oh, there are some damn good cops, don't get me wrong. I've worked with guys I really would put my life on the line for, but there are also way too many that are jerks who think they're king shit—and really are just plain shit.

Anyhow, as a kid I loved cop shows. I read True Detective fanatically—and not just because they had these sexy women with torn blouses on the cover. For a wannabe-cop, those were good years. Every other show on the tube was a cop show. Yeah, some of them were P.I. things, where the regular cops were portrayed as friggin' idiots, but that didn't bother me. This Dr. Krantz had it right. All I cared about was the idea of crime, of those outside the law struggling with those within the law.

Meanwhile Jimmy played with fire. He was always burning something. In spring he'd burn the grass, claimed it was good for the soil. More like good for his soul. In the fall, burning leaves was his joyous compensation for having to rake the lawn. And he loved fireworks. If I came into his room late at night to chat, he'd light a sparkler to honour the occasion. Only when the sparkler had burned out to a reverent silence would he bring out the forbidden cigs and we'd light up. (The Old Man smoked like a chimney, but had no problem with hypocrisy: he'd kick our asses if he caught us smoking. 'Do as I say, not as I do' was his policy: we got sent to church, not taken.)

.

When Jimmy was about ten he got this book from the library that explained how to make an incendiary bomb, and I'll be damned if he didn't pull it off. (It really is true you can make a bomb from the stuff in your kitchen. We should be given the right to arrest the jerks that publish the recipes.)

.

Anyhow, there was this old asshole on our block that was always yelling at us kids for no apparent reason. He had a real mouth on him. I realise now he was just one fucked-up old man, probably loony-tunes from Alzheimer's or something, but when we were kids we just hated him for being an asshole. In our neighbourhood, every block was cut in half by an alley, and the garbage cans were these concrete things built into the backyard fences. Jimmy planted his bomb in old man Fargo's garbage can. The night he blew it, my respect for my little brother went up more than a few notches. But so did my gut feeling that the boy was dangerous, was already heading out to where the buses don't run.

.

I remember the look in his eyes as we stood watching the firemen hose the mess down. Most of Fargo's fence had gone to ash, and it was only the speed with which the fire department responded that kept the fire from spreading to the old, dead elm in his backyard, maybe even to his clapboard house. Jimmy's eyes were aglow.

.

"Don't pull any shit like that again, bro," I said to him as he passed me his pack of Marlboros, this big sparkler now gone out.

.

"Hey, ya gotta keep them on their toes or they'll get soft" was his reply.

.

.

We both managed to graduate. Jimmy did better with the grades, because he worked harder. He knew the Chicago cops would take any dumb fuck with a good physique and the proper bad attitude. But for some reason the fire department actually expected applicants to have some kind of education. I don't know why. Pissing on a fire requires fewer smarts than dealing with the street scene.

We both worked for a few years before Viet Nam interrupted our 'careers'. As cops and firemen we probably both could've gotten exemptions, but the Old Man had us brainwashed about 'protecting democracy', so we both went off to the stinking jungle to fight a war everyone finally decided was as stupid as pissing in the wind. Frankly, I really don't remember much about my tour of 'duty'. I was stoned most of the time and didn't really see much action, although I think I might've actually killed a gook on one night patrol a week before they shipped me home. Anyhow, Jimmy wasn't so lucky. He came back much more fucked up than me.

.

I first suspected Jimmy was playing both sides of the line when one night I responded to a call on Stony Island. This wasn't too long after Martin Luther King was shot, and sometimes firemen responding to calls on the South Side found themselves targeted by locals. Don't ask me to explain it. I got nothing against black folk, but it sure seems stupid to me to attack white fireman for trying to keep a black neighbourhood from burning down.

Anyhow, in this particular case, our car arrived after the trouble-makers had split. But I chatted with the Fire Chief while his 'boys' (including Jimmy) made sure the ashes of the abandoned warehouse weren't still smouldering. He said it was clearly arson—one of those 'incendiary bombs you can make in your kitchen'.

At that time Jimmy and I were sharing an apartment, so later that night when he got home I asked him about the fire. He said: "Hey, it was good exercise. Things have been pretty dull for the last couple a weeks. Gotta keep them on their toes." He smiled as if to say "Just joking, bro." But my gut told me he wasn't.

After that I made a point of keeping tabs on the activity of his station. More than a few fires matched the m.o. of the Fargo garbage can episode. I can no longer pretend I didn't really know that Jimmy was not just putting out fires, but I didn't say anything—to him or to anyone else. Ever.

.

Ever! Yeah, 'ever' until I found myself spilling my guts to this shrink—excuse me, Dr. Kranz, this psychologist—plunked on a bar stool next to me. After I'd thrown open this family closet so he could see the skeleton, he told me a little about this *Fahrenheit 451*. As he described it, it sounded a bit preachy. I've had to listen to the free-speech freaks only too often. I used to drag up the 'shouting fire in a theatre' argument, but I don't anymore—for obvious reasons. Now I just shrug and let the bleeding heart liberals exercise their 'free' speech. As the Old Man used to say when my brother and I were old enough to get on his case for a change: "Thanks for the free advice. It's worth every cent."

.

But I appreciated the twist which made my new confidante think of the book. The 'firemen' in the book didn't put out fires, they started them.

.

"They burned books because that was their job," Krantz said, "but they also burned them because in their hearts they didn't understand books and so thought them a threat. We always want to destroy what we don't understand."

.

I said something to the effect that my brother didn't understand the world and maybe he found it threatening for that reason."

.

"None of us understands life, but for some people this ignorance is excruciating. Your job as a policeman is to quote clean up the streets. Maybe he was purifying those same streets in his own confused way. Purification by fire has a long history."

.

Maybe this was psychobabble, but it made sense at the time. For some reason, he suddenly reminded me of Father Anthony. I asked him if was Catholic.

.

"No, why do you ask?"

.

"You sort of remind me of our priest at St. Joe's."

.

"Well, I do sort of take confessions," he replied, smiling. "I guess you might say I'm a secular priest."

.

"But you don't do last rites."

.

"No. Someone die recently?"

.

"Yes," I said. "Fifteen days ago."

.

Someone also died a few months ago. A junkie. The neighbourhood had two kinds of houses: crack houses and crash houses. This crack house wasn't just condemned by the city. It was condemned by God. The rats would dine on your privates if you were stupid enough to pass out there. There was a perfectly respectable (by the local standards) squatter house to crash at just down the block. The guy shouldn't have been where he was. But he was. And he went with it when it went—up in a blaze of glory.

Dead guys, even junkies, prod the arson investigators to get off their asses. It was inevitable, of course. Eventually someone had to clue in. Jimmy was put on suspension. Word on the grapevine was that arrest was imminent.

Jimmy called me when the shit finally hit the fan. All he said was that he was "a fired fireman."

Two days later, it happened. By the time I got the call and made it to the service station on Jackson, there was already a crowd scene. They weren't getting too close to Jimmy, though. I think they realised he was dead serious. Jimmy was standing there, his fireman's suit shining wet and clinging to his body, standing in this pool of gasoline underneath the SELF-SERVE sign. The stench from the gasoline was keeping the 'I-wanta-see-him-die' crowd at a distance. He had an unlit cigarette in his mouth, a lighter in his hand. A crudely lettered placard was leaning against the pumps that read: "FIRE ME? YOU DON'T HAVE TO! I'LL FIRE ME!"

I pushed my way through the goof gawkers and started to walk right up to him.

"Freeze," he said as I approached.

I did. I'd been down this road before. You don't test the would-be suicides. Nine out of ten times, if you push them they'll jump whether they really intended to or not.

"Relax, Jimmy," I said.

"I am relaxed."

"Good, so what're ya gonna do now? Should I tell these assholes to go home. Tell 'em the show is over?"

"Ain't over! Hey, bro, I'm gonna get all fired up! I'm going to flick my Bic. Light my fire. Go up in a blaze of glory."

"That ain't funny, Jimmy. Put your lighter away." I took a tentative step forward.

"Don't make me rush it!" He put his thumb on the lever of the lighter.

I froze.

"You're being an ass, Jimmy," I said.

"My friends call me James."

"I'm not one of your sicko friends. I'm your big brother."

"Well, big bro, I guess that gives you certain privileges, but you ain't the Old Man so don't try to tell me what to do."

"I thought your so-called friends called you Flame."

"Sometimes."

"Look, I know it's been rough, but this is crazy."

"What the fuck do you know about crazy?"

"I was in Nam too. I know crazy."

"Fuck you do! My buddies there called me The Fireman, but you know why? Not cuz I was a fireman by trade. Because I'd fire the villages. That responsibility was always mine. Hell, I probably burned babies alive. Your little brother burned babies alive."

"That's horseshit, Jimmy, and you know it. Stop being melodramatic. You told me you never flamed a village until it was evacuated. It was a war, kid, one real fucking ugly war. We all did things that it's best to forget about, but you're cleaner than most of us."

"And that goddamn junkie? Should I just forget about that stupid, deep-fried freak?"

"You need help, Jimmy. We'll get you some help."

"Hey, you're the copper, I'm the bad guy. Why're you so concerned about my welfare?"

"You're my brother."

"No fault of mine," he replied. "Blame the Old Man!" Then he flicked the lighter.

It didn't take. These lighters weren't as reliable as the ads claimed. Thank God!

I lunged at him. When I hit him he collapsed like a soggy rag doll. No struggle. I lay on top of him, the stench of the gasoline and his rubber suit making me gag. He still had the lighter in his hand, but I knew that now he wouldn't flick it. I was his brother. We lay there until backup arrived.

After telling this to the good Doctor, he looked perplexed. "So your brother is okay?"

"Okay?! Fuck no! He's not okay, God knows he's not okay! But he's alive. It's the Old Man that's dead. One of the ghouls watching the whole thing gave a graphic recounting to the first reporter who showed up. The old man quite literally had a stroke when he heard about his two boys on the evening news. He might've survived the stroke, but he dropped his cigarette on the sofa when he passed out. You can guess the rest. Ain't that ultimate stupid? Jimmy didn't do himself in. He did in the Old Man. Sent him off in a real funeral pyre. One more load of guilt for Jimmy to carry the rest of his pathetic life. So now they got him in the State loony bin."

To this the good doctor replied with his final bit of psychological wisdom. "Life is shit!" he said.

I seconded that emotion. Then we had a few more rounds. Then my memory gets a bit fuzzy.

I'm still a working cop, still drink in upscale bars and always head home alone to my bachelor apartment before last call so I'm fresh for the morning roll call. Never talk about Jimmy to anyone anymore, although I did strike up a conversation with another shrink a while back. (The guy was an ass, and it was a short conversation.)

I visit my brother once a week, but he doesn't talk anymore. And every Sunday I light a candle at St. Joseph's for the Old Man—though I guess it's really also for Jimmy. Seems somehow appropriate.

~~~~

NO PLACE LIKE HOME

"The tree of deepest root is found
Least willing still to quit the ground"
— Hester Thrale Piozzi ("Three Warnings")

Johnny Washington was an odd old man, very odd indeed, according to his then neighbours. You just don't order out for groceries when you're trying to survive on the public dole. Ain't sensible. They felt this extravagant: good money going to delivery boys.

Some of them swore they'd never seen him venture further than the once-white picket fence that marked the perimeter of his yard. Oh yes he did have company occasionally: his sister, who lived across town, visited at least once a week, and sometimes he'd have some of the neighbourhood men over for poker. He wasn't a hermit, no. He was just a homebody.

Alphaville was deemed an eyesore by the municipal government. If thy eyesore offend thee, pluck it out. Relocation, it's called. They moved the residents' possessions in big open trucks once used for hauling trash. The people of the community were scattered like hand-sown seed into new high-rises and row-housing—ugly 'compact dwellings' designed by men who lived in big sprawling homes on five acre lots and specialised in space-efficient housing construction.

Most folk didn't want to leave, no. Even those who'd, just days before the announcement, bragged about getting out, about going to

Toronto or The States, even they complained that the relocation stipend was ridiculously small. But what poor people want and what poor people get bear no relationship to each other, unless it is an inverse one.

.

So most people moved, did as they were told. And the bulldozers came in. Most people, mind you not everyone. Not Johnny Washington. The workers swore at the inquest that they'd checked his house, and there really was no reason to doubt them. These bulldozer drivers weren't goons or murderers, just working stiffs doing a job.

.

Washington's house was empty, they said. Empty as a robin's nest in winter. Not a stick of furniture, not a cheap calendar on the wall, not even old newspapers or any of the junk almost everyone left behind. In fact, its very barrenness is why they remembered it so clearly. Most of the clapboard buildings they'd metamorphosed into rubble had blurred in their memories, but they remembered well the very, very empty house with the yellowed picket fence. Sure they'd checked the house; they checked every house, for some of that old junk was worth saving. One man's junk is another man's treasure—or divorced people wouldn't remarry. These workers brought some little treasure home almost every evening.

.

It is hard to imagine where Johnny Washington had hidden. The workers insisted they'd looked in the closets and the attic. There was no basement. It was possible he was under the house, in the crawl space. But it was late November, bitterly cold, and they couldn't have been expected to look there. No, it wasn't a case of negligence, so went the ruling. Johnny Washington simply opted to stay home. His choice, no one's fault.

.

Two days after the demolition, kids playing in the rubble came upon part of his right arm, the elbow, sticking up through the soil like a tree root exposed by erosion. It was quite rigid, like his conviction that there is no place like home.

~~~~

THE HEART OF A RAT

"I hate ye: I feel my heart new open'd"
                                    —William Shakespeare (*Henry VIII*)

The rat was in a large, glass, cookie jar. On the front of the jar a ragged piece of masking tape had been attached at a careless angle. On this tape, scribbled in large, crude letters were the words: "GAS CHAMBER".

.

The cookie jar had a raised floor constructed of wire mesh. The rat, an albino with bright pink eyes, stood on this mesh floor staring out at the two men. The two men stared back. One of these men, the other one would surely argue, was unbalanced.

.

"So this is your victim. He's almost cute," Lane said.

.

The other man released a short, unpleasant laugh as he went over to the door of the laboratory and shut it. He removed a lab coat from the hook on the back of the door and put it on.

.

"That lab coat really is you, Noah."

.

The psychologist smiled wryly. "Why is it everything you say comes out sounding ironic?"

.

"I don't know," Lane replied, his expression unreadable. "I really don't know. I'm usually deadly serious."

109

"Yes, I guess you are. Well, I just hope you don't take this procedure too seriously, too much to heart, one might say—even if it is deadly." Noah opened one of the numerous cabinets that lined one wall of the lab and removed a can marked "Ether". "So your flight's at two?"

"Yes."

"I'm glad—although I'll miss you."

"You're such a civilized and rational man."

"Is that irony I hear again?"

Lane treated the question as rhetorical. "You know something, Noah, I won't miss you one bit. The only person in this whole fucking city I'll miss is your wife."

"I'm sorry to say that I'm sure Michelle will miss you too."

"Such a civilized and rational man! How can you even stand to talk to me?! Why aren't you reaching for that scalpel over there and going for my throat?"

"Don't be melodramatic. You're still my friend."

"Strange, that. I'm sure you must know that I've come to dislike you very much."

The psychologist shrugged. "I don't know why. We've been friends since Grade Six." He walked over to the cookie jar, held up the ether can histrionically. "Well, Lane, this is it: the moment of truth. Are you sure you really want to watch this?"

"Remember what you used to call me when we were kids?"

"Lane."

"Very funny. So you don't remember?"

"Sorry. We've been grown-ups for a long time now. My memory obviously isn't as good as yours."

"Mister Experience."

"Oh that. Yeah, I remember that. Good nickname. Was Michelle a good experience?"

"Yes she was."

"And this little procedure is just something you'd like to add to your ever expanding collection of experiences?"

"Something like that."

"I'm afraid that this is only an experience the first time through; after that it's just a damn unpleasant chore."

"This is my first time."

"Right, you're a virgin—of sorts." The psychologist smiled at his friend. "Don't suppose you want to stay and help me all day? I have a dozen of these fellows to do."

"Nope. Just want to lose my cherry and go on my way."

"Figures." The psychologist looked at his friend and for a moment something fierce was there in his eyes, but then he blinked twice and it was gone. "I'd better get started." He removed the stopper from the ether can and then, lifting the lid from the cookie jar, quickly poured the ether down the glass sides of the jar. He deftly replaced the lid before the rat could scramble out. The ether mixed with rat urine and five raisin-like turds to form a murky soup beneath the wire mesh floor.

"What a stink!"

"The mesh floor is to protect the rat from direct contact with the ether," the psychologist explained as he replaced the stopper on the ether can. "It'd burn his eyes if he sloshed around in it."

"Oh, I see, for humanistic reasons."

The psychologist gave his old friend a look of contempt. "Don't go feeling too superior and self-righteous. Remember that you are here for the experience, which is nothing more than a euphemism for cheap thrills. I'm here because this is part of my research."

.

"This is a part of a sort of research project for me too." Lane paused. "I'm studying my lover's husband in his natural environment."

.

"Is that really how you see me now? As your lover's husband?"

.

"Does that hurt your feelings?"

.

"How could it? You've told me a hundred times I have no feelings."

.

Lane shook his head slowly. "Noah, you know you're..."

.

"Look!" The psychologist bent over the cookie jar. "See! There, he's starting to panic. This'll be the last bit of activity. The ether works fast; it usually takes only a minute or so."

.

The rat was now frantically rearing and scratching at the glass. It could reach the lid when it reared, but the lid was far too heavy for the animal to lift. The rat's claws made soft clicking sounds against the glass.

.

Without lifting his gaze from the frenetic rat, the psychologist reached over and picked up an egg-salad sandwich from the counter and began eating.

.

Then as suddenly as it had begun, the frantic activity ceased. The rodent dropped back to all fours. Totally immobile, the creature stared out at the two men. Its breathing became very shallow. Soon the movement of white fur around its rib-cage was barely detectable. (Shallow inspiration; shallow expiration.)

.

Then the rat toppled over onto its side.

.

The psychologist set his sandwich down. "Now watch carefully for the precise moment of cessation."

.

"Cessation?"

.

"Of his breathing."

.

"Of his life you mean."

.

112

"Not really. Of course it all depends on how you operationally define death."

"I would think that once the poor thing has stopped breathing you could say he was..."

"You're forgetting about his heart. You, Lane, of all people, forgetting about the heart! Ah, but you'll see in a moment." The psychologist bent closer to the jar. "Ah, here we go! One, two, three..."

The fur still seemed to be moving ever so slightly. But so very slightly it was hard to be sure it wasn't merely an optical illusion.

"..five, six..."

"I think I still see movement," Lane said.

"...eight, that's his heart, nine ten." The psychologist lifted the lid. A sickening smell compounded of ether and urine, a strangely sweet and cloying odour, wafted out.

Lane gagged slightly. Then, perversely, he remembered the scent of Michelle's perfume.

The psychologist grabbed the rat and quickly tossed him onto a wire-mesh cage that was upside down in the lab sink. He then quickly replaced the lid, but the air was already thick with the stench.

"Is that rat cage your autopsy table?"

"You might say that." The psychologist turned on the tap and adjusted it so the water ran down the side of the sink next to the inverted cage. "The running water keeps the smell down a bit. Besides, it flushes away the blood."

"I see."

The psychologist picked up a scalpel from an instrument tray next to his half eaten sandwich. "We want his heart to keep on beating so it can pump the rinse right through his circulatory system."

"Then he is still alive!"

.

"Like I said, it all depends on your operational definition of alive. You can define death any way you want."

.

"Oh. Well, that's good to know."

.

"Even after the heart stops, the brain 'lives' for some time. But I think the definition of death most suitable for someone like you would be the moment his heart stops."

.

"When his heart stops or when his heart stops feeling?"

.

"Your brain feels, not your heart. The heart is just a dumb muscle." The psychologist leaned over the sink and carefully, neatly slit the rat's belly from just below the neck down to its (his) genitals. An obscene red gash opened up behind the blade as it travelled down. The gash resembled a horrible mouth, toothless, bloody, infected with some unspeakable cancer, a nightmare mouth of some ugly, lascivious and diseased witch. To the lips of this grotesque and hideous mouth the psychologist attached surgical clamps, ramming them in deep around the ribcage. Then forcefully he pulled open the wound and exposed the inner body cavity. The heart was there: a surprisingly small, dark-red thing (no valentine) pulsing with perfect regularity. The psychologist glanced up at Lane. "You feeling okay?"

.

"My god, the poor thing really is still alive!"

.

"Look, if you feel sick, get outta here now. I don't want you vomiting on my subject's innards. I warned you that it looks gruesome, but damn it, you insisted you wanted to see a perfusion."

.

"I'm all right."

.

"I hope so. I've got to work fast now." The psychologist stuck the scalpel under the running water for a second, then replaced it on the tray. Taking what looked like manicuring scissors, he made a small cut at the base of the heart. Blood poured out, gushing into the body cavity, filling it quickly, then overflowing and trickling out over the edges of the wound, over the clamps, down the white fur in sticky, straggling rivulets, to drip, drip down onto the stainless steel of the sink—where the rushing water softened the red to pink before swirling it away into the drain. And still, amazingly, the heart beat on.

.

"That was to allow the blood to flow out," the psychologist explained as he lifted a huge glass syringe with a thick three-inch long needle, "and this contains the saline solution we use to flush out the blood. The heart will do most of the work for us, pumping the rinse through the circulatory system." He inserted the tip of the needle into the top of the heart and began slowly depressing the plunger on the syringe.

The needle was so large and the heart so small that for a moment it seemed the heart would explode like an over-inflated balloon. But hearts are not so fragile as they appear.

Suddenly the rat began to convulse, his limbs twitching wildly, and then moments later his intestines, like long, grey night-crawlers, began to uncoil and tumble from the body cavity. The twitching and writhing became more and more intense as the plunger descended slowly. The intestines continued to unroll and tumble out of the gut that could only contain them while they were docilely coiled up. A rank smell of shit and rot and death rose from the sink. (The running tap water seemed to be failing miserably at controlling this odour.)

"Sweet Jesus!" Lane exclaimed, grimacing.

"The saline rinse solution is causing all the motor neurons to fire at once. The effect is similar to a grand mal seizure," the psychologist explained as he continued the steady pressure on the plunger. It sank lower and lower forcing more salt water through the rat's arteries and veins.

"You look like a madman. You are a madman. Have you any idea what a sight you are, standing there jabbing that gigantic needle into the heart of that poor animal? Have you any idea of what you're doing?"

"I assure you I know precisely what I am doing."

"You are one cold-hearted bastard. No wonder Michelle hates your guts."

"Again, my friend, it is a matter of operational definitions, which you might paraphrase as 'the proof is in the pudding'. Unlike you, I wouldn't presume to know what she feels, but I do know that she is staying with me, not leaving with you." The plunger finally reached the bottom of the glass cylinder.

"Thank God you're finished."

"Sorry, not quite yet." The psychologist deftly detached the needle from the syringe tube, leaving the actual needle dangling from the heart. He refilled the glass barrel from a vial marked "Formalin" and reconnected it to the needle. "Like I said, don't be so god damned self-righteous. Yes, she had sexual intercourse with you, but she's had sexual intercourse with me for eleven years. And she is staying here." He began depressing the plunger again, and, as he did so, the convulsions (which had just begun to subside) returned with even greater intensity.

"Sexual intercourse! I don't believe you, Noah, I just don't believe you. We made love; we didn't have 'sexual intercourse'." The violence of the rodent's convulsions reached a point where it seemed the beast would flip right off the cage and into the sink. "What the hell are you pumping into it now?"

"Formalin, a preservative, the basic ingredient in embalming fluid. And call it making love or call it fucking or call it anything you want, the fact remains: she is staying with me. I know you asked her to leave, but she is staying with me."

Lane stared at his friend, or the man he had once considered his friend. Then he looked down to the rat writhing on the inverted cage. The regularity of the heartbeat was finally faltering, becoming more and more spasmodic. The intestines continued to tumble out. The beast was spilling his guts. The heart of the beast was breaking. Ah, the roots of our metaphors! Especially our dead metaphors.

And then at last the injection was over.

The psychologist withdrew the syringe from the heart. He glanced at Lane (whose lean face had become pale), and then, so quickly his companion would've missed it had he momentarily turned away, took large shears from the surgical tray and snipped the rat's head off and set it upright on a paper towel.

The heart was still beating irregularly. The convulsions had almost subsided but not entirely. Two signs of life, perhaps, but without the head, it was not really a living thing there on the wire mesh. It was— offal. The psychologist took a large paper towel and scooped up the body of the rat and its viscera and deposited them in a green plastic garbage bag under the sink.

.

"We call this," he said slowly, "the separation of heart and head."

.

"You're skilled at it."

.

"You are too, Lane, you are too. If you weren't so damn good at it you never could have—slept with, shall we call it—your friend's wife. Nor could you hate me so much for what you did to me."

.

Lane stared at the rat's head on the counter. Its eyes were no longer pink. They were a dull, milky colour. The left one closed for an instant, then reopened: a wink. No, just an illusion, a flash of insanity. A refusal to accept something as finally, irrevocably dead.

.

"You know what Michelle told me this morning when I told her you were coming to see me before you caught your plane."

.

Lane shook his head.

.

"She said that while she'd felt passion for you, she never loved you."

.

Lane continued to stare at those milky eyes. He was damned if they didn't seem to possess some vital spark of animation that signals life. This was, obviously, absurd: the heart and head of the creature were most definitely and permanently severed—and that was as good an 'operational definition' of death as anyone could hope to come up with. The carcass, the guts, lay in the garbage bag amidst soiled paper towels, bloody gauze, cigarette butts, discarded syringes. The disembodied head lay on the brown paper towel, the empty (empty empty empty) eyes open to nothingness. Death.

.

"She also said," the psychologist continued as he put on a pair of thin plastic gloves, "that contrary to your arrangement, she will not be meeting you at the airport to say goodbye." He then picked up the head and with medium-size surgical scissors began cutting away the flesh. The ears came off first—snip, snip. Then the flesh, looking like uncooked chicken, pale and sickly coloured, was clipped off in small chunks that were dropped onto another paper towel. There was no blood, for the perfusion had been most expertly done. The psychologist's face grew serious with concentration. In five minutes he had exposed the cranium and was once again changing

117

instruments. Using small, curved, blunt pliers, rondeurs, he began methodically picking away bits of the cranium.

Lane watched Michelle's husband carefully snap off bit after bit of the bone that surrounded the once living brain. "You do love her," he said after the long silence. "You do, don't you, in your own heartless way?"

"Yes, Lane, I love her."

"You are amazing to watch."

"Thank you. One has to be careful not to nick the cortex with the bone chips as you lift them out. It is delicate work."

"I can see that. But why do you do it yourself. Don't you have some ghoulish assistant who could do this sort of thing for you?" Lane hesitated briefly before giving into the temptation to add: "Or do you like doing it?"

"Yeah, it's lotsa fun." He paused. "Actually, my research assistant is sick, the flu. I need the brain sections by Monday. Besides, it's good to keep one's hand in—so to speak. Ah, there, take a good look. See how smooth the cortex is?

"Yeah."

"Ever seen a human cerebral cortex."

"I don't hang around autopsy rooms. I've seen pictures of course."

"Well, then you know it's convoluted, full of winding valleys and ridges. It's like a labyrinth. It gives us humans more cortical surface area, this convoluted structure. And that, my friend, is exactly what does make us human: more cortical neurons, a greater ability to think, to reason, to be reasonable."

"You have it all figured out, don't you?"

"No," the psychologist replied, returning to his task, "not at all. Which is why I do this kind of research." A few minutes later the brain was out. The head and brainpan joined the body in the garbage bag. Holding the tiny, pale object on his palm, he studied it for a few seconds, then held it out for Lane's inspection.

Lane looked at it. It looked totally insignificant, completely uninteresting; it had no connection with anything.

"Please note," the psychologist said, noticing Lane's lack of interest, "that there isn't a single nick in the cortex." He held it closer to his wife's lover's face."

"Yeah, just lovely."

"Yes, it is a nice brain." The psychologist smiled, hesitated for effect, then added: "I picked it myself."

Lane grimaced. "Jesus, Noah! Is that a standard little joke of yours?"

For the first time since Lane arrived, the psychologist dropped his professorial tone. "Why don't you cut the crap? We grew up on the South Side, remember? I certainly don't remember you having any particular sympathy for all the alley rats. In fact, what I do remember are those little hunting expeditions with air rifles. You've killed a few rats in your life too. You did it for 'sport'. I do it as part of my profession. Exactly when did you join the Animal Rightists?"

"I've grown up."

"Bullshit. All you're doing is elevating personal squeamishness to a high moral principle. Mister Experience, ha! Mister Gut-Feeling. Watching this makes you a little queasy, therefore this is wrong. Ethics by tummy-ache." He set the brain down on a paper towel. "And, I might add, the converse seems to be true with you too. If it feels good, it must be the right thing to do. Morality by penile erection."

Lane looked down at the tiny, pale object. "I didn't come here to be lectured," he said softly. "Are you done now?"

"I can't help but wonder exactly why you did come here. But to answer your question: yes, I'm done for now. I'll put the brain in a formalin solution for 24 hours to toughen it. Then I'll quick freeze it and section it using that microtome over there." The psychologist pointed to an instrument that looked like a refined cousin of a delicatessen meat-slicer. His voice had taken on a pedagogical tone again. "I'll prepare the slides from 30 micron thick sections. Then I'll be able to determine if the electrodes where in the right place; I'll be able to tell if the original operation worked."

"The operation was a success. The patient died."

"You might say that."

"And this whole gruesome ritual was just to flush out the blood from the brain? You like your brains bloodless."

"Right."

"Heartless."

"Are you referring to me or the rat."

"Disembodied brain."

"Me or the rat?"

"Both, both."

"Lane, I think you're a fool."

"Noah, the feeling is mutual."

"Goodbye, Lane." Noah put the rat brain down, removed his plastic gloves and held out his hand.

Lane did not shake it. "Goodbye." He turned and went to the door. He hesitated for a moment before opening it and leaving.

After the door shut, Noah picked up the brain again. He stared at the small, pale object lying in the palm of his hand. It felt strangely cold. Then he made a gentle fist around it, cocked his arm, and flung the brain as hard as he could at the laboratory wall.

It bounced off like a little rubber ball.

~~~~

AQUA REGINA

"Bluid is thicker than water."

—Scottish Proverb

Life's a bitch and then you die. No, life's a bitch and then you marry her—and then your son dies. No, life's a beach and then you drown.

.

Another large wave crashes ashore.

.

Let's start again. The meaning of life is in the meanness of life. The meanness of life is because nature is stingy. Mother Nature is a god-damned, mother-fuckin' Scot. Like my dad.

.

Another wave breaks on the beach, this one darkening the colour of the sand right up to my heels, but my feet do not get wet. My feet are cold. I have cold feet. I bet the water is warm. But, no, I will get up now and go home. The bottle is empty and the tide is coming in.

.

They have nice psychobabble catch-phrases for it, one being 'premature loss syndrome'. I hate that kind of labelling. My job is labeller, so naturally I hate labels.

.

I can see the lights of the Belmont Marina from here. My wife's name is Marina.

.

Marina. What kind of name is that for a woman? A place to dock your boat. A slip. A safe harbour. Like hell. Like hell is harbour.

Hank, my colleague at the university, thinks women are coves. Hank is a bloody fool. Hank is taking antibiotics for some kind of minor STD. He hasn't noticed that the harbour waters are polluted. He's been harbouring illusions.

I don't usually give advice, but I'll make an exception. Don't ever do it. Don't ever trust a woman. Don't ever trust life. Don't ever try to return to the sea.

.

Let's start again. My name is Richard. My friends call me Rich. I'm not.

I am a biologist, specialising in aquatic taxonomy. I live in Richmond, in a rather ordinary but well constructed, three bedroom, red brick bungalow with a swimming pool in the backyard and a large aquarium in the rec room. The Pacific Ocean is three blocks away. I know you expect me to tell you the sordid details of how I fell from grace with the sea. Sorry, but I usually fail to meet people's expectations. Ask Marina. She'll tell you.

My son is dying. That is central to all this. His name is Jason. He is no Argonaut. He has hair as dark as 20,000 leagues. He hasn't the sense God gave plankton, or he wouldn't be dying.

We have a 'love seat' in the rec room with broken springs. If you sit on it, you sink into a cavity and strange metallic noises are emitted from beneath you. I am sure that one day the dislocated spring will totally snap loose from its moorings and shoot up, impaling someone in their genitalia. Life's like that. Life's a bitch.

Jason's illness was originally diagnosed by a doctor who had hair in his ears. It isn't right that a doctor who hasn't the decency to trim the hair in his ears should be allowed to pass a death sentence.

This doctor said the disease was "progressing very rapidly." I thought that was an inappropriate verb and told him so.

.

Let's start again. I love my son. I used to love my wife. When I first started going out with her, my friends told me she was a cold fish. I didn't believe them. I specialise in aquatic classification, so for their labelling I had the contempt of a professional. Ironically, she is a Pisces.

.

.

Let's start again. This is Marina explaining life to me. She has tried to do this many times. I have a Ph.D. but I'm a slow learner. I've never understood her explanations.

.

"You can't expect life to be fair."

.

"I can expect anything I damn well please."

.

"You know what I mean. If you expect fairness, you're going to be disappointed."

.

"So you're not disappointed that Jason is going to be dead in three months? Just because you don't expect fairness from life?"

.

"I love him too."

.

"You love him, but you've never shed a tear?"

.

"Richard, what is—is. I can't remember ever crying, even as a child. Even when my mum died last year, I didn't cry. You know that. There just isn't any point to crying. Do you think that means I don't care?"

.

"Frankly, yes."

.

"People are different."

.

"Yeah, homo sapiens should be further divided into homo calidus and homo frigidus."

.

"What does that mean? You know I don't know Latin."

.

"It means I'm going to walk down to the beach."

.

Let's start again. I specialise in algae. There are seven phyla of algae. Algae. Pond scum. The filmy, translucent stuff at lake bottoms. Giant seaweed, meters in length. Algae, like suffering, can take many forms.

.

I recently published a paper on the classification of Cyanophyta, the so-called 'blue-green algae'. Some biologists class these with the bacteria, even though they are much larger than most bacteria. Their classification is moot. Cyanophyta resemble bacteria in structure and most functions and, unlike most algae, are single-celled, lacking organelles such as a nucleus and chloroplasts. However, they contain both DNA and chlorophyll, and furthermore, produce oxygen as a waste product. So are they plant or animal or bacterium? Labelling things is harder than most people realise.

.

.

Let's start again. My son is twenty-five. He'll never be twenty-six. He doesn't live at home any more. He lives at Martin Hill Presbyterian Hospital in the terminal ward. They don't call it the terminal ward, but everyone knows that is what it is. You can see the pity flood into people's eyes as soon as you hit the elevator button for the fifth floor.

.

The doctors say he will drown in his own bodily fluids. His lungs are filling up, like the tide coming in. The nurses say he won't suffer. In this particular case, I think the doctors are telling the truth and the nurses are lying.

.

The young woman who gave him this disease will also die. But not for quite a while, I'm told. Women are tougher, live longer. Water is their natural element. Women can breathe underwater for longer. If you look closely, you'll see that women have gills.

.

.

Let's start again. Algae can be harmful. The so-called 'red tide' of certain dinoflagellates produces a deadly nerve toxin that kills millions of fish in temperate and subtropical waters. In lakes where there is too much nutrient, blanketing growths of green and blue-green algae smother fish and plant life. Shellfish feeding on the Gonyaulax take in large quantities of an alkaloid toxin, and then some time later a number of seafood lovers die.

.

.

Let's start again. This is my father. He paid for my education—and only charged me 5% interest in paying it back. I never understood why news reports on fatal traffic accidents ended with an estimate of the damage to the vehicles. I'm sure my father never found this strange or disturbing.

·

"The bills must be horrible. You should renegotiate your mortgage. Interest rates have gone down again."

·

"Dad, my only son will be dead within three months!"

·

"Three months in hospital is a long time, a lot of money. Do you have any idea what this is costing you?"

·

"I don't care what it is costing me!"

·

"You'll care when the bills come in. Just because you're emotionally distraught, you shouldn't be fiscally irresponsible."

·

"Dad."

·

"Yes?"

·

"Fuck off."

·

·

Let's start again. When did sex become dangerous? It didn't seem dangerous when I was young. But I suppose it always was. Syphilis killed millions. Loving a woman killed part of me. I won't talk about my son.

·

Algae reproduce in three different ways. Vegetative reproduction is accomplished by division of a single cell or fragmentation of a colony. Asexual reproduction is accomplished by the production of zoospores. Sexual reproduction involves the union of gametes. Many species of algae reproduce by an alternation of generations, requiring separate asexual and sexual organisms to complete a life cycle. But some are totally asexual.

·

But what do you care if algae fuck or not?

·

·

Let's start again. I think we should, we really should. And this time with totally asexual reproduction and no siren memories of the womb or the primordial sea to lure us to our death.

·

125

Let's start again.

~~~~

PEELING

*"No mask like open truth to cover lies.
As to go naked is the best disguise."*
                    —William Congreve ("The Double Dealer")

Last night, while doing research, a new acquaintance of mine and I were almost raped by three drunken bikers (with life-threatening halitosis) in the parking lot of a strip club on the outskirts of Barrie. I talked our way out of it: convinced them not to ruin things, because we'd willingly party with them the next night. They were so pissed and stupid, I could've sold them the Brooklyn Bridge.

.

Afterwards, Alice, the naïve Social Welfare student I'd dragged to this joint, said: "Julie, maybe you really do know something about psychology."

.

This made me laugh.

.

This made me laugh because psychology is laughable—a fact I perhaps too often point out publicly. I ended up majoring in it more by default than intent. (I couldn't hack the difficult math in Physics or the even more 'difficult' Profs in English Lit, though science and books were my real interests.) So I ended up with a worthless B.A. in Psyc. Having always had the sense God gave a cantaloupe, I decided

127

to throw good time and money after bad and applied for grad school. Naturally my friends were shocked when I told them I intended to continue 'studying' what I had told them repeatedly was ninety-nine percent bullshit.

.

"Julie, you're crazy," they said.

.

"You ever met any one with a degree in psychology who isn't crazy?" I always replied. "Besides it runs in the family."

.

My explanation, if you can it call it that, has to do with this idea (idée fixe, actually) I have for my master's thesis: the psychodynamics of strip clubs.

.

Oh and it also has to do with my father, with understanding him.

.

.

My father is good man. It was totally unfair what happened to him, no matter what anyone says. He was silly sometimes, but it was almost always because his intentions were so good. I don't know if the road to hell is paved with good intentions, but good intentions definitely create a road with steep grades and dangerous curves. Pity. Dad so wanted his life to be a highway straight and wide, with high, reinforced guard rails, where he could race his classic Carmen Ghia. Instead it was more like a back road in the Appalachians designed by a drunken engineer and built by a corrupt contractor.

.

When I was only thirteen or fourteen he came home late from one of his drinking bouts while I was sitting out on the back deck looking at the lake and daydreaming about a boy in my Geography class. Dad spoiled me, so I didn't really expect to catch hell for still being up, but when I heard the roar of his 'antique' sport car's bad muffler in the driveway, I crouched down in the wooden lounge chair and was very still. I knew that no matter how drunk he was, his first mission upon arriving home was to "check in" on me. When I heard him enter my room, which is just off the deck, I got up and quickly went in. I didn't want him to freak out when he saw my empty bed.

.

I caught him just in time. He had a wild look in his eyes when I came in behind him and turned on the light. I'm sure he was just about to start yelling to wake Mother up. I quickly told him in hushed tones that I couldn't sleep and was just sitting out back feeding the mosquitoes.

"Can't sleep. Oh, I hope you haven't inherited that from me, Julie. It's a hell of a legacy."

I assured him that I rarely had any problem sleeping—which wasn't entirely true—and suggested he just go to bed and let me be. But he wouldn't have any of it.

So we sat out back and, with waves lapping the shore as accompaniment, he gave me one of many well-intentioned lectures on what I should do with my life. He was surprisingly eloquent, given that he was having some trouble shaping his words. At least it seemed eloquent to this pubescent girl.

The gist of his advice was that "you've got to go for it" and "when you finally find what matters, devote your life". Not deep, admittedly, but nor is it really bad advice. I guess one might say his tragedy was that he didn't follow his own advice until he was too old to get away with it. I wish I knew where he was now so I could tell him this, but contrary to what the cops seem to think, I haven't heard from him since he fled.

Dad was an immigrant kid and rather strangely proud of it. Finnish. Now Finns aren't exactly your typical discriminated-against minority. I don't even know what the derogatory, racist term for a Finn is. I think the worst stereotyping Finns have to put up with is the belief that they're all good carpenters—hardly something to get seriously indignant about. (And, in fact, Dad actually was a good carpenter. He designed and built our rather elaborate deck in two weekends with the help of his brothers.) Still he seemed to like the idea of humble beginnings and outsider status. I suppose it was the romantic in him. That, of course, was another fatal flaw, one that often accompanies good intentions and "going for it, devoting your life."

But, at least until he was pushing fifty, he'd definitely suppressed his natural romanticism. I can't say for certain whether or not he'd always been faithful to my mother, but I tend to think so, for he used to speak with contempt of any of his friends who 'fooled around' on their wives. And I never heard him say anything negative about my mother—which I suspect is a pretty exceptional characteristic in a husband. In fact the only time he ever got really angry at me was when, in adolescent pique, I said something nasty about Mother Dear. He almost struck me (well, he lifted his arm in a threatening

129

gesture) when I called Mother Dear "a tight-assed shyster bitch". (This is an evaluation I, at the ripe old age of twenty-five, still think quite perspicacious for a teenager.)

Now I sincerely wish he hadn't been such a loyal and devoted husband. A few quick and dirty affairs might have acted as a kind of emotional inoculation. But maybe I'm psychologizing. And I hate people who psychologize.

He married Mother when she was in law school and he in business school. The wedding picture on the piano shows a woman with a very pretty face, but if you look closely you can see hints of what was to come. Even then she had that pinched look that so perfectly defines her in my mind's eye, even though it was well disguised by that proverbial bloom of youth.

Still, I have to admit she was a fairly attractive young woman back then, and I am sure he was madly in love with her back. Actually, I suspect he's still in love with her, but it is a very different kind of love. Stained and tainted. Tired and old. More comprised of loyalty and memory than affection and passion.

Middle-age hit my father hard. He was a bit of a jock as a young man, and he used to run in the Ottawa Marathon until affluence and age caught up with him. Heredity gave him a stocky body type and a fondness for food and booze that started to take their toll on his looks by the time he was forty. He finished the last marathon he ran, but he spent half an hour puking his guts out afterwards. He didn't run the next year because he claimed his knees were bothering him. Middle age changed him from a runner into an occasional jogger—a decline similar to the classic marital sliding down from passionate lover to comfortable companion. He used to say that joggers are to runners as masturbators are to lovers. He gave up the saying after his last marathon.

When someone you care about gets into trouble you feel they don't deserve, you want to blame somebody and usually someone you know. I blame Mother Dear, of course, but I blame my father's friend, Mike, even more. The guy was a bad influence. (Funny, but my father never said that about any of my teenage friends, some of whom I now realise were pretty sleazy. Now here I am doing the role reversal bit. Rather presumptuous, I know.)

Mike was a bachelor. And he was, like Mother, a shyster, specialising in quote Family Law. In fact Dad met him at one of Mother's mandatory social functions. They hit it off immediately. Both my father and Mike had pretensions to liberalism, even a waspish, diluted libertinism. With my father it was all talk, for he was at heart a hopeless Puritan. With Mike it was a bit more real—if being the male equivalent of a slut is more 'real'. Sad to say, my dad envied Mike for this. If Mike had been married, Dad would've been contemptuous, but because Mike was 'free', any outrageous thing he did was somehow perceived as admirably roguish.

.

They'd go out drinking together maybe once or twice a week. Dad drank too much, but usually he just did so at home, and it never interfered with his workday world or the decency with which he treated me and everyone else, even Mother Dear. Mike lured him away from the rec room bar. Our lakefront home was twenty minutes out of town so it was especially crazy for my father to drive back into town to go drinking with good-buddy Mike. I'm sure Dad's rebuilt fire-engine red, '65 Carmen Ghia must have been extremely conspicuous to the cops waiting roadside to make their monthly drunk-driver quota. That he never was stopped was a minor—and probably, in the long-run, unfortunate—miracle: not a blessing, but rather a curse, in disguise. It might have terminated his visits to The Adam's Apple.

.

I don't understand why Mother Dear let Dad get away with these escapades. I guess she just didn't care—as long as it didn't interfere with her well-ordered life. Still one would've thought she'd worry, if not about his safety, then at least about her own reputation should her respectable husband get nailed for impaired driving. But perhaps she was shrewd enough to give him just enough free rein so he'd be willing to come home to pasture every night.

.

Mike and Dad frequented a sleazy strip-club on the far side of town. Dad made no bones about this with me, his only daughter, the light of his life. I think he rather revelled in this small act of non-conformity to Upper-Middle-Class mores. He often referred to himself as a 'feminist'—something which came to annoy me as I grew older—but apparently he saw no contradiction in visiting The Adam's Apple almost weekly to watch young girls take their clothes off. I don't think any the worse of him for it, but I doubt if most feminists would concur with his description of himself as one of them.

It was The Adam's Apple, of course, where he fell from grace, but it seems inappropriate to try to lay the blame on a business as old as business itself. I went there once. Dad, and especially Mike, would wax eloquent about its "ambience", so I figured I'd see for myself. Since Dad and Mike were both so well-heeled there is no question that they were slumming, but they obviously thought highly of themselves for their open-mindedness. In reality the place is a depressing dive. I've subsequently seen far more "ambient" clubs, but then, also worse dives.

I went with my friend Gloria when we were both eighteen. It isn't the sort of place young women go to alone, unless they're working there or were raised in a very different social stratum than was I, but it wasn't a dangerous den of iniquity either. Conscientious girl that I was, I did my homework first: I grilled Gloria's older brother, who'd often bragged about being a habitué of the place, about strip club protocol. He was amused by my interest.

"Chemistry and physics too tough for you, Julie? You want to investigate some other career choices? Well, you do have nice legs, but I've never seen your breasts."

I coldly informed him that he never would. This didn't seem to break his heart, and since he liked to talk, I soon learned more than I really cared to know—at the time. I learned that only a very few of the dancers were hookers, although a few more did rather intimate massage. I learned about the differences between 'show girls' and 'dancers', between table dances and lap dances, between Yankee clubs (the vast majority of which are really very straight-laced with girls always wearing g-strings and many where it is even illegal to serve liquor) and Canadian ones (where full nudity is the norm and the beer flows heavily). I learned that the euphemism for stripper is 'exotic dancer', although the women always drop the adjective 'exotic' in describing themselves. I learned that guys called them 'peelers'.

Armed with all this information, Gloria and I ventured out to the edge of town where the buses don't run, but boys will be boys. I remember that I found it all rather depressing. I remember that I was surprised at how subdued it was, how the men were so quiet. I remember being surprised that nobody hit on us, the only two women in the place who weren't parading around half-naked. And I still remember that one of the dancers that night was named Veronique, a bad dancer with a stunning body; I especially remember this because her name was the same as the child bitch who later fucked up my father's life.

.

.

I met my second Veronique, the alleged victim, only once, a year and a half ago. I was coming home from university for the Thanksgiving weekend, a luxury many of my fellow students couldn't afford. A man my father's age with thick nasal hair sat next to me on the plane and kept trying to engage me in conversation.

.

When Dad picked me up at the airport, I knew something was seriously wrong. He'd been drinking, but that wasn't anything new. What was strange was his lack of enthusiasm at the sight of me. Usually he beamed at me from the terminal window like a beacon, a beacon intended to guide me from the airplane to the shelter of his arms. This time the guiding light was dim, his smile forced.

.

I knew immediately that he had something to tell me, something painful for him. Having no more than carry-on luggage, we promptly headed out to the parking lot after a clumsy hug. When I didn't see his red Carmen Ghia double parked out front (begging to be ticketed), I knew for certain that something was wrong. (Whenever I came home from university, he always came alone to pick me up and always took me for a spin at illegal speeds before bringing me home to Mother Dear.) I wanted to ask him what was bothering him, but instead I merely asked him where his car was.

.

"I brought the wagon."

.

As he spoke I spotted it in the regular parking lot—and then understood why he'd brought the Ford station wagon (which he referred to as "the boat"). His sporty VW only seats two.

.

"I want you to meet someone, Julie. And I want you to be polite and friendly. It is very important to me that you are nice to my friend. I'll be dropping her off downtown and then I'll explain who she is and..." His voice trailed off. "I'll explain."

.

I did a lot of thinking during the time it took to walk the twenty or thirty meters to the car. It'd finally happened. Dad had found someone else. As far as I was concerned that was just fine and no reason for him to be glum. I was an adult; my parents needn't stay together for this kid's sake.

.

Certainly Mother's life wouldn't change very drastically. My parents had been effectively living separate lives for years. They just shared a nice house on the lake and the duties of acting as escorts for each other when fulfilling social responsibilities (primarily hers, since business managers, unlike lawyers with political aspirations, aren't expected to do anything more than what is indicated in their job descriptions). Dad was no fool: one would think that he would know I'd be happy for him if he found someone to really love him.

.

But when we got to the car and saw his "friend", I began to understand his apprehension. He wasn't worried about my disapproval of what he was doing. He was worried about my disapproval of with whom he was doing it.

.

And he was justified in worrying. She looked like the archetypal bimbo.

.

Bimbo. I know that is a silly word, but in this case it fit perfectly. In fact, to be more precise, she looked like a teenage bimbo. She looked like one of the East End girls from my high school. Her makeup, laid on with a trowel, made her look even younger, made her look like a little girl who got into her mother's makeup kit. Her eyeliner, in particular, was comical. Had she used magic marker?

.

I was going to get in the backseat, but my father took my arm and guided me to the front passenger door. He virtually shoved me into the front seat next to her, and so I quickly discovered that she was as intemperate in the application of perfume as of eyeliner.

.

Veronique was "delighted" to meet me. She had a cloying French Canadian accent.

.

The 'conversation' as we rode downtown was a question and answer period. She did the asking. I did the answering—at least as best I could, for the questions were either rhetorical or unanswerable.

.

How does one answer questions such as "What's it like to be a brain?" I thought about that one a long time before muttering something inane about not really being very smart, just industrious. What I should've done is met question with question: "What's it like to be a vagina?"

Every kid with older uncles and aunts learns early how to pass the social quiz that most adults think of as conversing with the young. So, although she was ludicrous in the role of adult, I responded with the same pat, empty answers I used on my old Uncle Ed. But I took to replying (mentally) in a more creative (albeit bitchy) fashion.

"Where did you find such a wonderful father?" Under a cabbage leaf. Where did he find you, under a rock?

"I wish I had a childhood like yours. What was it like?" Fine, but don't worry you still have lots of time.

"Doesn't it feel strange to still be in school at your age?" No, doesn't it feel strange to be out of school at your age?

When we got downtown and Dad pulled over to the kerb, I quickly jumped out and occupied my eyes by scanning the cumulous clouds scudding across the sky. I didn't want to know how she said her farewells to my father. Probably she stuck her tongue down his throat and patted his balding head.

After she got out and we stiffly shook hands, I climbed back into the Ford and whispered angrily: "Drive, she said."

He didn't say anything until he'd negotiated our way out of the midtown traffic snarl.

"Well Julie?"

"You ask questions which are about as meaningful as hers. Well what?"

"You obviously have something to say. Say it."

"First let me ask a few questions."

"Shoot."

"I'd like to." I opened my bag and took out, not a gun, but a cigarette. "Is she your lover?"

"Yes."

.

"Are you crazy?"

.

"Julie, you're prejudging. You just met her."

.

"Dad, I don't have to give her a battery of psychological tests to know she's a loser."

.

"She's an artist."

.

"An artist?! Yeah, and I'm an astronaut."

.

"She is, really. A painter."

.

"Dad, you've never been in an art gallery in your life. You wouldn't recognise an artist if he—excuse me, if she bit you on the ass. Which doesn't, incidentally, mean that if Ver-on-ick performs that little bit of foreplay on you, she is thus an artist."

.

"Julie, I don't like it when you talk that way." He looked at me with those hurt eyes that in my childhood did far more to punish my misdemeanours than any of my mother's various formal 'disciplinary actions'. "And I don't like to see you smoking."

.

"And I don't like it when you act the way you're acting. My God, Dad, she's just a poor, dumb teenager. You're forty-seven years old. Have you lost your mind?!"

.

"She's twenty-one."

.

"Yeah, and I'm an astronaut."

.

"It would mean a lot to me if you could accept her."

.

"Turn right here!"

.

He was startled and confused, but he swung the lumbering car down Engles Road without thinking.

.

"Stop the car."

.

Again he did as he was told. Anything for his beloved daughter. Only when I opened the door, grabbed my bags and jumped out did he notice the Greyhound Bus Station a little ways down the road.

"Julie, don't be crazy."

"It isn't me that should be institutionalised. Say hello to Mother Dearest. Make whatever excuses you want. The flight was cancelled. Whatever. Call me in a week or so. Maybe your mental illness is acute and self-limiting, and you'll have recovered by then."

I slammed the door and started walking toward the bus station. I expected him to pull up next to me and try to dissuade me from returning to Montreal, but he must've simply turned the car around and gone home. I never heard from him again, because a week later the proverbial shit hit the fan.

That spring I graduated. He wasn't there, although some plain-clothes cops were. And now it is spring again. And still no birds sing.

I have no inside information on what happened. All I know is what I read in the papers—and what I could get Mike to tell me. And both I view as very unreliable sources of information. Veronique won't return my calls. And the other day the cops called and told me I shouldn't be trying to contact her.

I wasn't surprised to learn Dad's love was a stripper. Mike said she was a real master (mistress?) of this unappreciated and socially unacceptable art. However, this wasn't what Dad had meant when he said she was an artist. Apparently she painted abstracts when she wasn't painting her face. Action paintings, a la Pollock, no doubt.

Dad and Mike used to occasionally come home from their nights at The Adam's Apple and talk about "a goddess" they'd seen. They had some kind of casual rating system, and maybe twice a year a dancer would so fascinate them that she scored right off their scale. These dancers were referred to as "goddesses", twelves on a ten point rating scale. Veronique was, in their eyes, one of these goddesses. Probably a thirteen for my father.

I once, to my sophisticated teen-age embarrassment, actually heard my father say he didn't know art but damn it he knew what he liked. Well he certainly didn't know female beauty either, but again I guess

137

he knew what he liked. He took to worshipping this V goddess.

.

When I try to recall exactly what she looked like under all the makeup, I can't. In the stage lights the makeup may have magically transformed her face into something startling and enchanting, but I cannot imagine how. As for her body, I can't say. She was wearing jeans and a sweatshirt when I met her, and I only remember her as having a typically slim teenager girl's figure. Maybe those jeans and sweatshirt covered an Aphrodite body. Or maybe it was primarily her dancing that was magical. Being a straight woman (and one who doesn't even like dancing) I'm no judge of what makes a man think a skinny teenager stripper is a "goddess". But both Mike and Dad obviously thought that she was indeed no mortal woman.

.

Well whether mortal or immortal, she was some kind of enchantress. Apparently Dad headed out to The Adam's Apple every night subsequent to first seeing her. Mike, the supposed libertine, couldn't stand the pace, and Dad started doing what he'd never done before: going alone. I wonder how many table-dances he bought, how many drinks, before their relationship moved beyond the confines of The Adam's Apple.

.

.

Veronique was found lying unconscious on the Guelph entrance ramp to the 401. The driver who 'discovered' her had to swerve so suddenly that he hit the guard-rail and his 1995 Honda Civic, according to the local papers, "suffered several thousand dollars damage". She didn't regain consciousness until she was in Emerg, and then she told the cops that she was drugged and raped by an older man she had considered "a friend". She claimed that after sexually assaulting her, he threw her from his car.

.

She named my father as this person. Blood tests confirmed that she was under the influence of LSD. Vaginal smears confirmed that she had recently had sex, although there was no evidence of forced intercourse. She did, however, have a number of bruises on her body. Computer database searches uncovered the fact that she was only seventeen years of age, a run-away from a small town in Quebec since she was fifteen, and her real name was Michelle La Blanc. A visit by the police to my home revealed that her alleged assailant had not come home that night.

.

Dad didn't come home the next night either. Or the next. Or ever again. If he were really innocent, why did he flee? Or so goes the local judgement.

.

I don't know what really happened. I do know that my father hated drugs (alcohol excepted), and so if she were stoned, it was almost certainly her own doing. Hell, he wouldn't have a clue where to get acid. I also know my father is not a violent man; as a kid, I was never even lightly spanked. Finally, I know they were lovers—although I choke on using that word for whatever was going on between them. So I'm sure he didn't drug and rape her. What happened is probably mundane and banally sordid.

.

To me the deeper mystery is why my father hasn't contacted me, the apple of his eye. Not a word in almost two years. Is it shame? I am convinced that if I could only get to understand the context, I will finally understand how he could so completely disconnect from me, his only and most beloved daughter.

.

I guess this is all by way of explanation for hanging out in strip clubs, sometimes very unsavoury ones. I began this 'preliminary research' while still finishing my course work because I found a thesis advisor who was so very enthused about my initial prospectus topic she told me I could set to it as soon as I wanted. I know I'm using her. She's a militant lesbian feminist, so she probably isn't going to like the perspective I take in my final paper. Oh well, if she doesn't like my conclusions, that's her problem, not mine. I'm doing this for myself (and my father), not to get an M.A. in a discipline I really can't take seriously.

.

So what have I learned? Not much really, but I have quite an impressive collection of tapes. Most of the dancers, surprised to see a woman in the audience, don't mind talking to me, rarely objecting to my petite, discreet little recorder. Sometimes I have to reassure—or disappoint— them regarding my 'sexual orientation', but that's rarely a big issue. Sure, a few of the dancers are hostile or speak a patois French I can't follow, even after living five years in Montreal. And a few are too stoned to make any sense. But most of them are as willing to talk about themselves as they are willing to show themselves—naked, peeled.

.

And the men, I talk to them too. Once I make it clear I'm not working at the place nor am I some kind of social reformer, they are surprisingly friendly and civil and frank. The propositions I do get are so genteel as to be almost ludicrous, and their acceptance of my demure rejections is rarely less than gracious. Oh, a few of the men are two-neurone types who ride Harley Hogs (since biker clubs have their hirsute hands on a lot of the clubs—and the women who dance there), but most of the people at these places, both the men and the women, seem more, not less, civilised than those you'd find at any singles bar.

So I have no conclusions to draw yet and only a marginally better understanding of this whole strange scene. Just the other day I confessed to one of my friends, a former Psyc Major herself, that even if I never get any insight into this milieu, I still feel a compulsion to explore it. She then confirmed me in my belief that psychology is dangerous hokum. She 'brilliantly' analysed my behaviour as a hidden desire to find my father. Hah! There is nothing hidden about my desire to find my father, but I'm not so stupid as to think he's hanging around strip clubs anymore. I just kind of like the nakedness of the places. The women take off their clothes. The men take off their more metaphorical covering. When both are peeled, interactions are a lot more honest, if more obviously base—or, to use a nicer word, basic.

The other night I was asked by one of the dancers, for what must be the twentieth time, if I'd ever consider doing what they're doing. The pay is great, they always tell me. Usually I just sort of shrug off the question. This time I felt witty and said: "Hell, I can't dance."

"Neither can I," she replied. She waved her arm at the audience: "They don't care, honey, they just want to see you naked. I once worked at club in Ottawa called The Bare Facts. Well, that's all they want, girl, the bare facts."

Odd. I have to admit that's all I want too.

~~~~

THE MAN WHO CREATED WOMEN

"Imagination is a jealous mistress."

—Hippokrites

.

"In dreams begin responsibilities."
            —Delmore Schwartz ("In Dreams Begin Responsibilities")

.

"May all your dreams come true!"

—Traditional Blessing (and Curse)

Dennis Culroth created his first woman in 1970, when he was a mere twenty-three years old. Her name was Barbara, and she was the corporeal manifestation of his favourite adolescent fantasy: a tall, slender blonde with a fine-featured cover-girl face. She was, he realised in retrospect, actually a rather conventional type of beauty, almost completely lacking in mystery and sensuality. Her lips were too thin, her smile too wide. She was not the sort of woman whose appearance would hold the attention of a mature male, but then Dennis Culroth was not a mature male. While Barbara was attractive, one might've expected more from a person of Dennis Culroth's tremendous imaginative powers: a creation more original, more individual, more bewitching than this typically All-American girl with long legs and a friendly, vacuous smile. But this is not a fair expectation, for it must be remembered that Barbara was his first creation, and imagination needs to be exercised before it can develop into complex maturity. Dennis Culroth was a genius, but his dear Barbara was only his first piece of juvenilia. This is not to belittle this impressive accomplishment by a young man without any formal training in the relevant arts; it is only to point out that finer things were to come.

Like many people of extraordinary creative powers Dennis was blessed (or, some would say, cursed) with an exceptionally passionate nature. For most of us, whether or not forewarned by parents or peers, the hard reality of puberty comes as a surprise; for Dennis it came as more than that: it came like a juggernaut, a whirlwind, a cataclysmic flood. No doubt part of the problem was a certain physiological abnormality: Dennis Culroth was incapable of spontaneous nocturnal emissions. The 'playmates' from the Playboy magazines he kept secreted in his bedroom, the sweet smelling girls he passed in the corridors of Evans High, the long-haired, long-legged beauties he saw on TV — all these angelic temptresses fuelled the easily stoked fires of his libido. But no matter how hot his furnace became, he was never permitted that intense and glorious release that other boys experienced in the dark of their dreams. By the time Dennis Culroth was fifteen he was in such a state of inner turmoil that he thought he would soon go stark raving mad.

He had no close friends at Evans High, for his family had packed up and moved the summer of his grammar school graduation, relocating him in a 'nicer' neighbourhood where he knew no one. That same summer puberty struck. Simultaneous with the appearance of his pubic hair came a stutter and a forehead full of pimples. The raging sea of new faces he encountered his first day at Evans High terrified him. This sea of young humanity was composed of three elements: 1) the neutral and indifferent of both sexes who brushed past him in the halls or filled the blank spaces unoccupied by the other two, more active, elements; 2) the boys with power and an accompanying destructive vitality who tormented and mocked him at their leisure; and 3) the girls with that magical something that weakened his heart and hardened his organ, the girls sweet girls who held him in thrall with their vibrant sexuality — and paid him no attention whatsoever. These three elements formed a compound as corrosive to his self-esteem as sulphuric acid is to human flesh.

His escape was, naturally, fantasy. His natural gift (or curse) of imaginative power was given the most vigorous of exertions in the quiet of his bedroom. But because the focus, the theme, that informed his rich fantasies was sexual while his physiological abnormality prevented nocturnal catharsis, he experienced only the anguish of creative effort without the small compensations usually associated with it.

Until, that is, he discovered masturbation. Glorious, glorious masturbation. That selfish joy. That private glory. That introverted ecstasy. That wonderful carnal communion with self. That pure, pure pleasure untempered by responsibility, caring, untempered happily by any of the adult virtues. How many things are there both harmless and selfish? Praise be to masturbation! The adolescent's salvation.

Except in Dennis Culroth's case. For in his case, Ma Nature was oh so contrary, both in the ordinary and the logical sense of that word. Just as in unconsciousness he could not come to orgasm, so it turned out that in conscious orgasm he became unconscious. It terrified him.

This is not to say he never masturbated. The urges that drove him to the brink of irrationality were stronger even than his terror, and so he would, although never without fear and trembling, avert the ultimate crossing over into madness by a late night rendezvous in the privacy of his bed with his dear friends: imagination, four fingers and a thumb. In the morning he would wake to guilt, fear and a certain stiffness of the sheets. Fortunately he could experience the full pleasure of orgasm before some neural circuit in his brain clicked like a relay and shut off his consciousness. Only after the last spurt of ineffable pleasure would the dark curtain descend. Talk about the little death!

A friend from grammar school days came to visit one weekend halfway through Dennis' freshman year. This friend had even less understanding of the physiology of sex than Dennis, so when Dennis in a fit of confessional fever told of his experiences, this friend promptly warned of the alleged danger of the 'solitary vice': madness. These warnings took a very graphic form, replete with descriptions of bizarre operations on the brain and the genitals. It seemed that madness lay wherever Dennis turned. (He felt he was trapped between getting his rocks off and a hard place.)

His friends' misguided warnings acted as a deterrent for over a month — during which time, ironically, the abstinence itself pushed poor libidinous Dennis toward the very insanity he foolishly believed he was preventing. Fortunately he fell off the wagon, so to speak, one night after what the school officials quaintly termed an "activity night". Marjorie Barb, the most wonderful creature in Freshman English, arrived at the school wearing a sleeveless, white blouse and the tightest pair of jeans Dennis had ever seen painted on a high school girl. But it was Marjorie's bare arms, not her small, rounded bum or high firm breasts, that stoked his fires. No, lovely as Marjorie was in every aspect, it was those downy arms, so very very naked, that enthralled him. He managed, in what he hoped was a casual and discreet fashion, to be near her all night. When she was leaning over the billiard table gracefully missing almost every shot, he was casually leaning against a locker pretending to talk to Arnold, the only boy he actually felt downright superior to. And when she was in the gym playing volleyball, he was in the doorway, trying to appear the disinterested spectator. All night he followed her around, the pain of longing searing his body. Those beautiful, naked arms! He imagined doing strange and wonderful things to those arms, caressing them, licking them, sliding them over his chest, his stomach, even lower. The soft, nude crook of her arm...it would, could — hold him. Oh, how he suffered that night! His penis, semi-erect, strained against the tight jockey shorts that bound it. And it hurt. But his physical discomfort was nothing compared to the mental anguish he suffered. So when much later in the insomniac dark of two a.m. his hand went against his will and better judgement to that imperious dictator of desire, he knew he was about to experience a very special orgasm. In a mystical mixture of terror and lust, amidst images of Marjorie Barb's soft, sensuous arms, Dennis Culroth came — and went...

.

...into a deep sea of unconsciousness.

.

.

After that night, Dennis Culroth resigned himself to a life in institutions, ministered to by gorgeous nurses his frontal lobotomy prevented him from lusting after. Each morning he woke surprised to find reality intact. Like a chain smoker convinced of the destructiveness of his habit, he tried to control it without for one moment believing he would ever conquer it. He rationed out masturbation sessions like a heavy smoker might try to limit his daily consumption. And like most such schedules of restraint, his was impossible to maintain.

.

It was not fear of madness, but the fear of embarrassment that finally drove Dennis into a life of total abstinence from his delicious, allegedly deadly sin. It was his first year at university. It was his first "mixer". His pimples were under control, as was his stutter. A beautiful co-ed he approached and asked to dance had accepted. He was drunk (or he never would have approached such a goddess) and he danced poorly. But she didn't seem to notice. In fact she seemed to like him. In a moment of unprecedented temerity he asked her if she'd like to step out for a breath of fresh air. She nearly convinced him that he really had finally gone mad and had begun to hallucinate, by saying coolly: "Yes, yes, it is awfully stuffy in here."

.

They had barely stepped out into the crisp fall air when lust unleashed by demon drink reared its satyric head. He reached for her. He kissed her. She kissed him back. She pushed her tongue into his mouth. And then the needles on all the valves buried themselves. Then the critical values were exceeded and a million red alerts were sounded. The next morning he was unable to remember exactly what he'd done in response to that warm probing of her tongue, but some brazen action performed seconds afterwards had frightened and appalled this apparently experienced and wanton co-ed. Mere seconds after the ultimate ecstasy had seemed imminent, he stood alone, his cheek stinging, the angry and profane words of his goddess echoing in his head.

.

It was a drunk and despondent young man who stumbled to his car, and once inside the dark security of the old Ford, began to cry. Then the anguish of his ravenous desire drove him to do something he knew, even in his drunken and lust-maddened state, was more than merely indiscreet. His hand went to his zipper. He closed his eyes. Instantly a perfectly and fully detailed image of the rejecting goddess formed. He clutched himself. The goddess began unbuttoning her blouse. He felt that subtle, barely detectable sensation, like a switch clicking, deep in his lower abdomen. And he knew what was to come even before he saw the image of his goddess's naked breasts.

.

He awoke to a blinding light.

.

"Christ, they get more disgusting every year!"

He realised his pants were down around his knees. The light moved from his eyes. He looked down at what now was in the spotlight.

.

"Disgusting!"

Oh my God, he thought, what have I done!

The light moved back up into his eyes.

"Wake up kid! Pull up your fucking pants and get the hell outta here pronto! Or else, buddy, we're goin' haul you in for indecent exposure. Bet your parents'd be impressed if their son got a police record as a sex offender. You hear me, kid?"

He struggled to pull his pants up, hurting himself on the zipper. The two campus cops laughed as he yelped in pain.

"Look, I don't know who you are, kid, but I just hope I never see your...", the cop paused, spit out a truncated laugh, then continued, "...your face around here again.

The key was in the ignition. As the car jerked forward, he heard their jeering laughter trailing after him. Driving into the night, this, his dark night of the soul, he sincerely wished himself dead.

It was after that profound humiliation that he ceased masturbating. He threw himself into his schoolwork, knowing he needed something to distract him from the tidal movements of his hormones. At first he thought psychology might hold the answers to his problems, but although he scored the second highest grade in his section of Intro Psyc, he decided against concentrating his studies in that area. Psychology seemed only moderately competent at understanding the behaviour of laboratory rats and hopelessly inept at understanding the behaviour of human beings. His sophomore year he registered his major as fine arts, for he had a natural aptitude for drawing and a highly romantic image of the life of an artist. But he disliked his fellow students, most of whom seemed more interested in sexual and social exhibitionism than in art. His talents lay elsewhere, although he did not at the time know where.

So it is he came to study applied mathematics. It was dry, intellectual stuff. And, most importantly, it locked his mind in a bear-hug of concentration that distracted him for whole, uninterrupted hours from his sexual longing. He did well — which wasn't surprising given the time and effort he devoted to his studies. Freudians call it 'displacement'.

After graduation he landed a decent position with a small, but rapidly growing investment firm. As he had thrown himself into his studies, he now threw himself into his job. However, he just was not permitted to work eighteen hours a day, and he found his employment less distracting than his studies had been.

It was in the lonely night hours he spent in his one room apartment that he began to fully exercise his imaginative powers. Everybody he got to know at all at the university had been into smoke, so along the way he'd picked up the habit of unwinding with a joint. He would sit in his stark room smoking up and day-dreaming about the mysteries of women's bodies.

Not surprisingly he'd developed an absolute, bottomless terror of women (real women, that is) and he knew that some of his colleagues at work suspected him of being gay. Little did they know that his passion for the opposite sex was a hundredfold stronger than theirs. The irony of this caused him bitter amusement as he sat alone in his apartment, his eyes closed, his mind carefully, lovingly creating detail after detail of his first 'ideal' woman. For, you see, Dennis Culroth had finally begun his serious training as an artist, a creative artist, a creative artist of the highest order. It would take two years of intense mental training before he would produce his first creation.

Twenty-three big ones. It was a few weeks after his solitary birthday that the idea came to him. Having just finished a lonely dinner at Marcus Pizzeria, it came to him in a flash.

A file! A portfolio, rather, such as he'd learned to create in Fine Arts. It would make his daydreaming more respectable — or at very least saner. His dopey dreaming had to be unhealthy. But writing a poem about, or painting a picture of, an imaginary woman was not considered bizarre or sick. It would be something like that.

He arrived at the stationary store fifteen minutes before closing and quickly bought everything he figured he would need: file folders, drawing paper and pencils, a new ribbon for his portable typewriter, even a good drafting lamp. Back in his apartment he carefully placed all his instruments on the kitchen table, set up the lamp, and took a blank file folder and carefully printed the name BARBARA across the tab. He was ready to begin. Nervously he got up and went to his stash and removed an already tightly rolled joint. Fighting back the urge to hurry, he sat down in his one reasonably comfortable chair and lit the joint. He tried to make himself smoke it leisurely, but actually he hurried it a bit. The urge to begin was overwhelming, albeit frightening.

Pinching out what was a still useable roach, Dennis rose and returned to the kitchen table. He'd already decided exactly how he would organise his first portfolio, Taking a piece of lined paper, he neatly listed the major components:

I. Physical characteristics (in graphic representation)
    A. frontal facial portrait
    B. profile facial portrait
    C. frontal full-body (nude) portrait
    D. profile full-body (nude) portrait
    E. rear full-body (nude) portrait
II. Physical characteristics (in written representation)
    A. hair (colour, type, style)
    B. eyes
    C. height
    D. weight
    E. measurements (i.e., breast, waist, hips)
    F. clothing sizes (dress, slacks, bra, shoes)
    G. unusual marks
III. Biographical data
    A. date of birth
    B. place of birth
    C. formal education
    D. unusual experiences
IV. Psychological data
    A. personal goals
    B. turn-ons
    C. turn-offs
    D. favourite intoxicant
    E. favourite movie
    F. favourite book
    G. favourite music
    H. secret dream
V. Sexual data
    A. previous sexual experience (amount and type)
    B. favourite foreplay manoeuvres
    C. favourite sexual position

D. average arousal time

E. orgasmic potential

After he'd completed this organisational plan, Dennis took out his portable typewriter and began to type up neat data sheets for the last four categories. It startled him how very, very easy it was. It became obvious as he quickly filled the pages that he had virtually completed the creation of Barbara in his head. He was only taking the impalpable idea and transcribing it. He'd read that Mozart wrote his symphonies the same way: just writing down what was already fully formed in his brain. Nevertheless, this was important, this actual giving of substance to a dream. Very, very important. No mute inglorious Milton, he!

It was easy. Easy as giving in to temptation. Only a few data points had not been determined before he began the transcription. (For example, he hadn't thought about what Barbara's favourite movie would be.) But strange as it might seem to one who has never imbibed the cool waters of that secret wellspring called the unconscious, the needed information came forth without strain or effort. It did not feel like invention; it seemed more a matter of, well, remembering. (Her favourite movie was Love Story, a film Dennis had never even seen.)

The first category, which required all of his moderate artistic skill, was not completed that first night. It was not a case of incomplete visualisation; the problem was drawing accurately enough to capture on paper the extremely vivid, mental image he had of his Barbara. Tearing up his fifth effort at a facial profile, he wondered if working with a live model wouldn't have been less demanding, for the mental image he was attempting to copy was so intense, so noumenously vivid, that he felt he was seeing more clearly with his mind's eye than he had ever seen with his own 'real' and slightly myopic eyes; and so standards were more stringent than they would've been in a life class. Clarity of vision does not ensure clarity of representation, and getting these drawings just right seemed inordinately important.

All weekend he worked on the drawings. He drew dozens of eyes, a hundred breasts, an uncountable number of pubic regions, before at last he had a set of five drawings as close to perfect as he felt he could manage.

The completion of the portfolio brought on post-partum depression.

He put the file away and tried not to think about it or Barbara for several weeks. He sat around his apartment at night watching vacuous situation comedies on his twelve-inch black-and-white TV. He smoked so much dope he developed a cough. He even found his eyes getting watery as he lay in bed awaiting sleep's deadening kiss.

.

Then abruptly the depression lifted. With a sudden, totally atypical burst of optimism and self-esteem, Dennis Culroth rose from his TV Dinner one Saturday night and, donning his best 'casual' jacket, went forth into the Nightworld. He was, he told himself as he shut his apartment door behind him, no ugly duckling — at least not any more. He wasn't Robert Redford, but neither was he the Elephant Man. Hell, he'd grown into a moderately attractive young man: well-dressed, well-groomed, well-educated. And he was no longer a naive adolescent convinced masturbation would produce madness and hair on one's palms. He'd read innumerable books and magazines on sex — everything from Masters & Johnson (the whole bloody book) to the *Penthouse Forum*. If given a multiple-choice test on SEX, he'd surely score in the ninety-ninth percentile. (Albeit he knew he'd fail terribly any practicum examination.) It was true he still did not masturbate, but this was not because he believed it harmful; his abstinence was based on what he knew (intellectually, at least) to be a neurotic phobia. He was terrified of being found dead in his bed, his hand, frozen by rigor mortis, locked onto his penis, the dried jism flaky on his cold, bare abdomen.

.

In all his extensive reading he'd never come upon any reference to his particular affliction. Oh, there were passing remarks about men and women collapsing "joyously" into sleep after an especially fervent bout of love-making, but never anything about a physiological abnormality that caused a victim to lose consciousness every time he had an orgasm and at the same time never being able to have an orgasm when unconscious. He told himself his was a, if rare, quite harmless problem. But whenever the temptation was upon him, whenever an erection stayed for hours, and he at last reached for himself — the memory of the two cops and their flashlight would return with eidetic intensity. The magic wand of fear made his wand wither.

.

Dennis decided to drive over to Angel's, on Ninth Avenue, to see if he could — as the guys at the office put it — "get lucky". He'd tried going to singles bars a few times, but he'd always come home alone and uncomfortably aroused, but he'd never tried Angel's. Mark

Hampersmith, a co-worker, had been bragging about his success at picking up women, and in the course of one of his lengthy and erotic tales of sexual adventure had mentioned this place. Hampersmith had a nose like an Evening Grosbeak and a voice like a crow, and Dennis remembered thinking that the women at Angel's must be very desperate if they really went home with the likes of this odd bird.

.

The place was packed. As Dennis made his way to the stand-up bar, he felt his self-confidence begin to wane. These women did not look at all desperate. And the number of males was easily twice that of the opposite sex. Many of these guys were incredibly good-looking, a bit plastic in their perfect grooming but intimidating nonetheless. Glancing around at the men, he wondered why they needed to go to a singles bar; surely with the looks and charisma some of them possessed, they'd need only walk down any busy street to get propositioned by some horny, liberated lady.

.

Wedging his way between two quarterback-types, he ordered a glass of white wine, the only alcoholic beverage he really liked. Behind the bar was a long mirror. In it he surveyed the sea of faces and bodies that surged and heaved behind him. The air was electric with urgent sexuality. Suddenly sweat was running down his ribcage, his heart pounding in his chest. He felt what he knew from previous experience to be the beginnings of a full-blown anxiety attack, and he wanted to rush from the crowded room. Instead he gulped down his wine, caught the attention of the bartender and placed his second order: a double-scotch on ice.

.

When the drink was placed in front of him, he stared at it for a full minute. He'd only tasted scotch once before. Then, nervously conscious of the presence of the two macho males flanking him, he lifted the glass and poured the entire contents straight down. It wasn't pleasant, but he didn't cough or gag. He stared at the empty glass, waiting for some physical effect other than the warm flushing sensation that had accompanied the actual swallowing of the liquor.

.

"Another?" The bartender was looking at him coldly, clinically.

.

"Yes, please."

.

"A double?"

.

"Yes.

The bartender moved away. Dennis lifted his head to look at the mirror. The two quarterbacks seemed totally oblivious of his existence. The sea of young humanity behind him had not noticeably changed.

The bartender returned with his drink. He looked down at it. He did not want it. He looked up.

And there she was, directly behind him. (Or else a ghost in the mirror; the madness having arrived at last.) She seemed to be trying to catch the attention of the bartender.

There was no question of it. Dennis spun around, a completely involuntary action. There she was, her face no more than six inches from his. Her face, her perfect, fine-featured face, the face he had laboured over with his drawing pencils, the face he had sketched again and again in a hopeless attempt to capture its perfection.

"Barbara!" His voice came out husky.

"Do I know you?"

"Your favourite rock group is The Eagles."

"Huh? I mean — yes, yes it is." She looked puzzled.

"Your favourite movie is Love Story."

"Yeah?! But..."

"You wear a size six shoe."

"Hey, how do..."

"You were born in Toledo, Ohio."

"Okay, okay, do I know you?"

"I doubt it, but I know you. You like empty beaches at dusk."

"This is certainly more impressive than guessing my sign."

"You drink white wine."

.

"Yes. Now do you want to tell me how you're doing this?"

.

"No, no, I ... I can't tell you that. But, uh, you like Italian. That's right isn't it?" He was grinning.

.

"Huh?"

.

"You like Italian cooking."

.

"Yes, but..."

.

"No buts!" Suddenly he felt confident, in complete control. He heard himself say in a self-assured tone: "Well, I know an Italian restaurant where the owner makes her own pasta. Great place. Not far. What'd you say?"

.

"Are you asking me to dinner?"

.

"Not dinner, a feast."

.

"Well...

.

"Please don't say 'But I hardly know you!'"

.

She laughed. "I don't you know at all. Or at least I don't think I do, but what the hell — okay."

.

They made their way through the warm bodies and out to the cold street. The world was perfect.

.

Every word Dennis said exuded self-confidence. In his daydreams it was always like this. Oh yes, he had practised being the self-assured man, practised it a thousand times in his dreams. And this had to be a dream, so it came naturally. Only when he tripped getting out of the car at the restaurant did he momentarily doubt that what was happening was a perfect miracle and transformation.

.

But the pasta melted in their mouths, the sauces were heavenly, and they talked easily, comfortably, like old friends. And when after coffee he asked her if she'd like to come back to his apartment, she said yes without a moment's hesitation. 'Twas a dream come true.

Unfortunately his apartment was left over from harsh reality: a stark and uninviting place. Still Barbara seemed to find it acceptable. She went and sat on the worn sofa. He just stood in the centre of the room, staring at her. It was almost impossible to believe that she, who was quite literally "the-girl-of-his-dreams", was there on the sofa looking at him with sky blue eyes that said yes-yes-yes.

"You know," she said, "you still haven't told me how it is you know so much about me."

"Does it matter." He looked into her deep blue eyes. She knew nothing about him. Nothing. Yet he knew everything about her. Everything. Not just the sketchy facts outlined in his portfolio on her. No, much much more than that. That was a mere crude transcription of the symphony in his head. All he had to do was think, remember, and he could tell her almost anything about herself. And she knew nothing about him. This gave him a tremendous sense of power, endowed him with infinite self-confidence. He was in control at last. And she was susceptible. Easy.

He knew she would like it when he nibbled on her ear. He knew she would start to breathe heavily when he rubbed her lower back just above her beautiful ass. He knew she would ask him if he loved her before she removed her panties. What he did not know is whether his answer was a lie.

And he also did not know, as he slid gently into her, what would happen to him when he came. Nor did he know what would become of her.

He did know, as he began to move in the rhythm that would suit her best, that he was at last, at long, long last, losing his virginity — and losing it to his ultimate dream-girl. And, like another creator in another time, he knew that it would be good.

The alarm went off at 7:00 a.m. He was alone in bed. He quickly scanned the room for any evidence of the night before, but there was none, no note, nothing. Dennis got up and went into the bathroom to shower. As the hot water massaged his neck and shoulders he tried to make sense of the events of the previous night. The whole incident was so preposterous, so contrary to reality as he understood it, that the only sane explanation seemed to be that he had hallucinated — that he had gone temporarily mad. To believe in what he remembered of the previous night would be to give in to permanent insanity; he could not permit himself the luxury of that delusion. Better to admit momentary insanity than to deny it and so sink into chronic madness.

But then there was a third alternative: he could simply avoid the issue. There was that old saying: "Never look a gift horse in the mouth." Hell, the only thing he did know for sure was that the she had been great, incredible, beyond belief. Beyond belief? Well, yes, that problem would remain. He wanted to know how — or if — what had happened could be explained. Yet, damn it, what did it matter ultimately? The sex had been great. He'd never felt happier in his life. It was insane, most insane of all, to worry about the "reality" of it all when he'd just experienced the best night of his life.

Nevertheless, after Dennis dried himself and started breakfast, he became obsessed with the idea of checking things out. He could retrace his steps of the night before. Angel's was closed on Sunday, but he could go to La Strada and talk to the waitress who'd served them last night. He could bring his drawings (the facial portraits, not of course the nude studies) and ask the waitress if she remembered his date. With the eggs still frying in the pan, he went into the living room and retrieved Barbara's portfolio. But when he opened the file a strange thing happened: he felt a profound lack of interest. The once beautiful face seemed dull, vacuous, even ordinary. Even the full body nude drawings left him cold. He read the data sheets and shuddered. Now he was feeling something, but it was not pleasant: he felt vaguely disgusted with himself. How could he have found this woman attractive? She was so obviously simple and commonplace, with little to recommend her besides her rather vulgar good looks. His interest in her seemed a blatant example of immaturity. How could he have lowered himself to lusting after a woman as fundamentally uninteresting as she? And she'd been too easy. Good Lord, he hoped she didn't have some social disease! But no, he knew that she didn't.

Dennis put the file away, turned off the eggs, and went to get a joint. His interest in confirming (or denying) her existence had completely disappeared. He put on a record, sat in his one comfortable chair, and lit the joint. He thought about the sex again. Ah, yes that had been good, very good. But, he realised slowly, he felt absolutely no desire to do it again. That is, he felt no desire to do it again with Barbara. He felt, for the first time in a long time, like he really wanted to be alone. He was free, for a while at least, from the driving lust that had filled his life since puberty. It would be nice to spend a quiet day at home alone. Perhaps he'd watch a football game. Ah, the peace that passeth all understanding.

.

And lasts for so short a time.

.

.

The image of Rebecca began to form itself on Monday. Over the next two weeks it gradually grew. He didn't do any drawings or data sheets. Instinctively he knew to wait, to let his new creation ripen on the vine of his unconscious. Then one night he knew she was ready to meet the world. As before, he did the written sections first, and, as before, they came easily—more easily in fact than they had with Barbara. The drawings once again took longer, but even they seemed easier this second time.

.

Rebecca was tall with dark curly hair. Unlike her predecessor she had full lips and lively eyes. She was a bit of a highbrow, a lover of Bergman films and a reader of avant-garde novels. She'd done some amateur theatre, could play Chopin on the piano, and had attended Bennington for several years. She worked as a legal secretary, and was thinking about going to law school, but was hesitant because she didn't like most lawyers. She did occasional auditions, although she knew acting as a career was unrealistic. She was luscious and fascinating.

Although Dennis put the finishing touches on Rebecca one Wednesday night, he waited until Friday to go to Angel's. This was partially superstitious behaviour and partially a deliberate attempt to add to the excitement by allowing his sexual tension to mount.

.

When he did walk into Angel's the second time, it was with a totally different attitude. Already he was feeling confident. He knew he would find her there. And he did.

.

She was standing at the bar talking to a wimpy, little guy with the most ridiculous moustache Dennis had ever seen. She was exactly as he had envisioned her.

.

Without hesitation he walked up to her, squeezed in between her and the wimp, and addressed her coolly: "You know, Rebecca, the reason you like Camus so much is because he's really a romantic optimist. All the posturing about whether or not to commit suicide is just that — posturing."

"Who the hell are you?!"

"It's because you are fundamentally a romantic that you did such a good job as Laura in *The Glass Menagerie*."

"You saw that play? I did that two years ago in San Francisco."

"You were great."

"Why, thank you."

The wimp was tapping Dennis on the shoulder. Dennis ignored him. "I have a recording of the *Marat-Sade* performed by the Royal Shakespeare Company." (He'd bought it on Thursday.)

"Really?" Her eyes were lively.

"I'm sure you'd do a superlative Charlotte Corday."

"Why, thank you again. But would you mind telling me..."

The wimp was still tapping on Dennis' shoulder. Dennis continued to ignore him. "If you'd like to hear the recording, we could go to my place."

Her mouth fell open. She stared at him in disbelief.

"But if you'd prefer to just listen to Chopin, I've a beautiful recording of the nocturnes by Rubenstein."

Her mouth closed. "Who are you?"

"My name's Dennis. Well, so what do you say?"

"I say yes, Dennis. I say yes."

The wimp stopped tapping on Dennis's shoulder and dissolved into the crowd.

.

And when they arrived at Dennis' apartment, Rebecca said yes again. She didn't wear a bra. She wore black, bikini panties. She behaved very, very histrionically when she came: much moaning and crying out. She even clawed his back. She had three orgasms before he did, which was nothing short of miraculous. The last one preceded his by a matter of seconds. The last thing he remembered was her murmuring: "Yes, yes, I say yes, yes." She was a very affirmative woman and had seen the film version of Joyce's Ulysses.

.

.

"In dreams begin responsibilities."

.

.

The next morning brought a pleasant surprise — or at least at first it seemed pleasant. As Dennis inspected his scratched back in the bathroom mirror, he wondered how to interpret this evidence. Was he completely mad, so completely mad that he was now living completely in a fantasy world? Or was he really creating women? And if so, where did they go after they came — so to speak. Did they fade back into nothingness? Or did they live on to old age and death, oblivious of their spontaneous generation? He tended to think they faded back into nothingness, for he had created them only for his own pleasure; once they had served, they would, it seemed to him, just disappear. What use could their continued existence possibly serve now that he no longer had any need of them?

.

And, honestly, he didn't particularly want them to continue living on their own. The idea of it was, for some reason he couldn't pin down, distinctly unpleasant, spooky even. So as he shaved he decided that they were no more. After they came, they went, so to speak. Went back to limbo.

.

That morning he didn't have to go to the file on Rebecca to realise he no longer lusted after her. Once again his memory of the sex was luscious (in fact, it was considerably better than it had been with Barbara) but a repeat performance held no attraction. And why should it? He could create a different woman any time he wanted. The next one wouldn't be as pretentious as Rebecca. The next one would be a girl from a small town. He tried to determine what her name would be, but he couldn't. Or else he didn't want to. What he did want was a hearty breakfast. Then a quiet afternoon watching the football game on the tube.

·

·

A week later he knew her name: Joan. It was a nice simple name, but she wasn't a nice simple girl. As the information on her began to surface, Dennis felt impelled to revise his data system. Although he felt the five sketches would suffice, the other parts seem woefully simple-minded. This Joan needed, deserved, more substantial documentation. He was appalled at how long it took him to make the revisions: a whole night just to lay out the format without filling in any of the information. He suspected she was going to take longer to create. He was right: it was almost a month before he marked the file complete and set off for Angel's.

·

·

She was a complicated woman, full of ambivalence and ambiguity, and it was reflected in the long conversation that preceded her going home with Dennis. For awhile he even had the feeling he was not going to be successful at luring her back to his apartment, but a few empathetic remarks about the problems an intelligent farm girl has in dealing with Bible-thumping parents eventually won her confidence.

·

Their lovemaking, too, was complicated — full of false starts, switchbacks, teasing, coyness and eventually a ravenous lust that almost precipitated the ultimate disaster: premature ejaculation. He had to withdraw several times. When he finally felt that familiar sensation in the lower part of his abdomen that signalled imminent orgasm, he cursed aloud his inability to go on for hours. Joan laughed a throaty laugh. And then Dennis pulsed into the bottomless dark.

·

·

"In dreams begin responsibilities."

·

·

The next woman's name was Jennifer; she took six weeks to create. She wouldn't come home with him, but eventually agreed to a late night snack. Then over coffee at an all-night bar and grill she suddenly changed her mind. She was acrobatically inclined. Dennis pulled a ligament that night and had to wear an elastic bandage around his knee for a week afterwards.

·

·

"In dreams begin responsibilities."

159

The next woman was Marsha; she took two months to create. He had to once again elaborate his portfolio system—especially to do justice to her complex sexuality. She was into bondage — which somewhat frightened Dennis. He almost decided against going to Angel's to meet her, but then he developed this fear that if he didn't, he would never again be inspired to creation. He felt he had to consummate each relationship before he could move on to a new creation. Marsha wasn't coy; she went with him readily, for he knew she gave in easily to men who came on strong. Back at his apartment he complied with her request that he tie her to the bed, but he tied slip-knots and moments before coming, freed her. She cursed him when he unbound her, but he feared for her safety once he'd lost consciousness. Besides, he didn't want to find her still in his bed when he awoke. Maybe she'd disappear anyway as his consciousness did, but he wasn't taking any chances.

Once her arms were free she suddenly went completely limp. You're a strange creation, he thought, as the familiar dark curtain descended.

"In dreams begin responsibilities."

And then there was Helen who loved oral sex. And Janet who was black and beautiful and had an intimidatingly high IQ. And then Sylvia. And then Erica, Beth, Vanessa, Rita.

And then there was Noreen.

Noreen.

There is the danger that responsibility will destroy the ability to dream. Dreaming is irresponsible, fundamentally irresponsible. No matter how much it may be laboured over.

Dennis Culroth hadn't failed to notice how each creation took longer and longer to complete. Nor had he failed to notice that each woman seemed more real and substantial than the previous one. Furthermore, he found that each time he created, met, and bedded a new woman he became more emotionally involved. The emotions weren't always positive ones. (For example, he actively disliked Beth.) Initially the women he created had been interesting but in a cool, intellectual sort of way. Now he found himself feeling the full gamut of emotions in response to the various creatures of his invention.

A strange thing, too, was happening regarding the sex. The actual sexual encounters had consistently gotten better and better, but it was a case of diminishing returns; Rebecca had been much better than Barbara, but Rita only marginally better than Vanessa. And most important of all, he had developed a suspicion that something was missing, some unknown factor. It didn't seem to matter how complex his documentation was (and it had become extremely complex, including such things as percentile scores on personality traits such as introversion/extroversion), nothing he seemed capable of adding to his technique or style of creation did anything to alleviate this feeling that something was missing. What it was, he had no idea. Still a feeling such as he imagined existential *ennui* to be soon overpowered him. You're just jaded, he tried to tell himself, but the feeling threatened to deepen into a severe depression. So it was that after Rita he decided to stop creating women. He didn't really feel much like sex anyway. He just wanted to feel normal.

One night he forced himself to go out and try to pick up an 'ordinary' woman. Perhaps it was the unreality of it all that was depressing him. He had feared losing touch with reality as long as he could remember. Creating women was certainly one way to court insanity. So he went to the Stagedoor one Friday night.

He couldn't go to Angel's: that would've been wrong, a form of infidelity. As he entered the bar he surprised himself with his confidence; all his successes had made him self-assured. But as he stared around the crowded room he felt another, less positive, emotion: disappointment. None of these women looked even slightly interesting. They all seemed two-dimensional, unreal. They were props in a grade-B movie. Plastic mannequins. It was only shortly before closing time that he forced himself to approach a woman who seemed perhaps a shade less unreal than the others. She rebuffed him rudely. He went home depressed.

But the next night he went back. He sat at a small table in the back. Before he had a chance to — before he felt any desire to — survey the scene and decide on a woman to approach, a woman approached him. She had long raven hair and dark eyes. She wore tight jeans and a tank top. She smiled a hard, tight little smile as she, without a word, sat down across from him. Dennis Culroth forced a smile. He told himself that she was a very desirable woman. "Hi," he said. "Wantta fuck?" she said. "Yes," he lied. The answer to her next question was—his place.

.

It was not a good night. Dennis Culroth of the exceptionally passionate nature was unable to achieve erection. The lady was not one of those oh-so-understanding women who say: "It's okay. It happens to everybody sometimes." What she said, among many other things, was that Dennis was "a bastard" for "wasting" her time.

.

.

Reality has its responsibilities too.

.

.

After that unfortunate adventure, Dennis Culroth slipped into the deepest depression of his life. An all-pervading numbness invaded him. Food had no taste. His job bored him to tears. He felt not the slightest sexual longing. As the weeks dragged by and the depression failed to lift, he began to seriously consider seeing a shrink. But he didn't believe in psychology; his one year of it at university had made him a confirmed sceptic of the efficacy of that pseudo-science to help anyone. Besides, he was afraid that a full confession of his experiences could only lead to his commitment to a psychiatric hospital.

.

Then one morning he woke with her name ringing in his head: Noreen, Noreen, Noreen. No, he told himself, no more women. That way lay madness. He went to work. Noreen, Noreen. He began to remember things about her. He tried to forget them. Noreen, Noreen. She was tall. No, no, he told himself. He spent the day trying to exorcise the name from his head. No Noreen, no. He spent the next day trying to exorcise the name from his head. And the next. The depression was replaced with obsession: the obsession with a woman named Noreen. He spent all his energy trying not to think of her. She had red hair. He denied her. She was fundamentally shy. She did not exist. She liked Marx Brothers films. He would not—no matter what—definitely would not document her. She'd quit smoking two years ago. Oh my god, Dennis Culroth thought to himself one morning, I am possessed. That morning he threw out all his old files and all his materials for creating women. He would not be tempted. Noreen was beautiful.

Noreen.

Two weeks after she had first surfaced to his consciousness, he went to Angel's. He told himself he was going there to distract himself from this woman who had taken possession of his mind. He'd given up the dark art of creating women. He was safe, even here at Angel's. He was, of course, fooling himself.

He'd been there about an hour when she walked in. She was with another woman. She looked extremely ill at ease. I will not approach her, he told himself. And to his credit he did wait almost half an hour before he got up from his seat and went over to her table.

Standing over her he marvelled at the familiarity of her face. He hadn't done any sketches of what her face would look like; in fact, he had tried his utmost not to imagine it. But here she was, every freckle exactly where he knew it would be.

"Do I know you?" she said as he stood staring down at her.

"Uh, no."

She squirmed in her chair.

He said at last, slowly: 'Please tell me your name is not Noreen."

"I do know you."

He moaned.

"Are you all right?"

"No, not really."

Just then Noreen's companion returned. She looked Dennis up and down, seemed unimpressed with what she saw, and then turned to Noreen. 'What do you say we split. This place is dead tonight."

Noreen switched her attention from Dennis's anguished face to her friend. "Okay, I'm ready to go. But I think I'd rather just go home."

"No, don't go yet!" Dennis spoke way too loudly and several people turned and stared.

.

Then he continued in a more reasonable tone: "Please, give me your phone number. I'd like to take you out for dinner."

.

Noreen hesitated. This fellow was strange to say the least, but there was something interesting about him. And she must've met him before, for how else could he know her name. She took out a scrap of paper and wrote her phone number hastily. Her companion frowned disapprovingly. Noreen handed the paper to Dennis and seconds later she was gone. Dennis returned to his table. He looked down at the scrap. She'd given him her correct number. He recognised it.

.

On the way home he had a vision: Noreen, seated at a table, looking through an artist's portfolio.

.

What followed could only be described as a courtship. Noreen was not sexually experienced, although she was not a virgin, and what Dennis Culroth felt for her was very different from what he'd felt for any of the other women he had created. He did find her sexually attractive — there was no question of that — but he seemed strangely satisfied just being with her.

.

They went out together more and more frequently as the weeks passed. They went to concerts, museums, movies, galleries, baseball games, plays. They did not go to his apartment, and they did not go to her apartment. An interesting thing was happening to his familiarity with her. What she told him about herself gradually blended with what he already knew about her. As the weeks passed he became more and more confused about her — her status. At first he'd been convinced she was another of his creations, albeit one he'd not intended and one he had not actually created on paper. But as he spent more and more time with her and the past became confused with the present, he found it hard to believe she was not 'real'. He had no portfolio, no documentation, no evidence that he'd conceived of her before she and he had met. All he had was the memory, and everyone knows memory is a lie to keep the soul together. He tried not to think about this too much, for he knew only too well what the ultimate test would be.

.

They'd been seeing each other for a month and a half when Noreen finally invited him over for dinner. He accepted. He had to accept.

Her apartment was real and, he rejoiced, totally unexpected and unfamiliar. She collected photographs of horses. The walls were covered with cheaply farmed pictures of every kind of horse imaginable, from Clydesdales to sleek thoroughbreds.

"I didn't know you were interested in horses,' he said, exulting in this wonderful ignorance.

"I'm not," she replied. "but I used to be, and I started collecting magazine pictures of horses when I was a teenager. Now I just collect mostly out of habit. It gives the room a kind of unity, having pictures of just one kind. Don't you think?"

"Uh, yes."

"I've moved around a lot, and whenever I move into a new place the first thing I do is hang these pictures. It makes it feel instantly familiar. It makes it seem like home." She looked at him and smiled.

"Why is it," she said slowly and softly, "that you've never kissed me?"

"I'm afraid," Dennis blurted out.

"Of what?"

"It's terribly difficult to explain."

"Try."

"To explain?"

"Either that or try to kiss me."

He went over to her. She was almost the same height as he. Kissing her was very easy. It was also very pleasant.'

She gently pushed him back. "I think I'm in love with you, Dennis," she said.

"I know I'm in love with you," he replied. And only in saying it, realised it was true. He felt terror constrict his throat.

.

"The hell with dinner," she said, her voice suddenly husky. "Let's got to bed."

.

"I...I can't."

.

She stepped back, startled. "You can't!? You mean you're..."

.

"No, no, not that. I can. What I meant is, well, I'm afraid."

.

"Of what? Me? Catching something?"

.

"No!" He shook his head. He wanted to run from the room. He wanted to be back in his apartment watching TV and smoking a joint.

.

"What are you afraid of? Please tell me."

.

"I'm afraid," he said, "I'm afraid that if I make love to you, I'll lose you."

.

"Dennis, if you don't make love to me you will surely lose me. Please don't worry, I'm not expecting something...spectacular. I'm pretty innocent. I love you, Dennis, and I just want to make love. It's what people in love do, you know."

.

"You don't understand. I'm not sure you're...real. I'm afraid you'll...you'll disappear."

.

She laughed. "I won't disappear, believe me. Let's stop talking." She began to unbutton her blouse.

.

"Tell me again you're real."

.

"Of course I'm real." She removed her blouse.

.

"Is this real?"

.

"What I feel is real," she replied. "If anything in the world is real, it is... " She hesitated, self-conscious. "...it's love." She unhooked her bra.

.

She had beautiful breasts, not large but graciously shaped and firm. And Dennis Culroth had an erection. Even in the grip of this terror, he did not suffer that kind of failure. There was no way out. This was reality testing. They would make love.

.

.

Dennis Culroth awoke. Noreen was there beside him on the bed. She was still there! The dim light from her clock radio illuminated their clothes piled on the bedside chair. It was ten minutes past the bewitching hour. He could tell by her breathing that she was awake.

.

"Dennis?"

.

"Yes?" He struggled to keep his voice steady, ordinary.

.

"You fell asleep right afterwards...you know?"

.

"Yes, I do that."

.

"I can't understand why you were worried. You're obviously an experienced lover."

.

He didn't say anything. There was nothing to say.

.

"Not that I mind. I certainly don't mind. I was surprised, but I certainly don't mind."

.

He stared up at the ceiling, desperately trying to sort out his feelings, desperately trying to understand why everything suddenly seemed so terribly, terribly ordinary.

.

"You're not saying anything."

.

"Sorry," he said, his voice neutral.

.

"You okay?"

.

"Yes."

.

"Can I ask you something, and will you promise to be truthful in your answer?"

.

"Of course."

.

"You promise?"

.

"Yes, yes, I promise."

.

"You weren't, uh, disappointed, were you?"

"No, no, of course not!" he answered quickly. Then searching for something to add, searching for something to give this sad lie conviction, he finally muttered softly into her silence: "I love you." It was a truth that has often been used as camouflage.

.

"I know that, but the sex, tell me the truth about the sex. Was it special? I'm pretty inexperienced."

.

"Special?" He paused.

.

"Yes, special. Was it special?" She sounded at the verge of tears.

.

"It...it was very, very..." He hesitated, not searching for, but already knowing yet afraid to say the right word — the most painfully apt word. He began again: "Noreen, believe me, it was very, very — *real.*"

.

Alas.

~~~~

TOM AND JERRY

"Friendship is a disinterested commerce between equals; love, an abject intercourse between tyrants and slaves."

—Oliver Goldsmith (*The Good-Natured Man*)

I wear glasses, teach high school English in a nice suburban school where turning to face the blackboard isn't an act of courage and have been married to the same woman since—as my friend Sergei would say—"dinosaurs trod the earth". I have two teenage daughters, both honour students, both of whom seem relatively unaffected by the hormones that must be pumping through them. I love my wife and—to quote Sergei again—"am monogamous to a fault". So Sergei laughed when, in the middle of his description of this bar for S&M types, I said I had some understanding of the phenomenon.

.

It was Saturday morning. We were in the kitchen. My girls were baby-sitting the neighbour's little boy, so I could hear cartoons blaring on the TV in the living room. Sergei was drinking a Bud, which, as a good Russian, he considers a soft drink. I was having a decaf but considering having a beer myself.

.

"Sure," he said. "I should've known you had a secret life. Anybody so straight that he could be used as a ruler just has to have a dirty habit. Take Fran on that saccharine kids' show: she just has to fuck

169

goats."

•

Sergei can be annoying sometimes, but we've been friends since university. I get to live vicariously a more adventuresome existence through his stories—which he is always willing to share. While he actually had a more genteel childhood than I did, he is rough around the edges and has attitudes which remind me of myself when I was younger and not so appallingly middle-class. He's a journalist, a bachelor, and has more balls than brains—and that is saying something, since he's a damn bright guy. His parents are from some place in the Urals, and I attribute his macho attitude, as well as his intelligence, to his Russian genes.

•

"Shit, man. I don't need to go cruising and answering cryptic personals to find out about the S&M world for my twisted editor," he continued. "I can just ask my old friend, the closet de Sade. He'll explain the whole scene to me." Yes, Sergei can be annoying.

•

"No, I won't claim that to be able to do that," I said. "But you seem to like stories about my childhood on the mean streets of Chicago. So let me tell you about the Stuckbauers."

•

•

I had a particularly perverse relationship with The Stuckbauers, two brothers named Tom and Jerry. ("Tom & Jerry" was also the name of a cartoon popular at the time.) Any reference to The Stuckbauers was not a reference to the Stuckbauer 'family', the other members of which seemed to have no substance: it was to Tom and Jerry.

Tom and Jerry Stuckbauer did have a timid little sister whose name I can't remember, but she was always in the distance, like a summer haze, her existence in this world not quite completed. If she had died, the euphemism 'faded away' would be the most apt way of expressing her passing. These three had no parents. They lived with their grandmother, who like Tom and Jerry's sister, seemed somehow unreal, ghostly, incompletely grounded in this world. I don't know what happened to their parents. Maybe they were both dead. Maybe they were both in jail. (Jailed parents weren't uncommon in our neighbourhood.) Maybe they never existed—Tom and Jerry just sketched onto the canvas of the world by God, The Omnipotent Cartoonist.

•

Tom and Jerry actually lived on the streets, although supposedly The Stuckbauers residence was a white frame house, which desperately needed painting, over on Wolcott Avenue. The house was usually dark, even though Grandma Stuckbauer was rattling around in there somewhere. Kids skipped the place on Halloween rounds, because it was always unlit and no one ever answered the door—even though everyone knew the old lady was home. The morning after Halloween their windows were always soaped. (Actually, waxed, which was harder to remove.) I was never inside the house, even though Tom and Jerry and I were street 'friends' for years.

Jerry Stuckbauer, a short, pudgy kid who wore glasses with scotch-taped frames, was a year or two younger than Tom. Jerry didn't talk much, a silent partner who generally followed his brother's lead. He wasn't docile, however, and the two of them would get into a scuffle at least once a day.

Tom was about my height and build, which during my high school days was a lean six-foot. His face was ordinary except for its pasty colour and the fact it was regularly redecorated with new scrapes and bruises. Given that Tom spent the whole hot Chicago summer on the street, it's difficult to understand how he kept so pallid.

Tom was one of my street buddies, although he was also a thorn in my side. For a long time I thought of him as a friend, but now I see our relationship somewhat differently.

Tom Stuckbauer was crude and ugly in a totally casual and unconscious manner. I realise now that he represented to me the profound ugliness of The Ordinary, what dull people call the Real World. He certainly epitomised The South Side of Chicago. I was learning to define being fully human as having passion, be it for a woman or for books or for science or—for that matter—for stamp-collecting. To imagine Tom Stuckbauer in love was impossible. He had no interests; passion surely lay way beyond his ken. But oh, he did things. He moved around.

And I, the kid with two lives, moved with him. We stole cigarettes off dashboards together, cruised Madelaine Avenue, shoplifted, played softball on the street. I got a thrill out of all of this, like acting in a play. But with Tom it was just something to do. I think that everything in his life was just something to do. Even the street corner softball games which filled up so much of the summer vacation sparked nothing in him. After a game, you could never tell from Tom's mood or expression whether he'd been on the winning or the losing team.

.

My relationship with Tom changed when I fell in love with my Rosa Giovanni. Rosa was fifteen, an honour student, with raven hair, who lived in a big house on the corner of Winchester and 57th. Tom made the mistake of noticing my infatuation—and commenting. It was this that contaminated our otherwise pure fraternal relationship. Unable to comprehend love, Tom naturally interpreted what he saw as purely sexual. It was, of course, very much sexual—but not, I believed at the time, in the way he understood sex.

.

Initially I don't think his comments were even intended to rile me. They were just passing remarks, just casual observations filtered through his eyes and expressed with his limited and vulgar vocabulary. "Nice tits." "Like to put it to her, huh?"

.

Well, Rosa did have nice breasts (although at the time I only knew their clothed shape), and God knows I did want to make love to her. But the way Tom expressed everything sullied it. Perhaps it was precisely because much of what he said was accurate that I became so upset by the way he said it. (I was a bit of a prude and very much a romantic at sixteen, playing at being a kid of the streets but secretly reading poetry in my room, anxious to escape what they now call 'the hood'.) After only quietly flinching the first few times he offended my young and tender sensibilities (and my girl's honour), I made the mistake of telling him to "shut the fuck up". Jerry was usually there, and he'd start to giggle, which would just encourage his older brother.

.

"Whatsa matter? Your little wop pussy too fuckin' pure to have a guy say anythin' bout her? Ain't getting any, are ya?"

.

"Shut up, asshole, or I'll rearrange your face."

.

Then he'd be backing off, but he wouldn't shut up. "Touchy, touchy. Maybe if she won't fuck ya, she'll give ya a hand job."

.

Then I'd go for him, while Jerry would start laughing out loud in a creepy high-pitched tone. Tom would run like the devil. He was so fast I could barely keep up with him, even though I was on the track team. In fact, initially he'd always pull away from me. But I also ran cross-country at school and had staying power, and Tom never used his initial lead to make a beeline for the safety of his house. Perhaps running away from me was acceptable, but running home was somehow cowardly.

It'd usually take a few blocks before he'd start to lose his wind, and I'd begin to gain on him. As soon as he realised I was going to catch him, he'd stop and face me.

It seemed strange at the time, but usually he didn't really fight back. The few times he did, I inflicted more serious than usual damage, so one might think his passivity was simple self-preservation. The trouble with that explanation is the way this scenario always ended.

I'd start by throwing body punches that he'd try to block—but not return. Then I'd manage to grab his arms, and the fight would become a wrestling match. Inevitably, I'd wrestle him down to the ground, pinning his arms with my knees, and slap his face. I wasn't a very tough kid by our neighbourhood's standards, but I could 'take' either of the Stuckbauers.

"Gonna watch your mouth, Stuckbauer?"

"Fuck off!"

Slap.

"Say you're sorry, shitface."

Silence.

Slap.

"Want me to knock your dirty teeth out?"

"Stop it."

Slap. By now the pallor on one side of his face had reddened from my blows. Red and white two-tone Stuckbauer.

"Say you're sorry?"

"Okay, I'm sorry. Let me up."

This is usually when Jerry would arrive, puffing like an asthmatic, sweat running into his eyes behind steamed-up glasses. Still laughing. He obviously viewed the whole thing as great entertainment. A born voyeur. He certainly never made the slightest move to help his brother.

So once I'd slapped Tom into reluctantly apologising, I'd get off him, and he'd stand up and brush himself off. If we'd gone down on the sidewalk or asphalt instead of someone's front lawn, he'd usually have a scrape on his arm which he would slowly and carefully inspect.

And then, every damn time, he'd say something like: "Your girlfriend fucks goats." And he'd be off and running again.

The first few times we acted out this ugly little scenario, I'd chase after him again. And a few blocks later we'd do a rerun—with the same ending. But I soon realised the futility of it all.

It was hopeless. Although I could get a begrudging apology from Tom while he was flat on his back and hurting, he would always retract it as soon as he was back on his feet. The only way I could see to break the pattern would be to escalate the violence, but I didn't really want to damage him. I never used my fists on him except for body punches before I got him down. I think I hated him at those moments, but not with a passion, and, oddly, he remained a friend of sorts. He was one of the gang, one of my street friends. It would've been totally unacceptable of me to really hurt him. The unspoken ethical code of my neighbourhood was that you only inflicted serious damage on hostile outsiders—or the black kids who lived on the other side of Western Ave.

So I found myself doggedly re-enacting this one-act drama over and over again. I was an actor in a play that I hated but which showed no sign of ever closing.

I arrived at a compromise. Once I'd extracted the first Apology For The Day by two-toning Stuckbauer's face, I'd ignore subsequent jibes—unless they were extremely nasty. This was my compromise between defending the honour of The Love Of My Life and conceding to the inevitability of the Real World dirtying my pretty picture of the world.

One Sunday afternoon Rosa and I were biking in Ryan's Woods. These 'woods' were actually a small treed area of a local park.

We came around a bend in the trail and there was Tom Stuckbauer, sitting on a tree stump, swigging from a quart bottle of Blatz. Nigger Beer we called it because it was cheap: three quarts for a dollar.

We stopped.

"Hi Tom."

He looked embarrassed, probably because Rosa was with me. The presence of girls seemed to make him uncomfortable. "Fats ripped off some beer. Wantta swig."

"Nah, thanks."

Suddenly five black kids came out of the trees. They were big, threatening. I recognised one of them from the halls of Pinewood High. He had a nasty scar on his cheek, and rumour had it he ran with The Rangers.

"She's nice," one of the black boys said, pointing at Rosa and grinning.

Rumour was it that a black girl had been raped in these woods the previous weekend by some guys from The Loafers, a white gang whose turf was just south of us. I knew our neighbourhood. I knew about the code of revenge. I knew I was scared.

Stuckbauer didn't even stand up. He just took another swig of beer.

"Look," I said stupidly, "we didn't have anything to do with what happened last weekend."

"Wha's that? Wha' happened?"

"Nothing," I said.

"Ya had nothin' to do with nothin'?"

175

"Right," said Stuckbauer, finally standing up.

"Yeah, she is nice," said one of the other black guys, the shortest of the lot. He had a particularly nasty grin.

"Well, you sure ain't nice, you ugly spear-chucker," Stuckbauer said, grinning like a crazy man.

"Ride," I whispered to Rosa.

She did.

"Come on, Tom!" I yelled, taking off after her.

I was so pumped up with fear that exactly what happened next is still confused in my mind. The five guys were off to the right of the trail. Stuckbauer was to the left. As Rosa raced off, one of the black guys started after her and Tom flung his beer bottle at him and struck him in the shoulder. He stopped immediately and turned, his face filled with rage. I went racing between Tom and the gang of avengers. This is when I yelled for him to run.

He said, "Just ride, asshole, ride!"

And I did.

To my shame.

The next day after school, I went looking for Tom. He and Jerry were sitting on the kerb in front of Golgotha Lutheran Church. Tom had a fat lip, and a black eye, nearly swollen shut.

"Hi Tom," I said."

"Hi."

"They worked you over, huh?"

"Not too bad. It's you and your wop broad they wanted. They punched me a few times and ran off."

"I want to thank you. I think they might've raped Rosa."

176

"Hey, no big deal. Now she'll wantta fuck me, not you. Besides she's probably disappointed she didn't get summa dat big black dick."

"Christ! Stop being an asshole. I'm serious. What you did was— brave."

"Asshole? Did you say Rosa likes it in the asshole?"

"Oh, fuck you, Stuckbauer!"

"What? You say she wants to fuck me? I know that! I'll let Jerry have her so she'll appreciate me more when I get around to her."

"Jesus Christ, Tom, will you just shut your fucking mouth! I'm trying to say thanks."

"My fucking mouth? I wouldn't use my mouth on her garlicky little twat."

And then I lost it. I'd given Rosa a *Selected Poems of Keats* for her birthday. She was refinement, civilisation, everything the South Side of Chicago was not. I didn't care if Stuckbauer had acted the hero, he had no right to talk like that about her.

I stepped forward, fists clenched.

"Jerry tells me she gives good head," Tom said, winking at his brother, and then turning and sprinting off.

I went after him. Either I was driven by more adrenaline than had ever before rushed through my veins or else, perversely, he wasn't trying as hard as usual to get away. I caught him in seconds.

I whacked him hard in the head from behind and he tumbled onto old lady Hartel's front lawn. I was on him so fast, he didn't have a chance. My knees pinning his arms, I leaned back and cocked my arm.

"Okay, shitface, you fucking apologise or I'll kill you!"

"Jerry says Rosa likes it when he cums in her face."

177

I pulled my arm even further back, readying to slap him harder than I'd ever done before, but something stopped me. Jesus, he had saved Rosa from being raped! I just couldn't hit him. God, but I wanted to! But I just couldn't do it.

.

He looked at me with surprise, perhaps disappointment. "Whatsa matter, don't you care enough to hit me any more?"

.

By now Jerry was standing next to us. He giggled.

.

I slowly closed my open hand into a fist. Then I punched Tom as hard as I could. Straight down into his nose. I felt cartilage crunch.

.

Through the blood and his tears of pain, Tom Stuckbauer smiled up at me—like a sated lover.

.

Jerry giggled.

~~~~

TRAVELING BECOMES MORE EXPENSIVE
WITH EACH PASSING YEAR

"Fly now! Pay later!"

—Travel Agency Advert

1: An Angel, This Angela:

.

"Her angel's face
 As the great eye of heaven shined bright,
 And made a sunshine in the shady place."

—Spenser (*The Faerie Queene*)

.

Image Angela. First a few physical parameters to warm you to the task: 1) height, five-nine; 2) weight, 123; 3) hair, blonde; 4) eyes, blue; 5) 35-24-35. She has a mellow coppery tan. She is twenty-two years old. She has legs that can only be described as perfect, even though she does have a small scar behind her left knee where a 'lover' stabbed her with a pen-knife. (This small scar is a gentle arc and lends a pleasing and subtle asymmetry that only completes her supple legs' perfection.) And her breasts—but wait: there is no point in further description. You can now create Angela on your own. It is better that way. You may even already have found my Angela's beauty too conventional for your taste. You may prefer raven hair. Maybe greater height—or less. Forget everything. I leave it to you now. You visualise the girl of your dreams—if, of course, it is girls of which you dream. Change these meagre 'facts' into ones of your own invention. Create in your mind's eye the sexiest, loveliest, most desirable young woman you can imagine. Her 'real' hair colour or height does not matter. What matters is the image in your mind of the most physically desirable woman conceivable. Image Angela. Image the ultimate young woman, unreal in her physical perfection. (Forget about the flaws that make one human. This character is a goddess, not a human. And if not a goddess, then at least an angel.) Now hold this angelic image in your mind. Give those fantasies swimming in your unconscious time to gradually flesh out this luscious creature. Do take your time. And when she becomes complete, hold her in your head, in your heart. Hold her there for a while. Hold her and weep. And if girls aren't your sexual preference, then weep for those for whom they are.

.

.

.

2: A Scholar Speaks Of Middle Age

.

"Halfway there is the best time for reflection."

—Hippokrites

.

I waited like a drunk philosopher
for the clarity of the morning-
after...

.

I travelled such a very long way
before meeting my personal limits
halfway...

.

I prepared like a vestal virgin
for the great sacrifice of my hopes
to time...
so thus

.

it is
this quiet disillusionment comes a surprise:
I'd expected so very much more

.

pain.

.

.

.

3: Ardour As A Point Of Departure

"Our schedule is rigid and tight. All aboard!!"

—The Stationmaster

Henry Innis came out the side door by the gym and felt it immediately: disappointment. That familiar emotion: a recurring motif, the thread that neatly tied his emotional life together. The sun was just visible over the lip of horizon, hanging blood-red and dying. He'd so hoped to have time for one lousy scotch in the refuge of his backyard before night descended (carrying with it hordes of blood-thirsty mosquitoes). Just one lousy scotch before darkness and dinner and domesticity with this wife's little agenda of "things we should do". He'd let his class out early with the expectation of out-racing the darkness home. Early maybe, but obviously not early enough.

As he walked to his car he reviewed the disappointments, the other numerous small disappointments that marked and marred the days of his fortieth year on this earth. There was the disappointment of having the A.P.T. Committee (that rag-tag collection of tenured dolts) refuse to approve his application for Associate Professor status. There was the disappointment of having his only son drop out of high school (high school, for Christ's sake!). There was the disappointment of having Marjorie (who was getting slovenly) telling him (after nineteen years of marriage) that she "never really enjoyed sex all that much, although it was all right." (She'd told him this so casually, as if she were talking about Greek cuisine or Danish Modern furniture!) There was the disappointment of having his book on the War of the Roses, his friggin magnum opus, rejected (especially after such an encouraging letter from that editor at U of M Press). And there was the disappointment of the bathroom scale, and of the bathroom mirror, each morning as he prepared himself for another dreary day of teaching those who couldn't care less. And now the goddamn sun was setting on him.

The waves of self-pity washed over him as he crossed the campus parking lot. Oh he knew it was virtually immoral to make a big thing of his piddling problems. He carried no great burden, suffered no horrible agonies. Hell, Fred MacIntyre in Geography, two years his junior, was in hospital with cancer. And the suffering and misery in the world outside his second-rate ivory tower made his own complaints seem like little more than the whining of a spoiled child.

But the starving-millions-in-Africa argument did not impress him any more now than it had when he was a young boy resisting a meal of liver and onions. In fact, it could be argued that precisely because his suffering was so fundamentally trivial and petty, it was all the more poignant. Tragedy has the redeeming quality of being large, significant. His suffering did not even have that.

.

He unlocked the car door—with some difficulty, for lately the lock tended to stick. Here was yet another disappointment: the car just about paid off and every other week some damn thing needed repair. Disappointment, disappointment. It could be a chorus, a refrain. State a fact of his daily life then chant: "Disappointment, disappointment." The night class he'd been saddled with. Disappointment. Disappointment. There wasn't a student in the lot who had the brains God gave a slug or the ambition God gave a turnip. There weren't even any reasonably attractive young women to soothe his eyes and feed his fantasies as he monotonously lectured from rote. Disappointment. Disappointment. His brother-in-law was coming to spend a week with them and would surely recount in minute detail the plot of every movie he'd seen in the last year. Disappointment. Disappointment. And those summer evenings in his backyard, his one bit of private, personal time—shot to hell, thanks to this summer night course. Oh how he'd tried to weasel out of teaching it, but no, they "needed" him!

.

"Like hell they need me, the bloody bastards!" Henry Innis actually cursed aloud (albeit softly) as he started the engine. "The bloody bastards!"

.

He pulled out of the lot and onto Fraser Road. He should count his blessings: tomorrow was Friday, a day with no classes and, this week at least, no meetings. Perhaps he'd finally catch up on his marking. But God, what a depressing thought! A 'free' day and he'd have to spend it wading through the turgid prose of freshman term papers. Disappointment. Disappointment. Shit!

.

Then he saw her. An apparition: an erotic angel. Wearing the tightest, the shortest pair of jean shorts he'd ever seen. Her legs were long and lovely, tanned to a rich golden hue; firm and muscular, they were displayed to great advantage as she walked along the shoulder of the road.

She turned in response to the sound of his car and stuck out her thumb. She was as lovely from a frontal perspective as from behind.

She was also, he noticed, familiar.

As Henry Innis pulled the car onto the gravel shoulder, he remembered where he'd seen her before: in the allegedly 'hallowed' halls of Academe. She was a student—not one of his, alas—by the name of Angela something or other. There wasn't a male faculty member under the age of sixty who hadn't, at one time or other, made some leering and lecherous comment about her. And from what he'd gathered from these occasional conversational bits, she was not only gifted with beauty but with brains as well. Which explains, he thought bitterly, why she'd never bothered to take any of his courses.

He reached over and opened the passenger door. Angela slid in beside him. She smelled of sun-tan lotion—which reminded him of his adolescence. Adolescence. Ah, if disappointment was the predominant, defining emotion of the present, well then lust had been the singing centre of his teen-age years—albeit unfulfilled lust. He remembered those years eidetically. He smiled at her briefly, afraid to look too long, afraid to make too obvious how totally enthralling he found her. Instead he focused his attention on the road ahead and put the Ford into first gear.

"You're Professor Innis, aren't you?" Her voice was deeper than he'd expected. Richer, more mature.

"Yes. How far are you going?" He tried to keep his voice casual, disinterested. He almost expected it to crack or waver. It was more difficult every year not to make a fool of himself by letting any of his female students suspect he found them attractive. There is nothing more ridiculous than a middle-aged, balding, slightly over-weight History Prof openly lusting after girls hardly any older than his son. It was unfair that with age came this requirement to assume a mantle of asexuality. He knew it bothered ageing women even more, for sensible-shoes Marsha in Social Welfare was always going on about it. (He suspected it was a bit of a come-on to her male colleagues.) But somehow she made her objections into some kind of feminist moral outrage. A middle-aged man saying the same things would be attacked by the likes of Marsha. Any middle-aged man publicly expressing the slightest sexual interest in a young woman was in serious trouble. He saw as an object lesson the awful Hawkins Scandal. The girl had cost Frank Hawkins his job—and worse than that, far worse, had made the poor man a public example of the immorality of dirty-minded, getting-old men.

Angela hadn't answered his question.

He took his eyes off the road for a second and glanced at his passenger. "Are you going downtown? If so I can..."

"No, I'm going farther than that. I'm going to Chicago."

"Chicago is over two hundred miles away."

"Oh I know where it is."

"But you don't have any luggage—I mean not even a backpack or anything. Are you hitch-hiking to Chicago with nothing more than the clothes on your back?" The expression suddenly sounded suggestive. He was feeling like a gawky adolescent, yet it was she who was the adolescent, or nearly so.

"Yes, just the clothes on my back and this." She held up a tiny leather purse on a long thin strap.

"Well, I suppose I could give you a lift out to the interstate."

She didn't say anything, not even so much as a thanks, although the interstate was a good five miles out of his way.

"Are you spending the weekend in Chicago?" He didn't know why he kept gibbering on; she didn't seem especially interested in talking. In fact, she seemed more interested in staring at him. He could feel her eyes on his profile.

"The weekend? Yes, I'm spending the weekend. Your first name is Henry, isn't it? You don't mind if I call you Henry, do you?"

What was he supposed to say? Yes, I mind; you must call me by my official title of Assistant Professor Innis? He glanced over at her again. "I don't mind," he said.

"I've seen you around the school, Henry, and I've heard you're a good teacher." Suddenly she sounded very warm and friendly; there was no irony in her tone.

"Really?"

"Yes. I bet you have large classes."

"Not particularly."

"That's strange, what with your reputation as a teacher—and your good looks."

Henry Innis threw a sharp look at his passenger. Was she making fun of him? Her voice had sounded warm and sincere.

She met his look with a smile, and there was nothing nasty or sarcastic in her smile. "I bet," she continued, "the women in your classes are always trying to seduce you."

This was too much! He couldn't help himself: he laughed out loud. It was too, too ridiculous. .

"If only it were true," he blurted out, immediately regretting his words.

"If it isn't, then you have fools for students."

Now he really didn't know what to say. He concentrated on the road. It was getting dark; at least she couldn't see his face clearly. He was probably blushing.

"Have you ever slept with any of your students?"

"That's a very personal question."

"I know."

He hesitated, then not knowing why he was admitting anything to this young woman he didn't even know, this young woman, a student, who might very well be mocking him, he nevertheless answered. "No, I have never slept with any of my students."

He should have stopped there, but something perverse in his nature made him add: "I haven't been with another woman since I got married almost twenty years ago." As soon as he muttered this confession, he knew for sure that he was blushing. His face felt very warm. He also knew for sure that he was going mad. And that he was making a total ass of himself. She'd probably be telling her friends about this conversation as soon as she had a chance.

.

"Really? Henry, I'm sorry, that's sad." She rested her hand lightly on his thigh.

.

And Henry Innis realised he had an erection. Her hand was resting on his upper leg only inches from it. Then suddenly for some reason he felt like crying. It was sad. Truly sad.

.

Pull yourself together, Henry, he thought, or you're going to completely lose it. Don't say anything. Don't do anything. Just drive.

.

They were nearing the interstate. She wasn't saying anything more either. When they reached the ramp that descended into the stream of headlights pouring west toward Chicago, he pulled the car off onto the shoulder. She removed her hand from his thigh.

.

But then she slid closer to him and kissed him, her tongue warmly probing into his astonished mouth. Simultaneously, she stroked the back of his neck. Then before he could respond in any way, she was leaning back against the passenger door and looking him up and down like he was some kind of specimen.

.

"Would you like to make love to me?" she said finally.

.

He didn't know what to say. To say no would be to lie. To say yes would be—what? Complicity, perhaps. Up until now he had done no wrong, had done nothing to encourage her, had made no improper move.

.

Finally he muttered: "Here?"

.

"No, not here, not in a car."

.

He didn't say anything.

.

"You think I'm putting you on, teasing you, don't you?"

.

"I don't know."

.

"I'm not. I want you to take me to Chicago for the weekend."

"You want me to drive you to Chicago?!"

"No, I want you to drive us to Chicago. Don't misunderstand me, Henry, I'm not offering a quick fuck in payment for a ride to Chicago. I'm no whore."

"I don't understand why you're...why..." He gave up trying to articulate precisely what it was that he didn't understand.

"It's just a whim, Henry, just a whim. You're sexy and I'm horny. So why not?"

He just stared at her. A car sped past, its headlights briefly lighting her lovely face.

"This is just a one-time, no-strings-attached arrangement. No big deal. And I don't kiss and tell, by the way. And Chicago is a very big anonymous place."

"Why are you...uh, making this...this offer?"

"I just told you."

"But..."

"You don't seem to think very much of yourself, but I can't understand why. You're an attractive man. I want you. I don't like boys. I like men, intelligent men. It's just karma that you happened to pick me up. Now I know I'll have a good weekend. And you will too, I'm sure."

"But my wife..."

She interrupted him by reaching over covering his mouth with her hand. "There is only one condition, Henry, only one condition. This isn't permanent or the beginning of something else, but it has to be intense, passionate, uncompromising. You have to prove to me you really want me, that you're willing to act on impulse, willing to give me your undivided attention. Guilt and second thoughts mess up this sort of thing ninety percent of the time. So, if you agree to my—as you put it—my offer, well then I don't want to hear a word about your wonderful wife and kids. If you agree, then from the moment

187

you say yes your family does not exist. You drive down that ramp and straight on to Chicago. You don't even call your wife to make some lame excuse. You can try to explain things when we get back to this dreary little town on Sunday." She removed her hand from his mouth.

"But..."

"That's it, my rules, Henry. All you have to say is yes or no. If you can't control your guilt and forget about your family, if you don't want me that much, then it wouldn't be a good time anyway and you'd best just say so now."

Dusk had advanced into night, but Henry Innis could see well enough by the lights of the interchange. He stared at her fine and sensual face. He'd just been propositioned. He'd never been propositioned before. Never. Not directly. Never.

"Well," she said, "yes or no?"

Never had a woman turned to him and said in plain English that she wanted to sleep with him. Never! Yet here was this gorgeous young creature, this sophisticated angel, offering herself to him, 'no-strings-attached'. It was an adolescent fantasy. (Or a mid-life fantasy.) She was a shadow. He did not know her. But he could see her, her beautiful legs, her high cheekbones, her breasts stretching the black t-shirt she wore. She was real. This was impossible, but she was real. Either that or he'd gone insane, finally cracked and moved out to where the buses don't run.

He thought of his wife, of his absurd fidelity to a woman who considered sex just tolerable—a fidelity without any religious or moral justification. He thought about the trivial sadness of his life. He though about how his friends bored him, how his students bored him, how he bored himself. He thought about the risk: perhaps she had some sort of venereal disease; perhaps she was mad and dangerous (for wouldn't she have to be mad to desire his doughy, unappealing body); perhaps she was leading him on, teasing him, playing with him, testing to see if she could get old Innis to admit unbridled lust for a student; or perhaps someone, a crazed colleague who for some reason wanted to get him, had put her up to this—but no, that was paranoid. And then he thought about his wife's reaction, what she would do when he failed to arrive home at his usual time.

He thought about her on the phone to the police; he thought about being discovered (unlikely as he knew it was) in a Chicago motel room with this young woman. He did a lot of thinking in a very short time.

.

.

4: Decisions Of The Body

"We feel sorry because we cry, angry because we strike, afraid because we tremble... Without the bodily states following on the perception, the latter would be purely cognitive in form, pale, colorless, destitute of emotional warmth."
—William James (*The Principles of Psychology*)

Pause here and image Angela again. One needs this goddess image to understand, really understand. One needs to understand idolatry, for it explains adultery. And remember that image is not thought. Henry Innis did a lot of thinking, but all this thinking, thinking itself, really had very little to do with his decision: what determined that was what he felt. And what he felt was passion, lust, craving, desire, desire, desire stronger than any emotion he'd felt since the tragi-comic days of his youth. Even the bitterness and anger he often felt toward his wife, his colleagues, the college administration, even that slow-boiling rage was a mild, restrained, watery emotion compared to the intense longing he felt for the young woman seated beside him. What he felt was the stuff that made rapists and martyrs and romantic poets. It was the stuff of suicide and sainthood, of revolution and creativity or atrocities and blind, self-less devotion. What he felt was feeling. "And only feeling can make a person alive," exclaim the thrill-seekers prowling every city's seamy underside.

(Oh yes, this does sound like a lecture, a secular sermon almost. And so now must we have the moral: the greater value of heart—or even loins—over head? Time to drag out the rhetoric of romanticism, drag it out kicking and screaming into the cool climate of our times—into a place where rationality, sanity, decency, a distant smirking irony prevail. Can it survive this climate? These are the years of middle-age, middle-road, bourgeois compromise. How absurd and dated sounds this clarion call to passion. How bathetic sounds this obsolete and anachronistic cry for vitality. How sad!)

Be that as it may, and choke, as well you might, over this call to carnal worship. Be that as it may, what Henry Innis felt was passion, an all-consuming and blue-flamed passion. No other word will do for this roaring blaze of ardour. What he felt was the resurrection of his body from numbness, the Novocain finally wearing off. At what cost? Don't be silly. You can't put a price on Rebirth.

(Oh yes, what nonsense, this glorifying of carnality! Certainly a very good argument can be made that dismisses what the good professor was feeling as nothing more than the lowest, commonest, most ignoble and animal of emotions: concupiscence. Listen carefully and one can hear the mockery of The Moralist, The High Puritan (of any religion, even or especially the High Church of Liberalism). Listen to the condescending tones of Common Conscience: "How very, very pathetic, a grown man, a scholar and teacher and supposed moral exemplar, falling victim to animal lust. He does not even know the woman. He does not even know the woman. He is only attracted by her physical appearance, her youth. She is a mere girl. How superficial! And how very demeaning for her—and truth be told, for him too. Tsk. Tsk." But the romantic will reply: "Tsk, tsk yourself to hell, to a cold, dank, unfiery hell which you'll probably mistake for heaven, so very weak is your imagination.)

And Henry's reply? "Yes," said the man who was not going home tonight.

5: Journey To The Centre

"We can expect it to get much warmer as we approach our destination."
—Jules Verne (*A Voyage To The Center Of The Earth*)

The drive to Chicago was three and three quarter hours of foreplay. When they'd begun the descent down the ramp to I-90, Angela had asked him not to say a word until they'd reached their destination. She said a strange thing for a young woman to say: "Silence is room to feel."

Oh, it was probably one of those pseudo-profundities young people find in Kahlil Gibran or one of his ilk, but well, if she wanted silence, she would have silence. And certainly, through the dark and silent drive, Henry had feeling. As the car moved steadily along the highway, he banished speech and thought and made plenty of room for sensation. He forced his mind to go blank—or more accurately: he made of his mind a receptacle to store the delicious flow of sensations streaming in from his peripheral nervous system.

.

She began by unbuttoning his shirt. This simple act was itself almost unbearably erotic. Then she ran her hands over his chest, lightly, gently. The palms of her hands grazed his nipples again and again, producing an electric, unlocalised tingling. He'd always considered his nipples exceptionally sensitive, and for a moment he wondered if there was some way she could have possibly known this—but then he realised it probably was not as uncommon an erogenous zone as he'd thought. He was just being caressed by a woman who understood male sensitivity—a new experience for him. As her palms slid lightly over his nipples he imagined a plexus of sensory neurones just under his skin pulsing in response to her touch like dancing lights of various colours.

.

She leaned over and slid her tongue into his ear while her right hand continued to caress his chest. For an instant he closed his eyes. But then quickly he opened them. It'd be the ultimate irony for him to die in a flaming car crash on his way to heaven.

.

There was something narcotic about the way the moist and muffled sound of her tongue exploring his ear made the outside world recede. Whether it was actually the sound or primarily the feel of her tongue that did it, he couldn't tell. But as the outside world receded, the universe of his own body expanded quickly to fill the void, to fill his consciousness.

.

He felt her hand travel down his chest to his waist—his unfortunately only too ample waist. And then to his zipper. He heard the faint scratching sound of the zipper being drawn down. He felt her fingers snake in—and touch him, although still only through the fabric of his shorts. Then, to his momentary despair, she withdrew her hand. Ah, but only to open his belt and the button on his pants. Then her hand was back on his stomach, sliding down, down, under the elastic of his shorts. And then she touched him, his erection. And the world receded into nowhere.

.

Suddenly her tongue was no longer probing his ear. Her hand was withdrawn. He opened his eyes—or, rather, focused them. He could see tail-lights off to the left. Why to the left? And he could hear the world again, hear the crunch of his tires on the gravel shoulder. He carefully guided the car back into the right lane.

"Henry," she said softly, "please be careful. If you aren't I'll have to stop touching you. And I don't want to stop."

Her hand was already back, this time on his neck, brushing the soft skin over his jugular, and then descending once again to his chest, to his nipples. Her left hand came up the back of his neck into his hair.

He concentrated fiercely on his driving. He quite literally gritted his teeth as he struggled to maintain a balance between the warm, engulfing sea of sensation and the hard, dark reality of the road ahead.

She began touching him again down there, but now only for a few seconds at a time. It was as if she sensed the precariousness of his position and could gauge precisely how far to push him before drawing him back.

"I don't want you to come yet," she said, "and I really don't want you to drive us into the ditch."

He balanced. He drove. For almost four hours she touched him everywhere she could reach with her long-fingered hands and in some of these places also with her tongue—but always lightly, always teasingly. She helped him maintain his balance by pulling taut the tightrope he walked. For almost four hours. For almost four hours he kept his eyes glued to the road unwinding before him, hardly ever even glancing at the woman who was methodically awakening every nerve cell in his body, making him exquisitely sensitive, raw and exposed and alive. All that time he resisted the urge to reach over and touch her, for he sensed it would be somehow inappropriate. He was to be passive, receptive—for now at least. Any active aspect of him had to be suppressed or channelled into the driving.

But when he saw the sign saying "CHICAGO - 10 MILES" he suddenly yielded and reached over to touch her knee.

"Not yet," she said, gently removing his hand, "not quite yet. We're almost there."

"No mortal man can survive four hours of foreplay," he whispered in a voice gone gravelly.

.

"Then I guess you are among the immortals," she replied.

.

.

.

6: Image

.

"Thou shalt not make unto thee any graven image."

—Exodus 20-4

.

Image, v.t. -- 1. To form a mental picture of; imagine. 2. To make a visible representation of; delineate. 3. To mirror; reflect. 4. To describe effectively in speech or writing, as with vivid comparisons or descriptions, figures of speech, etc. 5. To symbolize.

.

Graven image. Craven. Crave. Craving image.

.

.

.

7: Payment On Arrival

.

"C.O.D. is an acronym for a misnomer: They usually make you pay before they hand anything over to you."

—Hippokrites

.

Henry Innis pulled into the first place along the North Side's motel strip that had a vacancy. The Edencourt Motel looked neither seedy nor expensive.

.

As he stepped down on the parking brake, Angela quickly opened her door and jumped out. "This is my treat," she said already heading for the motel office. "I'll check us in."

.

Along the outside wall, next to a pop machine, was a phone booth that wouldn't be visible from the motel office. He watched the beautiful young woman go in. Briefly he considered dashing to the phone and calling Marjorie. Surely she must be worrying about him by now. But then he thought: to hell with her! Instead he would be faithful—to the woman he desired, that is, not to his wife. Let Marjorie worry a little. So what?

.

Desire. The woman he desired. Oh my dear God yes! Desired as he'd never desired a woman before in his life. His penis ached. His balls ached. (They used to call them 'blue-balls' when he was in high school, this aching in the groin resulting from unconsummated stimulation.) But even in his youth he'd never felt such intense desire. Desire, lust, craving, longing. It was exquisite to want so desperately. He now understood why 'exquisite' was sometimes used to describe pain.

.

He'd have to warn her as soon as they were alone that he would surely ejaculate prematurely. He'd been existing on the precipice of orgasm for almost four hours. There was no question of it, no avoiding it: he'd explode the instant he entered her. But it didn't matter, for he was equally certain he'd be ready again within minutes—like some virile young man half his age.

.

Angela came out of the motel office grinning broadly and holding up a key attached to a piece of hard brown plastic. In minutes he would be with her, in her.

.

She slid in next to him. "Room 42. It's around back. Drive that way." She pointed and her t-shirt stretched tighter around her breasts.

.

He did as he was told, parking the car in front of Room 42, ground level. He got out of the car quickly, as did she. But as soon she had unlocked the door to the room, she stopped and turned to face him. She kissed him—but lightly, almost chastely. And then she stepped back.

.

"Give me your car keys," she said.

.

"What?"

.

"Your car keys. Give me your car keys. I want to go find a liquor store and buy us a bottle of wine."

.

"I don't need wine. I need you."

.

She laughed. "I can tell, but I want to do this right. We've got all weekend. Now c'mon, give me the keys. I'll be right back. You go take a shower and wait for me in bed. This is going to be very nice, I'm sure, so let's not rush it. Believe me, I know how to make love to a man."

.

"I believe you," Henry Innis replied, his voice still an octave lower than usual.

"You're tense. It will relax you."

"I like being tense. I don't want to relax," he protested. But he handed her the keys.

The motel room was ordinary, cheap, but clean enough. He pulled back the covers on the bed and imagined himself there, between the crisp sheets, exploring the voluptuous slopes and curves of Angela's body. He pressed his palm along the pillow and closed his eyes. Then he shook himself and headed for the shower.

As he soaped his body he wondered how a woman could find him appealing. He wasn't exactly fat, but he was soft. He'd always been soft, even as a teenager. Of course he'd also always been smart. And everyone said that most women are more attracted by intelligence than physical characteristics. (However these alleged wise women didn't seem to cross his path very often.)

It was after he'd towelled dry and climbed in between the sheets completely naked that he suddenly remembered passing a liquor store about a block before the motel. If Angela had seen it too, she'd be back any second.

But she mustn't have seen it, for she didn't return within seconds— or within minutes. He lay waiting. He checked his watch. He conjured her image in his mind. And waited. After half an hour had elapsed he got up and dressed. She was a woman who obviously knew how to arouse a man by teasing, by holding off. It wouldn't be beyond a woman like her to deliberately delay her return just to increase his passion. Perhaps she was waiting to see him come out looking for her, perhaps she was waiting just outside for one more proof of his impatient desire.

As he was tying his shoes a darker thought crossed his mind but he banished it. She was a strange woman, but she wasn't a car thief.

He stepped outside to wait for her. And as he shut the door behind him he remembered that she had the key. Trying it immediately, he found it locked. Damn motel doors always locked automatically.

He started toward the street. Even along a Chicago motel strip, traffic is sparse at two in the morning, so if his car was around he'd be able to see it. When he reached the street, he turned north, in the direction of the liquor store.

.

It wasn't even a two minute walk. The manager had just locked the front door and was striding toward the back of the store, but pounding on the glass had no effect; the fellow didn't even turn around. Obviously in Chicago closing time was closing time.

.

A police cruiser turned the corner. Henry Innis quickly left the locked liquor store and started walking back in the direction of the motel. The cruiser was coming down the street behind him. He realised his back pockets felt funny and then he realised why: no keys and no wallet. Angela had his keys and he'd left his wallet in the motel room. No money, no keys—in the eyes of the police he'd be a suspicious vagrant loitering around a closed liquor store. He stepped up his pace.

.

Just as he reached The Edencourt, the cruiser drew up next to him. He glanced over at two stern faces and tried to smile causally. Then he quickly entered the office.

.

It was deserted. There was a small bell on the counter next to a "Ring For Service" sign. He didn't ring. He waited a minute, then went back out.

.

He found his car parked in front of Room 42 and cursed himself for leaving on his futile mission. She was back! Joy and adrenaline surged through his blood. He ran up to the car. The keys were dangling in the ignition, but he could see that all the lock buttons were down. That was careless of her; it meant breaking a window or getting a locksmith in the morning. But so what? She was back, waiting for him, and that was the important thing. He went up and tried the motel door.

.

Locked. He knocked softly. No answer. He knocked louder. Still no answer. He felt sure she was in there. Why was she ignoring him? He began pounding on the door as hard as he could. .

.

Enough was enough! What did she want him to do? Beg? Scratch at the door like a cat locked out of its house? Or did she want him to smash the damn door down?

The door to Room 41 opened and a large, hairy man stepped out wearing only a tattered pair of boxer shorts. "What the fuck do ya think you're doin' pal? It's two fuckin' thirty in the fuckin' morning!"

"Sorry. I'm locked out."

"Don't be sorry, pal. Just be quiet, okay? If there is anybody in that room, they're either fuckin' dead or they don't want to let you in."

Henry Innis backed away from the door, then returned to his car. He tried all four doors, although he could see clearly they were locked. The man he'd awakened hadn't gone back to his room. He was watching, shaking his head as if in amazement at the number of idiots in the world. Then, finally, he turned and went back into his room.

There was only one thing to do. He went back to the motel office. This time he rang the little metal call-bell, and an unfriendly-looking man with an eye out of alignment came out of a doorway at the back of the office.

"Yeah, can I help you?" The man's tone indicated he didn't really care if he could or not.

"I'm in room 42."

The clerk just stared blankly.

"My...my wife, uh, she left with the room key and I'm locked out."

"So?"

"Well, have you seen her?"

"Now, buddy, how would I know if I seen her? I don't know who your wife is"

"Oh, of course. We, uh, she checked in here just a little while ago, within the hour I'd say. She was wearing jean shorts and a black t-shirt."

"That's your wife!?"

"Yes, have you seen her?"

"Unfortunately not since she checked in." The man smiled an unpleasant smile.

"Well perhaps you could just let me into the room?"

The clerk frowned then looked down at something under the counter. "Did you say Room 42?"

Henry Innis nodded.

"She booked in as a single."

"Huh?"

"A single. Listen, buddy, I don't know what this is all about but..."

"It's none of your business what this is all about." Henry Innis was surprised at the anger appearing in his voice. "Just give me the damn key please."

"What's the name again?"

"Professor Henry Innis."

The man looked down again. When he looked up he was smiling nastily. "Funny, that's not your wife's name, *Professor*. You did say Innis?"

"Her first name is Angela. She may have used her maiden name." That the last remark was foolish he realised immediately; he didn't know Angela's last name.

"Which is?"

"Please stop being difficult. I want the key for Room 42. Angela in Room 42."

"We don't have any Innis registered and we don't have any Angela anybody here."

"Well... maybe she used a false name." As soon as he said this he knew he was bungling things hopelessly.

"Now why would she do that?"

"I don't know. I don't know. I'm in Room 42, I swear it! I took a shower in there not half an hour ago."

"Look here, buddy, I don't know what your kink is, and frankly I don't care. If the lady is a hooker, it ain't none of my business, but I guess your meter has run out. So I think you better get outta here..."

"Now hold on!"

"...before I call the cops."

It was at this point that Henry Innis, Assistant Professor of History, almost struck the man in the face. Instead some residue of rationality caused him to spin on his heels and storm out of the office. He tried to slam the door behind him, but one of those air-cushion contraptions sucked the violence from the gesture.

Damn her, he thought as he ran back toward his room. Damn her to hell! He knew with absolute certainty that she was there, the god-damned bitch.

Well, he thought as he once again tried the door and once again found it locked, well if she wants me to beg then I'll beg. If she wants me to crawl on my belly, I'll crawl on my belly. If she wants a fool, then she'll have a craven fool.

He began pounding on the door, began cursing and begging. How could she do this to him? .

He'd never reached such a fever pitch of desire for a woman in his whole life. What kind of woman could lead him into this altered state and then mock him so cruelly? He could imagine her lying in the motel bed, stark naked, listening to his desperate entreaties and quietly laughing to herself. Maybe playing with herself. Maybe it turned her on, this torturing of helpless male victims of her beauty. Oh, he was the fool all right! The biggest damn fool of all for thinking himself in control, thinking she was a gift from the Gods for which he'd not have to pay. Yet he continued to beg, to scream at that ugly number forty-two. The hell with pride, with self-respect!

The only thing that mattered in the world was the woman behind that inch and a half of wood. If she wanted him to grovel, he'd grovel. Humiliation is of no importance when the stakes are this high, the needs this strong. He hated her now for doing this to him, but he did not want her any less.

"Bitch," he screamed, "open the door and I'll do anything. God! Do you hear me?! Anything!"

The man in 41 came out briefly, but this time he said nothing, only shook his head and went back in.

Henry Innis noticed the police cruiser out of the corner of his eye. Oh shit, he thought, realising immediately why they were pulling into the parking area. He stopped pounding the door. He leaned forward and rested his forehead against the wood, closed his eyes, visualised Angela naked on the bed not ten feet away. Or perhaps she stood there just on the other side of the door, only a foot away, probably smiling with the satisfaction of knowing how easily she could raise a man from the dead and then send him to burn in hell. It was over now.

But then he opened his eyes, raised his head and again screamed at the door: "Bitch, open up!"

He turned around. The police were getting out of the car. He could tell by their faces that they were worried about dealing with him. He must've looked completely demented, and they know the insane are to be treated with caution. Well, if insanity is sensitivity, he was insane. So what?

Henry Innis turned and began to run.

"Hey, hold it, stop."

Henry Innis did not stop. He ran.

"Take the car!" he heard one cop yell.

Henry Innis went around the corner of the motel block and down the alley. He was amazed at how easily he ran, amazed that he even remembered how to run. He felt almost graceful as he sprinted down the alleyway.

To his left were the backs of motels, restaurants, parking lots, but on his right were the backyards of houses. All these yards were fenced, but some of the fences didn't seem all that high. He spotted a dilapidated chain-link one up ahead that was quite low. He began to angle toward it.

"Fucking bitch!" he screamed, much as a karate master screams some incomprehensible phrase before driving his hand through a stack of bricks. And Henry Innis sailed over the fence.

He landed on his feet in the grass of someone's backyard and hardly broke his rhythm. He raced toward the back of the house. There was a low metal gate out to the gangway between the houses. He would not stop to unlock it.

"Fucking bitch!" he screamed again and up he went.

And over. This time he landed not on grass but on sidewalk. This time he lost his rhythm and stumbled as pain shot through his feet and knees. But he did not fall.

As he came out from between the houses he saw the police car. It was slowly gliding down the street from the south. Drawing energy and nerve from some unsuspected and mysterious reserve, he kept running in a straight line: right out into the street, right in front of the police cruiser, and across to the other side. Then down another gangway.

As soon as he entered the deep shadows of the gangway a sharp pain cut into his left side, but he refused to slow his pace. He didn't slow even when he saw that the gate to this backyard was at least five feet high and constructed of heavy lumber. Instead he charged it, at the last second throwing his left shoulder forward and hurtling into it—screaming.

"Bitch!"

The lock clattered to the sidewalk as the gate banged open and Henry Innis came stumbling into the backyard. This time he fell, bounced, rolled. And then scrambled to his feet. There was a concrete garbage unit built into the back fence. It was easy to jump up on it and then over the rear fence into another alley.

After landing on the rough concrete pavement, he hesitated for a moment, deciding which way to run, and noted that a pain in his chest had joined the pain in his side and his knees. He had no idea how close the police were, so arbitrarily he began running south toward where another alley intersected this one before it emerged into a main street; at this intersection he turned left, half expecting to run into one of the cops.

Backing on this lane was a large food store and behind it three huge commercial garbage bins. The pains in his side and in his chest and in his knees were getting worse. He was having a difficult time breathing. And he decided that there is a time for running and a time for hiding. .

To every lover or fool there is a season, a time for living and a time for dying.

He partially ran, partially stumbled, toward the nearest dumpster.

He had to chin himself to get up the side and get a footing on a thin metal edge, and the effort doubled the pain under his ribcage. His arms almost gave out, but then his foot found the edging, and with one great final burst of energy he swung one leg over the top lip of the dumpster, rolled his weight up and hurtled himself over the top to tumble down into the bin.

He landed flat on his back, but he did not injure himself further, for he landed in a soft, complex blend of rotting produce. The air was thick with the stench of decomposing vegetable matter that filled the dumpster as liquid fills a vial. As he lay there spread-eagled on his back, he felt like he was afloat on some putrescent sea, a bather luxuriating in filth. Above he could see stars twinkling.

He lay quietly for some time like this, afloat on this rancid, fetid sea of garbage, lay and watched the stars. He listened as first his breathing, then the pounding of his heart gradually, ever so gradually, slowed. He attended to the various aches and pains that rose and fell in an almost musical counterpoint: a dissonant sonata for damaged muscles and raw nerves worthy of some Bartok of the body. The pain was everywhere: his side, his chest, his shoulder, his knees, his feet, his heart. But each pain was different in pitch and timbre and intensity. It was luxuriant, this suffering, exquisite. He was at a concert being performed in the nerve endings of his body. And he could see the stars.

.

He didn't worry about the risk of being found. It was impossible. He wouldn't even be recognised if someone did climb up and peer into the dumpster. He'd be seen as just one more piece of garbage in a bin full of garbage. Surely he neither smelled nor looked any different from the rest of the decaying refuse. He was beyond ripe, but at least he knew it now, was able to feel it—and so in some strange way appreciate it. He was at one with decay. He was at one with the entropic universe. Oneness. A mystical union of garbage with garbage.

.

Eventually he rolled over into a foetal position. As he unzipped his pants an image formed in his mind, an image crisp and fresh and wholesome. "Bitch", he whispered softly, lovingly, as he took his erection in his hand. Image Angela. "Sweet bitch," he whispered as he began to make love to her. Ah, she was such a beautiful, beautiful image: the image of an angel. He could tell it was going to be very, very good. She would not be a disappointment.

~~~~

FINDING GOD

"God seems to have left the receiver off the hook, and time is running out."
—Arthur Koestler (*The Ghost In The Machine*)

I skipped Sunday Mass, not feeling particularly grateful to God for the latest curve he'd thrown at me. Also, I'd slept poorly because there was still "a hole in the bed"—to quote a Roberta Flack lyric—where once upon sweet Susan lay her lovely body down. But last night, for the first time in a week, I slept a bit better. And the Monday morning mail was refreshingly—and atypically—free of any bills. There was only a single letter from my friend, the gonzo journalist, putative investigative reporter, and wannabe Biblical scholar, Gottlieb Schreiber—or Gotty, as his friends called him.

.

.

First Letter From Gotty Schreiber

.

Dear Thomas,

Me too. That's what me thought after your call last week. Me too has been diddling around too long. Time to make a change! It is synchronicity I think, your decision and mine. Your wife leaves you, and that is the impetus you need to decide to quit your cushy academic job and take a road trip. For me it also was a woman who knocked me out my rut. She was not nearly as lovely as your Susan, not by many miles, for she had imperfect skin, coke-bottle glasses, and a bad attitude. But hey, it was far less painful for me, for I wasn't emotionally involved with her. I am not so stupid as to ever get emotionally involved with a librarian. What man would want to compete with great authors, too dead to ruin romance by farting in bed?

I should explain. I had a little run in with the archives and this archivist bitch; it is this that convinced me it was time to leave the library and take my project on the road. But I'm sure both of us have been intending to hit the open highway for quite some time. (Well, I know I was.) So, let me tell you about my plans. (Of course I'd like to know about your plans, too, my friend, so, if you're leaving soon, give your itinerary to your brother, and I'll call him in a week or so. Assuming I can! Then I'll know where to write you next.)

Anyway, first the back-story. As you know, I think Nietzsche was wrong: rumours of God's death are greatly exaggerated. There are more plausible explanations for His apparent disappearance. So I was at the U of M library one fateful afternoon looking for an old article in the now defunct Journal of Teleology that elaborates on the Aristotelian and Thomistic "First Cause" argument. The library has this new, high-tech, automated microfilm viewer. As you know, hi-tech stuff hates me. Two minutes after turning the bloody thing on the God damned apparatus started eating the microfilm. I punched the hell outta the stop button, but the mechanism must've been nerve dead. I had my own mini-ticker tape parade happening: attractive little strips of celluloid confetti were fluttering out of the gears into my lap and onto the floor.

Well, you know methinks I am a religious man (in my own way) or me wouldn't be working on this project in the first place, and you know religious men are not afraid to get down on their knees. So that is what I did. Mind you, I wasn't praying to it to stop. (I know you think I'm mad, so I have to make that explicit.) No, I was just looking for the f'ing plug. All else failing, pull the plug, my stepmother used to say. So picture me crawling under the table, all this microfilm flutter descending on my behind as I searched for the outlet. Nice image, eh? Don't answer: that was a rhetorical question.

The power cord snaked out of sight behind the microfilm storage cabinet, and tugging on the cord did nothing. I tried wedging my fingers between the wall and the cabinet and pulling on it, but I was hardly in an ideal position to exert much leverage, and microfilm must be like paper: deceptively light when handled in small quantities, but actually very dense and heavy. (Remember helping me move my personal library last year? You kept referring to my boxes of books as boxes of trees. And you should talk! Good thing you're just leaving home, leaving your own processed tree collection with Susan, for you'd never be able to move.)

Anyhew. There was no way I was going to budge that cabinet full of compressed information. I'd just started backing out from under the table through this gentle shower of celluloid strips (the microfilm reader had by now completely transmogrified into an insane slice and dice kitchen aid) when I bumped into something.

Something. Something animate, if a librarian can be called animate. I knew *then that I was about to have an unpleasant interaction with another human being—if a university librarian can be classed as a human being. I won't go into the details of our little tête-à-tête. Suffice it to say, I now know more about the costs and inconvenience of replacing microfilm then I ever wanted to know— thanks to a shrill lecture from a bitch with a bun. And next time I'm in the library I'm being treated to a free tutorial on the proper care and feeding of microfilm equipment.*

But I don't expect to be in that library again for some time. After this little misadventure, I found meself a quiet bar, threw back a coupla rotgut bar Scotches and made my decision. The article I'd shredded was almost certainly superfluous. I'd been wasting my time in libraries long enough. I'd fallen into that age-old writers' trap of substituting preparation for action. Christ, for months now I've had more than enough information to make me move.

So here me sat in this seedy little bar sipping (well, guzzling actually) my Scotch (with water that had better credentials) and decided it was time to take the Big Step. (By the way, I think you are doing the right thing too. Another Big Step. As my stepmother used to say, moving is better than moping.)

"Face it, Gotty," I told meself, "you're procrastinating." I confronted the hard truth: I was as prepared as library research was ever going to make me. It's time to grab the proverbial bull by the horns. (I can hear you thinking: "'bull' is a good word." Well, we'll see.)

So that is what I'm doing: grabbing the bull. I went home, bummed a few hundred from Patty (who was too stoned to care), took my credit cards from the sealed envelope where I'd been (cleverly) hiding them from meself, and booked a flight to South Himmel. I didn't need any more scholarly confirmation to my belief that this was the place.

That was yesterday. At this moment I am high over Middle America (and believe me it is hard for me to get high over Middle America; it's like getting excited over PTA meetings). The guy sitting next to me is surreptitiously reading what I write. He just stopped. Now he's blushing. Now he's smiling, tentatively, sheepishly, and looking away.

I didn't look up or smile. He is now very uncomfortable, pretending to read World Travel Magazine. Shit, I can be such a bastard sometimes!

Enuf. You said you'll be passing through Toronto and paying your brother a visit. I lost his home address that you gave me on the phone, but I'll mail this both to you at what recently was your home, in case you're still there packing, as well as care of him at University of Toronto's Religious Studies Department. I don't have the address for U of T either, but I figure the posties there can figure it out. I'll write again soon. I want to use my letters to you as my notebook for this project. So although I'm keeping carbons, please keep my letters as a backup.

You may laugh, but what I am investigating really is very dangerous. So do keep my letters please! I'll keep in touch. I trust this or a carbon copy will reach you wherever you are.

Wiedersehn,
Gotty

.

.

.

I was, in fact, still at home packing. (I was taking my time, since I had till Monday to vacate, according to my arrangement with Susan.)

.

Since Gotty always had had a tendency to dramatize, I took 'dangerous' with a large grain of salt. I felt his months in Rehab last year hadn't entirely brought him down to earth. He'd always had a tendency to get himself into strange predicaments based on dubious ideas, so when the second letter arrived the next day, I tore it open with just a bit of concern for my old friend—and of course considerable curiosity.

.

Second Letter From Gotty Schreiber

.

Dear Thomas:

Let me begin by letting the cat out of the bag: I am certain God is not dead. He is in hiding. And I even know where! Here! South Himmel. Yes, South Himmel, Indiana, fer Kerist Sake!

I'm here too. Thank God, I guess, for the grace of omission. Cuz, you know, if God wanted to prevent my approach, he missed the modern classic opportunity. No thunder bolts, mysterious engine failures, nothing. My flight (flights plural actually, for it took several connections to get to this place) was completely uneventful.

It is eight o'clock, and I'm sitting at the tiny desk that comes with my tiny room. I didn't do anything today except 'explore' the town. Just getting here was enough for one day. Besides, I decided I needed a good night's sleep to work my nerve up.

So. South Himmel is not at all what I'd expected: it is too small, too common. Neither a nice place to visit nor a nice place to live. I've a room in a cheap motel along the town's fast food and neon strip, a strip identical to those in every North American town of more than ten thousand population.

I must say methinks this an unlikely place for God to take up residence. But then I'm not sure what I'd expected? Large billboards advertising daily House-of-God tours? Tourist shops selling plastic holy icons made in Taiwan? This place is as crass and ungodly as any place on the continent, except that, of course, it isn't really ungodly. Maybe I just expected the residents to be crass enough to cash in on that fact. Or knowledgeable enough. Maybe they really don't know He's holed up here? But that's hard to believe. I've no illusions about

207

having unearthed some deep secret. What I believe I know may not be common knowledge or admitted to by scholars, but, hell, even a rumour is usually enough to get greedy entrepreneurs scheming and the paparazzi reloading their cameras. I suppose God has just been very successful at keeping a low profile. From what I've been able to glean from my extensive research and my brief interview with the one man who seemed to be the real McCoy (i.e., a true prophet, albeit also a true wino), God is acting a lot like J.D. Salinger. He doesn't go out much anymore, keeps to himself and does whatever He does in private. (Frankly, I wish more people behaved the same way.) Also, there is the fact that most people, like you me friend, are too sceptical to accept God's presence down on earth without 'substantial' proof.

But low profile or no, Our Lord hasn't been completely successful in keeping His whereabouts secret from believers. Last time we chatted, I told you how I met this Jacob character down in The Bowery, and he spoke more sense than all the rabbis, priests, and biblical scholars I've ever talked to. I should have taken him at his word a long time ago.

So even if what I now know is no big secret, strangely it just doesn't seem to have really mattered. I wonder if we have really become a secular society? Then there is that fact I've discovered in my research that whenever some journalist or religious fanatic has discovered His whereabouts and travelled here, God has simply refused to grant interview or audience—and eventually the God seeker simply gives up and goes home. Naturally no one is going to take such claims seriously without documentation such as a taped interview.

God is clever that way. He doesn't really hide His identity (apparently He doesn't care much for deception anymore) as he goes about his daily business. But then He doesn't flaunt it either. If cornered coming out of a Ranson's Office Supplies and asked outright if He is God, He just says he really doesn't feel like discussing it with anyone and then slips past the intruder and hurries on His way. This tactic seems to have been effective; nobody yet has had the guts to try to physically detain him. Of course only a few of those who know that God has come to live down here among His creations have actually made the pilgrimage to South Himmel. If they know He is here, they also know He probably doesn't welcome visitors. Most people don't like to impose, especially on God, for if you can trust the veracity of the Old Testament at all, our Lord has a bit of a temper.

But to return to my question of why He chose South Himmel, I can only guess that any small town would have suited his purposes equally well. But maybe he liked the name?

There is, of course, the much bigger question: what is He doing? What the hell is God up to? My months of scholarly sleuthing have uncovered three particularly common rumours.

I call the first one the "Sequel Rumour": God is working on a new universe. (There is a variant of this theory I call the "New Edition Variation"; i.e., God is merely working on a revision, a second edition of sorts, with all the rough edges smoothed out, all the loose strings tied.) What is to become of the present world is, predictably, a central theme in the speculations of Sequellers. They all seem much less interested in what the New Universe or New Edition will be like than what will become of the old one. Personally, I prefer to speculate on the nature of an Improved Universe, for I find the debate whether He will discard this one when he finishes the sequel tends to be rather arid. Either we buy the farm or we don't. I can't find any meat for the imagination in either alternative: things go on or they don't. Ah, but the utopian in me loves to fantasize about the sequel.

Then there is the "Abdication Rumour": God has abdicated His celestial throne. The proposed reasons for His doing so are numerous. One that is quite popular in England is that He is secretly living with a mortal woman, perhaps a divorcee or an atheist. Another proposed reason for his abdication is that He became bored with the overview and decided to stop looking at the forest, opting to wander among the trees instead.

The third very popular speculation is what I call the "Delusions of Mortality Rumour": God has gone insane and thinks He is a mere mortal. I first encountered this theory in an article by a psychiatrist, and it wasn't hard to figure out what had inspired it. To a cop everyone is suspect. To a shrink everyone is nuts. An inversion of this rumour (I uncovered in the radical Jewish journal Jesu) is that God was insane when he created the Universe; but now He has come to his senses and is living in his own creation as a kind of penance. This idea reminds me of a line I heard somewhere: "There is no evil, just God when he's drunk." Who knows, maybe he has come to South Himmel to recover from one very bad cosmological hangover. Can you imagine his chagrin when he woke up one painfully sunny morning and saw what he had wrought millennia before?!

Of course, all the arguments supporting one or another of these explanations for God's solitary retreat in South Himmel are based on authority and deductive reason. And like all non-empirical philosophies, ultimately academic. You know me: I'm an empiricist to the bone. I am reserving judgement until I learn the truth from the Horse's Mouth—so to speak, no blasphemy intended!

Enuf. I'm going to have one drink, and then me is going to crash. (I use that word judiciously; the bed here is to "firm" as terminal cancer is to "under the weather".) Tomorrow I procrastinate no more. I'll mail this on my way to see God. And I'll write you again tomorrow night.

       Wiedersehn,

       Gotty

.

.

.

After reading this, I got up for another cup of coffee and noticed out the window that it was starting to cloud over again. I thought about calling Patty and asking if Gotty was—as the saying goes—'using' again, but then I thought she might think I was implying she was to blame.

.

The mail the next day consisted of a flyer for great deals at Topper's Pizza and the phone bill. But the following day there was another letter with a postmark from South Himmel, Indiana.

.

.

Third Letter From Gotty Schreiber

.

Dear Thomas,

So, I'm a breaker of promises—you know that—especially ones I make to meself. So I didn't write you yesterday! Bind me with binder twine and whip me with fresh willow branches. I have broken my vows yet again. I am a sinner.

Me, I am also giddy. It's the tension. I have made a major breakthrough.

I didn't write you because I was too busy -- sort of. Things are happening. (My, my, that last sentence was profound! Guess you can tell I'm an accomplished journalist by the casual way I drop profundities, like pearls, into the swill of my prose?)

Okay, Gotty, start at the beginning.

I got up yesterday well before dawn, for I wanted to be at my destination as early as possible. I shit, showered and shaved, put on a clean shirt and poured meself a stiff Scotch. The last is not a usual part of my routine—in case you're concerned about my "lifestyle"—just an emergency dose of liquid courage, more than justified by the day's itinerary. If you thought you might be talking to God, and probably an irritated God, by early afternoon, you'd probably feel justified in having a little nip in the morning too. (And, yes, if you're wondering, I've had a wee bit this fine morning also.)

After the grain warmth diffused throughout my body, I hopped in my rented Toyota and set off to stake out the House of God. Turns out that God doesn't actually live in South Himmel; He lives in the country just outside of town.

From what I've gathered, He only comes into town once or twice a month to pick up groceries and odd bits of hardware and office supplies. Other God-seekers who have staked out this territory have collected a surprising amount of data about these infrequent public appearances. One determined young man spent six months loitering about town and recording not only the frequency of God's visits, but the nature of his purchases. Strangely, this persistent and patient young fellow was too shy to ever actually attempt to approach God; he merely followed Him around, at a respectful distance, recording His every public action, and talking to the locals. I got my hands on his report (which he never attempted to publish) just the day before I left.

According to this young pilgrim's surveillance, God's occasional shopping trips usually involved a visit to Quigley Supermarket, Ranson's Office Supplies, and Home Hardware. Since there was no record of any serviceman ever being called to His house, His repeated visits to the hardware store would seem to make sense. It is an odd image however: God fixing his own toilet or leaky faucet. But then it was also odd to imagine him eating weirdly flavoured potato chips (which apparently He purchased in great quantities and are a staple in the South Himmelese diet). Perhaps God believes in that old adage my stepmother was so fond of quoting: "when in North Porcupine, do as the North Porcupiners do". South Himmel, North Porcupine, Rome, same principle. However His regular visits to the stationary store are odd; apparently He bought reams and reams of paper and dozens of printer ink-cartridges.

I set out at dawn. The road out to His House has a picturesque name: Concession Road 7. As I drove along this deserted two lane, I began to understood a little better how anyone could willingly chose to live out here in the sticks. Hell's bells, the landscape really is pretty. So pretty and peaceful as to be therapeutic. (I am not being sarcastic.) It is farming country, gently rolling hills spotted with those most peaceful of creatures, cows—who turned their heads slowly and serenely as I roared down the dirt road beside their fields. The sunlight was doing marvellous things to some wispy cirrus clouds, showing its true colours without modesty or coyness. If God were indeed working on a New Edition, He surely wouldn't mess with sunrises; it was one thing he got right the first time.

I'd decided that the best approach was a direct one. My plan was to start with a direct assault on the Old Man. I felt that I had bait (albeit, of a dubious kind) that gave me a slight edge over previous would-be interviewers: I would be spontaneous and so be ingratiating!

I've never really believed all the slanderous Old Testament stories about God's temper. I won't deny some nervousness as I drove out of town, but my reason told me that probably my temerity would at worse only result in a snubbing.

It took about an hour to get out to God's place. Again, as in my surprise at South Himmel, bad reasoning had given me false expectations. I don't know why I'd expected something more modest. Silly of me of course; modest by my standards wouldn't be modest by God's. This place was probably very modest and humble in His eyes.

The property was surrounded by a high wall constructed of fieldstone. It reminded me of some of the country estates I'd seen in the British countryside. The gates were approximately ten feet high, cast iron painted black—apparently some time ago, for the paint was chipping and rust showing. They were locked shut with a thick chain and ordinary padlock. There was no sign identifying the residence. No bell to ring.

The casual would-be visitor would be stymied right here, for without scaling the wall or gate, an overt act of trespassing, there was no way to let the resident know one's desire to speak with Him. Me suddenly got this image of a little trio of black-suited Jehovah's witnesses, their Watchtower pamphlets in hand, *standing outside these gates wondering at how they could get in to save the soul of the owner of this estate.*

Me, of course, was not going to be put off by this small barrier. I climbed the gates to the top of the wall. From my perch I could see a long paved driveway winding into a dense thicket of evergreens. Beyond the trees, barely visible was the top of a large manse. I descended the gate on the inside and set off down the driveway.

The house, like the wall and gates, reminded me of an English Baron's country estate. This mansion was as out of place in the context of rural Indiana as a Quonset hut would be in the Cotswolds of England.

I gathered my nerves in a tight bundle and knocked firmly on the door. As I stood waiting for some sound from within, I remembered a story about a brazen young literary journalist who was determined to get an interview with the then elderly and hermitic Ezra Pound. Ignoring harsh warnings on the gate about intruders, this intrepid journalist had gone up to Pound's door and knocked. He'd expected to be intercepted, as many before him had, by Pound's intransigently protective housekeeper. So he was rehearsing the speech he hoped would convince her to let him arrange to see the poet, when the door opened and there stood the great man himself in a tattered bathrobe. Caught off guard and at a complete loss for words, the journalist muttered an inane "Mister Pound, how are you?" To which the poet, with succinct wit that belied his answer, replied: "Senile." And then shut the door in the man's face. Allegedly this was Pound's last interview. Have you heard this story before?

But I am digressing. So. I waited what seemed a courteous length of time and then I knocked again, a bit harder this time. Almost immediately the door began to open, and I caught my breath. I may be one tough-minded, grit and muck journalist, as my taking that Satan's Choice biker club assignment last year should prove, but all those stories about what happens to He Who Looks Upon the Face of God would cause anyone in my situation a little trepidation.

A wispy young man with rosy cherubic cheeks stood in the threshold. He was wearing a white, cotton leisure suit of the kind you might see on a wealthy American tourist in Paris. "Yes," he said in a melodious and slightly effeminate voice. "Can I help you?"

Unlike the journalist trying to see Pound, me, I'd no speech prepared. I wanted meself to appear completely open and sincere, and I figured that whatever I stuttered would be better than a prepared spiel.

So what I stuttered was something like: "Is God home?"

"Yes," he replied, smiling condescendingly, "but he is not receiving." That was the word he used: receiving.

"Perhaps I could make an appointment?"

"Unlikely." His smile broadened.

"I need to see him." My improvisational approach no longer seemed so sensible. Perhaps I should have worked out some eloquent speech about the

importance of frank communication and spirituality in a troubled world .

"He used to answer everyone's needs, but it became too much for him."

"I'm not just a nosy tourist," I said stupidly. I began to feel my strategy was flawed; I definitely should have come more prepared.

But then, to my amazement, he asked me my name and, once I'd answered, told me to wait a "moment". Then he shut the door in my face.

The moment seemed like eternity. I suppose that if time is relative, mortal moments are bound to be quite different from immortal ones. I waited. I shifted my weight from leg to leg. I waited. I toyed with the idea of knocking again, and rejected it as pushy, as pushing my luck. I waited. I have no idea how long I waited, since the battery on my watch had died in its sleep last night. So, I waited and waited and waited. I probably would have stood there at least until the sun set, but eventually the door did open again. The cherubic face was no longer smiling.

"Tuesday at 10:03 a.m."

Then I was facing a closed door again. I almost let out a whoop of delight, but I stifled it. I did not want to appear indecorous in case there was video surveillance.

When I got back to the gates, I was a little disappointed to find they still were closed. I guess I expected they would now open magically, a minor miracle, to afford me a dignified departure. It was, as I was scaling them that it struck me: the date of my appointment with God was the first of April. But I quickly pushed the thought and its implications from my mind.

So now I have three days to kill in South Himmel. I know it is going to be the longest three days of my life.

Wiedersehn,

Gotty

.

.

.

Needless to say, I postponed my departure and waited impatiently every day for the mail delivery. There is no mail delivery on the weekends, of course, so when no letter arrived on Friday, I had to decide if my curiosity was greater than my desire to begin my personal journey. My bags were packed. I'd told Susan she could take (retake) possession and occupation of the house on Monday.

.

Curiosity turned out to be the greater motivation. I called Susan and asked for an extension of my stay in what was once our home—to which she less than graciously agreed.

.

I went to Mass on Sunday. Then I moped around the house, remembering the good times Susan and I had once had here.

Monday's mail consisted of a thick pile of advertising flyers that the local paper so generously distributes to everyone in the area, whether or not they subscribe to their rag—that and a gas bill. I'd already decided, in pique of pettiness, to just leave the bills for Susan, so I just threw the bill on the dining room table with all the other mail that had arrived in the last week—Gotty's letters excepted, of course.

Tuesday, finally, another letter came from South Himmel.

Fourth Letter From Gotty Schreiber

Dear Thomas,

Well, guess what? God is a black woman in a wheelchair. No, only joking. God is an old white guy with a beard and a stern expression on his face, very much the conventional image. No, still just kidding. God is dead, a corpse nicely preserved in a hermitically sealed glass sarcophagus—just like Lenin. Sorry, only fooling.

Enuf clowning around? I'd better get to the point, you say, or you'll start skimming me immortal prose.

Okay. As Aussie men say by way of foreplay: "Brace yourself, Sheila!" Are you sure you want the truth, the hard facts, the real dope, the bottom line? Are you absolutely certain you want to know (as talk show host Merv Griffin used to ask of guests he was pumping for gossip about other celebrities) what is He really like? Remember all the shit that happened when Adam bit into the Apple of Knowledge?! All right then, read on, me friend—if you're sitting down and have at hand a double-shot of single-malt Scotch.

The truth is God is a writer, leading his readers down the garden path to the final period at the end of the final sentence of the final page of his book. His shirt is schmutzy, his smile is smirky, and his plotting plodding. But God has a gadget: Deus ex machina.

Me shoulda known all along! Why else would people keep saying truth is stranger than fiction? We mere mortal writers can't compete. We have to beg for willing suspension of disbelief, but whoever doubts so-called 'reality'? Even atheists are taken in by his bizarre tales of life on this planet.

We had a great time chatting; as two hack writers we found much common ground. I'll tell you the details when I get back. Suffice it to say God is just as neurotic as the rest of us scribblers, and he too has a taste for good Scotch.

Wiedersehn,
Gotty

P.S. Incidentally, my letters to you are copyrighted, so don't get any ideas. As a fellow writer, God is on my side regarding intellectual property. You don't want to mess with Him. Sorry, didn't mean this to sound threatening. I know you're an honourable man. I'm just a little paranoid about getting scooped.

P.P.S. Oh also, since the Big Guy and I really hit if off, he's going to make a revision in one of the myriad subplots of his epic work, just as a favour to me— and you. Unpack your bags. Susan has decided the split was a bad idea and entirely her fault. She'll be showing up soon to cook you a wonderful meal and bed you down like you've never been bedded down before. (He told me he especially likes writing the racy bits.) Have a great day. God bless ya!

~~~~

DON'T MAGNIFY TRIVIAL INCIDENTS OUT OF PROPORTION

"Emotion is an unpolished lens. The stars twinkle brightest for a person with astigmatism."

—Hippokrites

1: OBJECTIVITY

.

.

Objectivity is one way of looking at things. However, some would elevate it to the level of a moral and aesthetic responsibility. It should not be taken to such heights, since it is only indigenous to—and suited to—the mundane plane.

.

.

2: CONSIDERATION OF X

.

Consider 'X'. X means unknown. X marks the spot. X implies mystery. X indicates the location of treasure. X is the deadly letter formed by the cross-hairs of a telescopic sight on a high powered rifle. X means time(s).

.

.

3: MOVING IN

.

216

1x. The shoreline along the Northside gives an entirely misleading impression of Chicago, an impression of almost pastoral tranquility and civilized leisure—if viewed from the window of one of the numerous high-rises that line the west side of Lakeshore Drive. No doubt this visual lie has a lot to do with why so many of Chicago's affluent choose to live in these towering apartment buildings known collectively as the Gold Coast. The view to the east from on-high: the old winding eight-lane known as Lakeshore Drive which rises and falls like small stationary waves as it rolls over the bridges at the interchanges; beyond it the quarter-mile wide strip of parkland that follows the lake shore from near downtown to fifty-five hundred north, looking all lush and manicured from this distance; and then beyond the park the blue expanse of Lake Michigan, today tipped with tiny streaks of white. From on-high the rich do not see muggers—or lovers. (From on-high the rich do not see a helluva lot.) If you look at a distant star, you are seeing that star as it was hundreds, thousands, or even millions of years ago: you are looking into the past. From the high window of a Gold Coast apartment the parkland below is still in the nineteenth century. We all have our treasured illusions; the rich are just more fortunate in that they can arrange their lives to support their illusions.

.

5x. Closing in. One can see the winding bicycle and foot paths cutting through the park near Wilson Avenue. One can make out a figure strolling along one of these paths. Disappearing from view momentarily as he passes some of the higher shrubbery. Reappearing again, his casual pace now quickening—apparently at the sight of another figure seated at a park bench further north along the path. At this magnification it is impossible to describe these two persons in any detail, but both are dressed in dark clothing.

.

10x. Now you can see, even in the diminishing light of dusk, that the man on the bench is a priest, a negro priest--dark, very dark, with a tiny patch of white at his throat like some ornithological marking. The walking man is white; he is wearing black slacks and a black leather jacket. He is now about ten yards from the priest. There is no one else in the immediate area. The priest is picking up a notebook from the bench and searching for a pen in his coat pocket.

.

20x. The pen is in his breast pocket. Directly over his heart. At this magnification one can even tell it is an old-fashioned fountain pen. Directly over his heart.

.

217

(No, I am no sniper. Nor you. It is all only metaphorical shooting: consider the camera, how it kills. Admire the view. Zoom. Focus. Click.)

.

.

4: FOCAL POINT

"Do you mind if I share this bench, Father?"

.

"No, not at all." The priest answered even before looking up. In truth he did mind indeed, for he'd just had an idea he wanted to enter in his notebook. The man would almost certainly want to talk. But then after all he was a priest first, a scholar second.

.

The man sat down and turned toward the priest. "Making notes on the wildlife?" His voice was unpleasantly sarcastic. He grinned.

.

"Huh?"

.

"It was a little joke."

.

"I'm sorry, I don't get it."

.

"Ha, don't you see, the only wild life here is human. More or less human." The man released a truncated sound that was closer to a grunt of disgust than to a laugh.

.

The priest studied the man's face. It was very ordinary; even the eyes were. There was usually some clue in the eyes, but this man's eyes gave nothing away.

.

"It's getting kinda dark to write, ain't it?"

.

"Yes, you're quite right."

.

"Is that a journal, a diary?"

.

The priest was mildly startled. It was not the sort of question most people presumed to ask a priest.

.

"Hey, I don't mean to be rude, Father, but I just wondered, you know, if priests ever kept diaries. I mean they hear so many juicy things. You guys ever write the stuff down? Sorta keep records of the good bits people confess to you? Or is that against the rules?"

"I don't know of any rules against keeping a diary, but this isn't a diary. I don't keep a diary."

"But some priests do?"

"I'm sure some do, but I wouldn't think very many."

"Well, I bet a priest's diary would be pretty funky reading. Your life must be pretty dull, but you do get to hear about all the exciting parts of other people's lives. It'd make a good book."

The priest didn't know what to say. The man didn't sound too stable.

"So, Father, what do you write in that notebook if it ain't a place to keep your secrets?"

"My secrets!?" Really, this man was outrageous.

"You know what I mean." He winked histrionically, grotesquely.

"I'm not sure I do. But to answer your question, this notebook contains the rough draft of an article I'm working on."

"An article? You write articles for the paper?"

"No, an article for a scholarly journal. It deals with a philosopher of whom I'm sure you've never heard."

"Hey, I ain't dumb. How do you know I haven't heard of him."

"Jacques Maritain."

"Huh?"

"Jacques Maritain, that is the philosopher's name. And I meant no offense. He just isn't a very well known philosopher."

"I guess you're right. Never heard of him."

The priest realized he was still holding his pen. He replaced it in his pocket and leaned forward on the bench as if to rise. "I should be going now."

"No, wait!" The man became agitated. "I want to talk to you. You're a priest. You're supposed to listen to people."

The priest leaned back. "Yes?"

"Are you a teacher or something?"

"Yes, I teach Theology and Aesthetics at Loyola University. But you wanted me to listen to your problems?" He smiled, partially to make the man feel more at ease and partially because of the implication of what he himself had just said: that the teaching of theology was a problem. It was, rather.

"Hey, I didn't say I had any fuckin' problems!" The man's voice was suddenly belligerent. "Why should I have any problems. Hell, I've got money. I'm in the fing prime of life—just turned thirty-four. I'm strong. I'm smart." He hesitated, and then continued in a more moderate tone, "Smart enough to know what people need."

"And what is it that people need?"

"Thrills."

It struck the priest as such a pathetic answer that he leaned toward the man, intending to gently touch his arm—but something restrained him from completing the gesture, some unworthy but uncontrollable distaste for this particular example of his fellow man.

"You thought I was going to say God, didn't ya?"

"I'm sorry, what did you say?"

"I said you thought I was going to say everybody needs God, or peace, or love, or some other bullshit."

"No, I had no idea what you were going to say."

"Well, let me tell you something, Father, let me give you a little advice. All people really need..."

"Hold on." The priest interrupted, surprised at the firmness in his voice, for the man was beginning to frighten him. "Let me give you some advice instead. Something is bothering you or you would not talk that way. Why don't you just tell me what the problem is. It will make you feel better."

The man's face tightened, the skin seeming to stretch tighter around the cheekbones, creating little dark hollows. "I just told you I don't have any problems. I'm young and strong and smart—and white! Unlike you, nigger!"

The priest felt his heart skip a beat. Immediately he tried to consciously regulate his breathing. Ever since his late twenties he'd been plagued by tachycardia whenever he became tense.

"Did you hear me, nigger?"

"Yes, I heard you. And since you have no problems, and I do have to get back, I'm sorry but I'll have to go now. It's getting quite..."

"Don't move, nigger, or I'll cut your fuckin' throat." The man now had a knife in his hand. Where it had materialized from, the priest had no idea.

"I have no money."

"I told ya I don't need no money."

The priest glanced around. No one had passed since the man had first sat down. This was strange; there usually were a few joggers panting along the path this time of day. Probably a few would show up shortly, although whether or not they would help was another question.

"Sit back. And relax!" The man's voice had deepened and become raspier.

"It is hard to relax with you holding that knife. What do you want if you don't want money?"

"A good time."

The priest looked up at the Gold Coast apartment buildings in the distance. Lights were coming on. Surely a hundred people were glancing out the windows, and none would be seeing him. His heart was beating fast and irregularly despite his efforts to control it.

"You're breathing funny."

"Sorry."

"You know what else I want?"

"No."

"I want practice."

"Practice? Practice at what? Terrifying people?"

"As a matter of fact, yes. You got it. You hit the nail right on the head. You're not such a dumb nigger after all."

"Thanks."

"You know why I picked you? Are you that smart?"

"I'm afraid not." In hearing himself answer the priest almost smiled. I'm afraid not, not afraid. Dear God, I am not afraid. Though I walk through the valley of the shadow of death, I will fear no evil. But that was not true. In his heart, his wildly beating heart, he was most definitely afraid.

"I picked you cuz I figured you wouldn't be easy to scare. I wanted a challenge."

"Why would you think me difficult to frighten?"

"You believe in God, don't ya?"

"Yes, of course I believe in God."

"So, there, you shouldn't be scared."

"That doesn't follow. Just because I believe in God doesn't mean I can't be frightened. God is a comfort, but I am human."

"So are you scared?"

"Yes, I am scared."

"Well, shit, that's no good. You're making it too easy." The man stared into the priest's eyes. "Or maybe you're lying. You're just saying you're scared!"

"No, I assure you I am very frightened."

"Oh, shut the fuck up!" The man leaped to his feet. Standing over the priest he leaned forward until the point of the knife was gently touching the clerical collar. "I want proof that you're scared. I want to see you wet your skirts or cry or beg. Hey, did ya know you're so black I'd better be careful or I'll lose you in the dark."

"Are you doing this because I'm black?"

"God Damn It! If you're so fuckin' scared, how come you sound so fuckin' calm!" He pressed the point of the knife more firmly against the priest's collar.

"It's my training," the priest replied softly, immediately and fearfully regretting the flippant reply.

Suddenly the man laughed a strange laugh, a laugh that fluctuated wildly in pitch. Then he put the knife in his pocket. When he spoke again his voice was as soft and steady as it had been originally. "You know, Father, I've got nothin' against black folk. I was just talking that way to scare ya. I'm not prejudiced. Now tell me the truth. Did I really scare you?"

"Yes." It was the truth.

The priest considered making a run for it now that the knife was again in the man's pocket, but curiosity was taking over from fear. He noticed his heart was once again beating regularly; the full tachycardia attack had not materialized. Oddly, he felt good, alive, energetic.

"Good. Well, I'm going now."

"Why?"

"Cuz I gotta meet somebody."

"No, I meant why did you do this to me? Why would you want to frighten people."

"I'm trying to become a saint. I wanna do good works."

"Terrifying people is your idea of good works?"

"Look, if I scare somebody, it makes me feel good cuz I feel powerful. And it makes them feel good cuz it gives 'em a thrill. A real thrill, not a phoney thrill like a horror movie. I never actually hurt anyone."

"Oh."

5: MOVING OUT

10x. A white man in black is walking away from a park bench where (5x) a figure sits in the shadows becoming (1x) just shadows: an abstraction, a study of shades of darkness before the sea-like expanse of Lake Michigan, timeless along the long horizon. The scene is peaceful.

6: OBJECTIVITY

Note: Two months later *The Journal of Christian Metaphysics* received a submission from John Berson, S.J., dealing with the aesthetic theories of several French philosophers. The main thrust of the article was a criticism of those thinkers who held that art was a way of taming the emotions. Berson argued, to the contrary, that art possess value in direct proportion to its emotional impact. Although the arguments were presented in a very dry, rational manner, and though they were accompanied by quotations from St. Thomas Aquinas, the editors were appalled at the aesthetic proposed and promptly rejected the piece as being too much on the side of Dionysus. As one of the editorial readers commented: "If one applied this man's criterion, horror movies would be elevated above the works of Chekhov. Art should not be equated with titillation."

7: CONSIDERATION OF X

Consider X. X is exciting. And ambiguity is its own reward.

~~~~

WHEN THE BLOOM IS ON THE ROSE

"With a gift it is the thought that counts, but only the thought of the recipient."
—Hippokrites

I wasn't drunk as I strolled up Bourbon Street. I wasn't sober either. Being completely sober on Bourbon Street is as inappropriate, sacrilegious even, as being drunk in church. In fact being stone cold sober after dark anywhere in New Orleans' French Quarter is socially deviant. They probably have a bylaw prohibiting it.

.

Bourbon Street was closed to vehicular traffic, as it usually is after dark, so it was like a large canyon through which flowed what was probably the most heterogeneous group of people on the continent. This murky river of humanity was more turbulent than even the trickiest stretch of real white water: complex swirling eddies, backflows indicating obstacles ahead (perhaps a drunk deciding he needed a good brisk sit), and curving fast-moving stretches past the clip joints, music clubs, strip joints. Suddenly a current differential brought this fellow up next to me and for a few meters we coursed along at equal speed. An odd occurrence, this momentary order amidst chaos.

.

He turned his head slowly toward me, his eyes heavy-lidded and uninterested. Then he did a slow-mo double-take.

.

"Hey man, you look like me," he said, snapping alert.

"I hope not," I replied—this delivered with a grin so he wouldn't think I was being hostile. But there was an element of truth in what he said. He was of similar build and, like me, a bit over six foot. We both had longish, unruly hair. My guess was he was my middle age, or maybe a bit younger, although he looked like he'd lived harder, faster. And we did have similar facial features, although I'd say he was better looking—except for his ravaged complexion. Dissolution had scribbled on his face. He had large pores.

"Fuck, man, you do, you really do." He spoke slowly, drawing out each word in a rising intensity that ended abruptly. But it wasn't a southern drawl. He was no native. "Same eyes."

I didn't wish to continue this discussion of our physiognomic similarities. I noticed he held in his hand a long-stemmed red rose, wrapped in thin cellophane, so I remarked: "A rose is a rose is a rose." I tend to spill out irrelevant literary quotations when at a loss for something to say.

"Gertrude Stein," he returned. "You a writer, man?"

I nodded.

"Me too," he said.

Had I been completely sober, I'd have been sceptical: everybody who has read five books in their life and has a few stories or poems stashed in their sock drawer is a writer, just as every waiter in L.A. is an actor. But I didn't ask for his C.V. I just asked what sort of stuff he wrote.

"Wrote for *The Ventura*," he said.

I had no idea what '*The Ventura*' was. Was he an out of work reporter? The New Orleans rag was called (of all things) *The Picayune*. It didn't matter. It was a sufficiently convincing answer to my not entirely sober self.

"C'mon, I'll buy you a beer," I said.

This atypically altruistic gesture requires some explanation. I was alone in the Big Easy, had been for days—alone and lonely. N'awlins is a fabulous city. Being there with people you care about is like attending a great, never-ending party. But being there alone can be hellish; one feels like a widower at a party where there are no other singles, and everybody knows everybody, and nobody knows you. A party can be the loneliest place in the world. I'd spent too much time talking to bartenders who told bad jokes. I was missing my wife and daughter with an ache that had become physical: my whole body actually hurt in a vague, undefined way. General malaise is the term doctors use in describing symptoms such as mine. Common to colds and flus, vitamin deficiencies and incipient cancer—and homesickness.

"Name's Randy," my new acquaintance said.

I told him my name and asked him: "What's with the rose?"

"From my daughter."

The image of my own daughter flashed in my mind. I wanted to be fourteen hundred miles north northeast of here, sitting with Kate and my wife at our dining room table, complaining about the snow but feeling warm inside. Somewhere along the years, I'd become domesticated. Being away from my family for even a short time made me feel like a young kid the first day at the summer camp that was supposed to be so very much fun. Somewhere along the years, I'd become a wimp.

The bar was in a court yard. I'd been there years before with friends, heard some good R&B, danced with two young women who worked for a travel agency in Milwaukee, and had only thought of home every quarter hour or so. That time the mulatto waitress had been so beautiful I asked to take her picture, and when she wasn't serving or taking orders, she'd be up dancing, by herself or with anyone who cared to join her. This time the waiter was short, ugly and surly and he didn't dance. The music was being supplied by a lone country and western singer who couldn't carry a tune in bucket but fortunately had a weak voice and a weak amp. C&W fits in New Orleans like New Age Music fits in South Central L.A. Not surprisingly, the place was nearly empty. But it would be a good spot to sit and talk.

Randy asked me who was my "all time favourite writer".

I declined to answer. Impossible to answer, of course.

.

He insisted.

.

"Listen," I said, "you'd only ask me that if you had your own answer prepared for when I ask you the same question."

.

"Right, man, right. Steinbeck's the best."

.

Synchronicity: my daughter had been reading *Grapes of Wrath* when I'd left on this trip. I told him this.

.

He looked confused. Then he talked about *Travels With Charlie*, and how he didn't like Hemingway but liked Fitzgerald. We tried 'literary' conversation for awhile longer, and I soon realized that Randy hadn't heard of, certainly not read, anybody I mentioned except Faulkner. Barth, Fowles, Updike, Nabokov, all drew a blank look. Then I remembered that the standard curriculum for a first year college survey course in Contemporary American Lit used to be Steinbeck, Hemingway, Fitzgerald, Faulkner. I asked about his own writing. *The Ventura*, it turned out, was his high school newspaper where he'd been the star reporter. Yes, high school! Randy was forty years old, if he was a day.

.

I asked about his daughter. Like I'd said to him, people often ask questions they want asked of themselves.

.

But I never did get to talk much about Kate. Randy went into a rhapsody about his eight year old daughter and how she had to be so smart and good looking because his wife was so beautiful, long raven hair with fine features, high cheekbones and very intelligent too. He was very articulate, even poetic when he spoke of his wife. Too bad she was a heroin addict.

.

"Oh," I said. A sympathetic oh.

.

His wife was in Monterey, California. His daughter was too, but she was living with his parents. His wife wasn't a fit mother. Randy was earning his daily bread working as a ship cook. He'd be heading out, a new gig starting tomorrow, for two months. It didn't pay much, only five bills a week, but on board there was no way to spend the money.

.

"California is a long way away. When did you last see your daughter?"

I asked.

.

"When she was two." Six years ago.

.

"Oh," I said. Another sympathetic oh.

.

Randy's folks were raising his daughter. Randy's Mom was an angel. His Dad, who had the same first name as me, was the greatest guy on earth, but had "gotten into money".

.

"He sells computer systems. Makes a bundle. When I was kid, we always had people over, making music, partying. But then Dad got into money, gave up the sax."

.

"Oh," I said. A third sympathetic oh.

.

Conversations always have mysterious underground passages, but this is especially true of those with strangers. One gets glimpses of the person's life, hints, clues, but these only raise more questions. You can ask about things, probe, but to do this too much is rude. This is why a few drinks help, because we're more willing to be rude when we've been drinking.

.

"I'm an addict," Randy said suddenly, apropos nothing.

.

The waiter came by. I ordered another beer. My companion had hardly touched his.

.

"You're a junkie?" I said after the waiter left.

.

"Clean. Been clean for years. Now I'm a drunk."

.

Then he told me about heroin. How he'd got hooked. He had a motorcycle and was making good money as a mule, running drugs from California to Vegas. Just a lark. The bread was good. No border crossings were involved, so the risk was minimal. One day a fellow courier convinced him to try the stuff.

.

It was a revelation. Not what you'd think. You just felt good. You just didn't hurt. It didn't fuck up your ability to think, like booze did. It was clean as a new razor. You could go about your business, be efficient. You felt "fresh as summer morning when you're five." His words.

He thought it felt too good, so he didn't do it again for months, but then he did. And it doesn't take long to get hooked. As long as you can get your fix, you could go about your daily business, smooth and sharp. Drunks have a hard time with daily life, usually end up losing their jobs, but not so for junkies with a steady supply. You get up in the morning, reach for the spoon and soon you're out there functioning at peak. He knew several big time executives that were junkies. No one ever suspected.

"But forget about sex," he said, no regret in his voice. "You can forget about sex."

I asked him how he beat it.

"Went to visit my grandparents in Wisconsin. Nobody could understand why I didn't fly, but I took the bus. Three fucking days on the bus, and no way I could get a fix. It doesn't hurt as much as they say. The hell is just that you don't sleep. I didn't sleep for three days. I drank the whole time, took downers, but still I couldn't sleep."

I asked how long it took to chill out.

"Forever. But I was in rough shape for fourteen days."

I wanted to ask a hundred questions, but I was starting to feel like a vampire. I was feeding on his blood, the misery of his life. It was renewing me. I was no longer feeling sorry for myself because I was briefly separated from my family and had to—gee whiz—try to have a good time all by myself. For a while I used to carry a card in my wallet that I'd read whenever I was out of sorts. I'd scribbled on it: "Half the world's population is starving, what did you say your problem was again?"

I'd had my fix at his expense, so I changed the subject. We talked about how everything was funny. Then about jokes. Naturally he asked me what was the "very best joke" I'd ever heard and then told me his best joke ever. Then he told me that people always said he should write a book, that he must be living the way he was for some reason. I replied with the cliché that yes, you can only take in for so long before you have to give back. We told more jokes—runners-up. We talked about the city. When in port, he usually drank across the river. Bourbon Street was one big commercial hustle.

.

I'd had three beers, he'd only had one, when I suddenly felt bone weary, so I lied and said I had to get up early. He picked up the rose, and we walked down the alley back to the roiling river of people on Bourbon. We shook hands and wished each other well.

"Oh," I said before I dived into the human current, "how'd your daughter get you that rose?" It was a cruel and stupid thing to say.

.

"C'mon, man." He looked me hard in the eyes. "Whatta ya think? They sell 'em in all the bars. I bought it for myself. But I know she'd want me to have it."

.

"I'm sure she would," I said.

~~~~

ABOUT THE AUTHOR

He believes that literature, like science, is a way of exploring different perspectives. The results of these literary explorations, like the results of science, are always inherently tentative. It is for this reason he calls all his books 'hypotheses'. *God When He's Drunk*, is Hypothesis 14.

He is also a visual artist and has paid his bills with a day job as a tenured university lecturer at Nipissing University in North Bay Ontario, where one of his courses is on the psychology of art and creativity. He has a wife who teaches philosophy, a daughter who is a theoretical mathematician, and a son who is website designer. He also has two dogs and no time.

Website: KenStange.com